DEATH
GODDESS DANCE

DEATH GODDESS DANCE

LEVI BLACK

TOR

A TOM DOHERTY ASSOCIATES BOOK
NEW YORK

DEATH GODDESS DANCE

Copyright © 2019 by James R. Tuck

A Tor Book
Published by Tom Doherty Associates
120 Broadway
New York, NY 10271

www.tor-forge.com

Tor® is a registered trademark of Macmillan Publishing Group, LLC.

The Library of Congress Cataloging-in-Publication Data is available upon request.

ISBN 978-0-7653-8252-8 (hardcover)
ISBN 978-1-4668-8762-6 (ebook)

Our books may be purchased in bulk for promotional, educational, or business use. Please contact your local bookseller or the Macmillan Corporate and Premium Sales Department at 1-800-221-7945, extension 5442, or by email at MacmillanSpecialMarkets@macmillan.com.

First Edition: July 2019

Printed in the United States of America

0 9 8 7 6 5 4 3 2 1

ACKNOWLEDGMENTS

I would like to acknowledge and thank all the staff at Tor who worked so hard on this book and the whole series. I truly enjoyed working with y'all and look forward to doing it more.

Thank you to Greg Cox for shaping this series and being an aces editor.

Thank you to Christopher Morgan for always being quick to take care of me.

Thank you to Lucienne Diver, best agent in the world.

Thank you to Robert E. Howard for taking the Mythos in a direction that really spoke to me as a young man and created a life-long enjoyment of weird gods and their machinations.

DEATH
GODDESS DANCE

1

HAVE YOU EVER been split down the middle, laid on the griddle, and fried, fried, fried?

Ever had your organs scoured in salt?

Ever been sliced in the center and left out in winter till you died, died, died?

Ever had your brain ground into malt?

No?

Me neither.

But I know what it feels like now.

Holy shit, did that hurt.

You try teleporting across the universe, see how you like it.

Snatches of memory crash into my brain, flashes that came through even the protective layer of my coat, the living skin of an archangel I wear—it's a long story; let's just leave that for that.

We roared through a cloud of starspawn, scattering them like a school of fish, their little cuttlefish heads and streaming tentacles suckering onto us as we passed only to be sheared away by our velocity. They tumbled along in our trail, a dissipated cloud, before reassembling and continuing on, leaving me only their tiny psychic cries of homelessness to feel in the wrinkles of my brain.

My skin still tingles from the scald of a malevolent sun that tried to roast us for coming too close to it, blasting us with its gaze and a throb of zeta-rays.

A color chased us to the end of the nebula, tumbling its way around a belt of asteroids we zipped through.

A colony of vast alien civilizations all the size of thin needles tried to embed into my skin with the intention of turning my body into their version of a home planet.

These were all outside me. Inside, my lungs pounded like hammers on steel for lack of oxygen and the blood, my magick blood, rushed through my veins like a river of rapids, crashing over and over and over while my heart felt like it had been frozen.

What a long strange trip it has been.

Gods and damned gods and goddamned gods.

I had a normal life. I *was* a normal girl.

Okay, not normal like most are normal, but I felt as normal as I think I ever will. I had a job and an apartment I shared with people who were becoming friends.

And I met a boy.

Daniel, with his green eyes and his quick mind and his almost bashful smile.

And I fell in love. I think I fell in love.

It wasn't quick or sudden, it just felt that way. It snuck up on me.

We had one misunderstanding, a big one, but still, it was good until in through the out door came Nyarlathotep, the Crawling Chaos.

The Man in Black.

He told me I would help him save the world from other things like him. He brought Daniel along to keep me on point.

It was lies.

I found out the Man in Black was using me to find and kill other gods so he could gain the power to free his father, who is way worse than him.

I've been trying to stop him, but the slippery bastard has been on the run. He got the power, the soul gems of other gods, and zapped his way here.

And I followed him.

And here we are.

I'm lying on something solid, my eyes are closed, and all I can do is breathe and feel the agony inside me. It takes a moment for me to make my brain work in some kind of order.

I'm cold.

Not *cold*-cold, but *cool*-cold. Gooseflesh cold. The front of me is cool. My arms feel swollen, heavy and sodden, as I reach and touch my torso. Bare skin over my stomach and soft cloth higher up. My shirt has ridden up. I tug it down.

I don't want to move.

I open my eyes.

Nothing changes. The darkness stays complete.

Are my eyes open?

I try again and they stay shut and now I feel them tugging against themselves, like they've been taped down.

Have my eyelids been taped down?

Eyelids . . . taped . . .

A scream of panic crawls up into my mouth, like a centipede from behind my heart.

Something warm and wet swipes over my face. It smells terrible. I jerk, pulling away, and something hard presses me back down by my shoulder. I'm pinned to the floor.

Pinned and blind.

Trapped.

Captured.

Panic slaps me across the mind. Every muscle I have jolts tight and I'm tipping over into going berserk. *I will fight! I will flail! I will not be taken like I was before! No, no, no . . .*

A strangled bark cuts through the rising panic like a beam of light through the fog.

It takes a moment for me to be able to speak. "Winnie?"

That warm wet slides across my face again, this time over my eyes. I put my hands there. My eyes are sealed with something gummy.

I wipe it away and it burns as my lids begin to crack open.

Sight returns slowly, fuzzy shapes to clearer shapes. Until I am looking at the skinless face of a hound. Muscles bunch around his jaws and the bone-cracking teeth part, letting a long pink tongue loll out as he begins to pant. He tilts his head and looks at me with one lidless egg yolk eye, the other an empty dark socket.

I pat his face, hands slightly sticking to his tacky lack-of-skin muscles.

My throat hurts as I try to speak, a line of bruising ache around my larynx. The Torc of Ashtoreth, *my* torc, lies heavy on my collarbones. The bruise is from it clamping around my throat as I used it to wish myself here.

Wherever *here* is.

I force the words out. "Hey, Winnie. Good boy. I'm glad you're okay." It is good to see the skinhound. He stands over me, his breath warm and moist on my face. I lift my hands and push his face, the thin, tough membrane that covers him in place of skin slightly latching onto my fingertips. He turns aside, blister-pink tongue lapping against my hand as he does. He seems to be fine from our trip across the universe.

I can't believe I was scared of him once. I mean, he *is* scary looking. The whole skinless thing was super-creepy the first time I saw him, but now I'm used to it. To be fair, the first time I saw him he was part of a pack of skinhounds sent to attack me by the Man in Black to get me to help him, to become his Acolyte. The Man in Black showed up and '"saved" me, killing all of them but this one here. He then convinced me to join him. The skinhound began trailing us, showing up anytime I began to question the Man in Black, a subtle threat that I should stay with him.

Anger at the manipulation and trickery flares hot once again.

The skinhound came at me directly after I turned on the Man in Black. I broke the hold over him, named him Winnie, and now he's mine.

The shape-shifting coat I wear, made from the still-living skin of an archangel, stirs around me, trilling in my mind.

You okay, friend?

A string of nonsensical noise, the coat's voice, rolls across my cerebellum in a dry tickle I want to reach in and scratch if it weren't inside my skull.

I am glad for both the coat and the skinhound. Both things that once belonged to him and now are mine.

The skinhound nudges my arm, then tosses his head. I look around.

I'm in a room so white it's impossible to see where the walls end and the ceiling and floor begin. It is seamless, the light not bright enough to make me squint but coming from everywhere at once. It feels like the room is about the size of an aircraft hangar, but I can't tell if that's real or illusion. I know there is a floor because I feel it beneath me, but for all I know I am just standing in some weird diffused light dimension with no boundaries. It feels like there is space around me with a limit. I don't have that small breath air pressure of a tiny enclosure, but there is room.

Then again, I could take three steps and run smack into a wall.

Or step off the edge of a crevice.

All this thought is giving me vertigo; my eyes feel like they are attached to wires and being tugged in a leftward spiral.

The only things marring the clean, pristine nature of the place are me and Winnie.

And the small trail of fluid about two feet away from my left hand that squiggles off in a series of dribbles and drops.

I put my left hand on Winnie to feel anchored, lean, and hold my right hand over the fluid.

Magick vibrates off it. The Mark on my palm tingles, glowing softly in response. This is familiar. My mouth goes dry with the taste of blackberries and grave dirt.

I know what this is.

This is the blood of Nyarlathotep.

The Man in Black.

The chaos god I came all this way to kill.

I know the rough part of his plan. He's going to use the soul gems he tricked me into helping him gather from killing other elder gods to free his father and set him loose on Earth. He and his father will then treat Earth like an all-you-can-eat buffet. I had to let him go before to buy some time for my family and friends and Daniel, the man I think I have fallen in love with. But they aren't safe, not until I stop the Man in Black.

He has a head start on me, but maybe not too much of one.

My hand lowers toward the blood.

Is this blood? Do elder chaos gods bleed blood? Or is it some essence, ectoplasm, or ichor?

It's something like unto blood, but the thing that matters is I can use this to track him.

Before I can touch it a voice comes from behind me.

"Do not smear that. You will just make a bigger mess."

2

I TURN AND use the movement to roll to my feet.

It hurts, but I've got a rush of adrenaline making me hot under my clothes from being startled that takes the edge off it.

Standing about ten feet away is a man.

A man wearing overalls and clunky brown shoes. He isn't much taller than me, if at all, and has the stoop-shouldered, splayed-feet stance of someone the world has trod on more than once.

There is a mop in his hand.

How fucked up is it that this isn't even weird for me?

"Who are you?" I ask.

He sighs and walks closer. "I do not see how that matters."

I turn my palm out, shaking magick down my arm and into my hand. I don't have much juice left, but the scar-tissue lines and squiggles that make up my Mark flare to life in a dark red, almost magenta, crackle of magick. "Believe me, it matters."

He stops short and stares at me. His eyes are wide by nature, not from surprise, and set in a matching pair of dark smudges. They're shimmery, as if lying in shallow pools of water, and the face they're set in is round and smooth but not clean shaven, more like it's never had hair. His skin looks like parchment, not in color but in texture, as if it might feel rough under my fingertips. His mouth lies under a nose that matches its width, ears tapering from cup to the end of his jaw without the separation of a lobe.

"You are threatening me." He says it with no inflection in his voice.

I don't say anything.

He shakes his head. "I cannot believe you are really threatening me."

"Take it as you will. Who are you?"

The skinhound leans against my thigh, just close enough to let me know he is there.

"I am a keeper here," the man says.

"You have a name?"

"You know better than that. You do not sign my checks, then you do not get my name."

"You get checks?"

His brow wrinkles. "What are you talking about?"

His mop moves. I look closer and see that the strings are actually long, thin tendrils. Small bumps cover their surface and under each of them is a thin leader of gristle that runs their length from their tips down into the midst of them. Tongues. They're tongues. They lick at the air, writhing against one another.

There's something . . . *off* about this guy and it's not just the mop. He doesn't feel right. He makes my palms itch.

"You aren't human."

"What?!?" He convulses around a chuckle. "No, no, no, what gave you *that* idea?"

"You look human, more or less."

Wide lips purse. "Now you are just being rude."

I don't have time for this. Every quip and line we exchange the Man in Black gets farther away.

I point at the blood trail. "I'm going to touch that before you do anything to it."

"Why on the moon would you want to do that?"

The moon? "To track the person that left it."

"Who left it?"

"Nyarlathotep."

"You think the Crawling Chaos left his blood lying around for you to find?" A laugh bursts out of him, making his cheeks shake. "You really are a human, are you not?"

Goddammit.

He's right. The Man in Black wouldn't be careless with his essence. Not with the magickal potential of a chaos god's blood.

He continues to laugh. "If you use that spoor to track, you'll end up somewhere you don't want to be."

"Already there, asshole," I mutter in frustration.

"What did you say?"

"Never mind." I raise my arms, indicating the whiteness that surrounds us. The coat rustles against me, caressing my torso. "Where is this?"

"You do not know where you came to?"

"I'm chasing someone. He came here, so I came here, but I don't know where *here* is."

"You are chasing the Whispering Man?"

Gods and their damned names.

"Haven't heard that one before. If it's another title for Nyarlathotep then yes."

He nods. "That is the one. I am surprised he came back."

"Back? He's been here before?"

The man nods.

"When?"

He looks off to the upper left nowhere, thinking. "Before the other day."

"He come and go often?"

"He swore he would never return. Said nothing would ever make that happen."

"He's here to free Azathoth."

The man says nothing at that, but his mouth makes a line hard enough to leave a bruise.

"Why'd he say he'd never return?" I ask.

"Things here what do the tricking do not like to be tricked themselves."

"He's a bastard."

"Not in the literal sense." He shakes the hand holding the mop, dislodging a half-dozen tongues that have wrapped across his fingers. "Stop that." He says it to the mop, still looking at me.

Not a bastard in the literal sense.

Things click in my head. The Man in Black is here to free his father, the Mad God Azathoth, Bringer of Insanity.

"Tell me where Azathoth is," I say.

He puts his hand up. A low growl rumbles from the skinhound as he steps forward. The man's eyes widen and I watch him tense across the shoulders. I've seen that enough in the dojo I know he's about to swing that tongue mop, not to hit the skinhound as much as to put it between him and Winnie.

"Don't do that." I let the urgency ring out from my voice. "Stay still. He gets very protective."

"I am not threatening you."

"Then don't act like you are and you should be okay."

"Should?"

"Most likely."

"That thing needs a leash."

I laugh at the notion; it just bursts out of me. Winnie hasn't been with me long, but I couldn't even conceive of trying to leash him. "Sorry," I say. "Just be calm and let's start over."

He nods.

I nudge the skinhound with my thigh and and make a motion with my hand. He whines once, a short, sharp note, but sits back on raw haunches.

My head hurts.

The Man in Black is getting farther away. I can *feel* that fact like I feel my own skin. I don't know what this place is, but before, when I was still his Acolyte, the red-handed bastard said his father was stuck in elder god prison by humans long ago and far away. Ashtoreth had elaborated on the story, when we were friends. Telling me that some people with names that have too many syllables and the man we now call Noah made the Flood happen to sacrifice all the world so they could lock the gods on the other side of the universe.

That was only like a day or two ago.

The conversation, not the Flood.

Damn you, Ash. Damn you and your whore heart.

It hurts to push the hurt of her betrayal away. Friends. Shit. I spend a long moment compartmentalizing the sting of what she did. As I move the pain, my old familiar friend anger stirs behind my breastbone and tries to slither in and fill the void.

But I'm aces at shutting down emotion.

I'm a fucking survivor.

The man tilts his head, watching me.

He can help me.

He's from here, wherever *here* is, and seems to be free to move around. He called himself a keeper and with that tongue mop and his desire to clean the blood on the floor . . . maybe he's a janitor.

Maintenance worker at an elder god prison. Prisons need people to handle stuff like that. Right?

Prisons also use trustees to do that. Trustees are prisoners who are "trustworthy" enough to do small tasks and jobs in the prison.

Jobs like mop floors. They might still be dangerous, but not the *most* dangerous.

In elder god prison I think dangerous is a wide river with a deep end.

All the weirdness I've experienced since signing on with the Man in Black swirls through my memory. The cancer god made of tumors growing inside people, humans eating pieces of Cthulhu in a sushi joint in New York, me using magick and wielding a cursed sword who wanted to drink the blood of everyone in the world, gaining a living coat that is the skin of an archangel and a skinless hellhound as a pet, becoming friends with a goddess of whores and being betrayed by her, visions of my world turned to blood and fire and ash, a Yellow King in a fiefdom of lunatics, and a fertility goddess captured by hillbillies, her offspring used to supply their barbecue joint in some backwoods holler.

Falling in love with Daniel, returning his soul to him, and then abandoning him to chase a chaos god here.

It's been a really weird month or so.

I have done things I would never have imagined.

I've killed things.

Gods.

Creatures.

And humans.

The thought is a barbed needle jabbed into the soft parts of me.

And I'm not done yet.

And there's the twist.

I shake it off.

I have a hunch, a feeling, a notion, that this trustee can help me find the Man in Black. I need his help.

He has to help me.

The coat responds to my thoughts, shifting around my body. It murmurs in my skull and I feel my weapons that it keeps inside its infinite folds. The Aqedah, knife of Abraham, which has thus far been able to cut through anything I've laid it against, presses in a hard line along my right hip. If I reach into the coat's pocket I will find it there.

If I laid it across this man-thing's throat would he take me where I want to go?

Weight settles against the left side of my body, from rib cage to mid-thigh. That would be the shotgun I took from Ephraim, the hillbilly high priest who planned to add me to the menu, the one featuring barbecued offspring from Shub Niggurath, the Black Goat of the Woods with a Thousand Young. It looks like a fancy pump-action shotgun, but it shoots gouts of balefire and brimstone. As far as I can tell, it doesn't ever need reloading.

If I pressed its barrel against this man's forehead would he take me where I want to go?

My right palm itches, the raised scars that form my Mark tingling and burning with desire to do violence. I also have magick, power, all my own.

And a skinhound I could sic on him.

If I did those things would he take me where I want to go?

All the things I could do to create the outcome I need to happen.

He stands there, with his mop.

My head really hurts.

I stick my hand out, the one with the Mark. "I'm Charlie."

He looks at my hand like it has teeth. After a long moment he reaches out and clasps it in his own. His palm is wide but short, the skin rough against my Mark. The magick in my blood surges, wanting to spill out and sample him, but I clamp it down. My stomach goes hot and greasy with the effort. The coat trills along my brain and I feel its concern.

It's okay.

The man opens his mouth and what comes out isn't English but some guttural string of consonants and noises, most of which a human throat could never replicate.

"Umm," I say, "run that one more time and a bit slower."

He does.

All I catch is a vague "*Mmmm*," "*ur*," and "*thun*."

"Sounds like 'Murthun.'"

He shakes his head but smiles, sort of. It's really awkward on his face. "Human ears are the worst."

"Mind if I call you Marty? You look like a Marty."

"If that is as close as you can get to my name."

"Feels like it probably is and I need to get moving."

"Good. Then I can get that mess cleaned up." He takes a step to the side to move around me.

I step to match him. "Actually . . ."

He sighs, deep in his wide chest, lifting slumped shoulders and letting them fall as the breath rushes out of his wide nose. "You are not going to ask me to help you, are you?"

"I'm trying something new."

"New?"

"Yeah, I just went through a lot of shit and I'm tired of threatening people to get them to do what I need."

Amphibian eyes narrow. "I do not think you want to threaten me."

"I don't. I said that."

"That is not how I meant it."

"I know."

Marty, you don't know what I'm capable of. Keep thinking I am just a harmless human.

"If I refuse will you go away?" he asks.

"No."

"If I do not help you . . ."

"I will get out of here and muck my way through this place."

"That sounds very much like a threat."

"It's not. It's a statement. I am going to find the Man in Black. Whatever it takes. I came all the way across the universe or dimensions or whatever that was to get here."

His eyes widen. "You came from Earth?"

What?

"I'm human; where else would I have come from?"

He waves away my question. "You do not know what this place is like."

"I don't, but I also don't care."

He sighs again. "Let me mop that up and we can get going."

The coat babbles at me.

No, I don't know if this is a good idea, but we'll see.

The noise it makes in reply feels like skepticism.

3

THERE IS A wall in front of us.

I can't really see it, but I *feel* it there, almost like echolocation, as if sonar waves are radiating out of me and bouncing off it and back to me, like a pressure, a resistance. But my eyes tell me that nothing is there, it's all just unchanging whiteness, so pure and unmarred that my eyes begin to try to color it, subtly, surreptitiously, giving light blushes of yellow and blue and gray to the white, but it rolls across my vision like a cataract, a sclera, that I can feel slide across the surface of my eyeballs, and so I know it is my brain trying to trick me into thinking there is more than the unrelieved paleness around me.

This must be what being snowblind feels like.

Not. A. Fan.

I've been nearly turned inside out with magick and whisked through the voids of space and other dimensions, but none of that is as disconcerting as being in this white room (god, I wish there were black curtains).

Marty shuffles around me. He's done mopping up the spoor and is now twisting the mop of tongues in his hands. It folds in on itself, becoming smaller and smaller until it is just a little ball of flappy things that he drops into a pocket of his coveralls.

The skinhound shifts beside me and I notice for the first time that we are the only sound in this space. I've grown so used to how his crescent razor nails click-clack on things that I didn't notice it wasn't happening here.

The only sound is our breathing and the soft rustling of the coat around me. No footsteps, no echoes, just any incidental sound made by us or us interacting with us.

"Ready to depart?" Marty asks.

"Yes. One hundred percent yes."

His chubby hand reaches into another pocket and pulls out a ring of keys. They don't jingle. He carefully selects one and moves past me. He stops where I feel the wall is and extends the key. It disappears into the white.

"Follow me," he says.

Before I can answer he turns his wrist and steps through a suddenly wavering oval. It shimmers like a heat mirage on a desert highway.

I look down at the skinhound, who raises his head to look at me with his one good eye, all egg yolk yellow in its socket. "You ready for this?" I ask.

He chuffs, the noise low in his throat, then up through his noseless snout.

"Yeah, me neither, but here we go."

My hand on Winnie's head, we step up to the wavering spot, and the white room tries to eat me.

4

EVERYTHING BECOMES A pulse of red mist. I can't even blink before something slithers through my belly button and wraps around my spine like eleven icy fingers in a clench. My hips flare with hurt, all the tendons and connective tissue in my pelvis gone brittle. The coat screams in my brain and begins flapping at me, slapping me with stinging hits of itself. It violently jerks and slews me sideways. All is red and black against my eyes, like they've been painted with ink, no, have become ink themselves; the sockets of my skull are now liquid reservoirs, inkwells. I drop to my knee. A grinding noise chews at my ears and I realize it's the skinhound. I reach for him, unable to see anything past the caul of crimson that has taken my sight, and I am yanked forward off my feet by the invader in my body.

The memory of my first time in the ocean roars against me.

Young, I am young, years before that night that changed

me, changed everything. Not the night the Man in Black arrived on my doorstep in a swirl of coat and murder but the first night my life was utterly changed.

My family takes a vacation, driving almost a full day to reach the coast. The hours so long once the exhilaration fades to just monotonous stretches of asphalt and trees and other cars. Bad pop music on the radio, songs from my parents' youth, songs I may have been conceived to. We went straight to the beach. I am a child still but old enough to cross a street without a hand. We park, piling out of the car onto the hot asphalt, skipping quickly over to the hot sand. A hill of sand and tall, swaying grass rise before me, a thin bridge made of gray wood climbing it. The sun broils down on my hair, heating me up and blasting back into my eyes from the sugar-white granules of the dune. Birds caw and cry as they wheel against a pale blue sky that shines like plastic. Even the air is bright in my nostrils and lungs, scrubbing my throat with molecules of water, particles of salt.

We climb that narrow, gray bridge, even my tiny footsteps making it vibrate with importance.

Cresting it puts us on a small deck staring over the beach.

The ocean looks larger than the whole world.

It stretches farther than my eyes can see, going from blue-green and white near the shore to a heavy, leaden gray that rolls on forever. Ships that look like toys move on its surface, and far off in the distance I can see an entire cloud turning a spot of it black with storm. I stop and I drink that ocean in with my eyes.

That is the first time I know magick is a real, living, palpable thing that exists.

My mother takes my hand, leads me down the stairs and across the beach. We leave my father behind as he places our things and go to the water's edge.

Up close the water is warm, and friendly.

Over my feet.

Around my knees.

At my waist I feel it pull, tug, as it sweeps in and out in waves, and I match my breathing to it.

My father calls out.

My mother turns.

My hand slips from hers.

The ocean seizes its chance and drags me with it, pulling me under as I exhale.

I am upside down and I cannot breathe; everything is dark around me, my eyes burning, my lungs burning, my skin burning, as I am ground against the sand on the bottom. The dank verdant taste of the sea fouls my mouth as it forces itself down my throat, seeking to tear me apart with pressure inside my body.

All is dark and fear and pain.

Until all is just dark.

I am yanked back like I was that day, dragged from the dark and the deep. Not by my mother this time. No, not her.

And this time when my vision returns and I can breathe again I'm not on a sandy beach but back in the pure white room I started in.

5

I'M KNEELING AWKWARDLY, off-balance, one leg under me, one splayed out to the side. Marty looks down at me with his wide-set eyes, and his hand clenching the collar of my coat is keeping me from being flat on the floor.

The coat growls in my mind. It does not like that.

Me neither.

We both shake off his grip and rise as he steps back. "You humans."

The sides of my throat stick together, but I swallow hard and make my voice happen. "What about 'us humans'?"

"I forgot how three-dimensional you are."

"We're made that way." When I'm off-balance I get snarky; it's a thing.

"Oh, I am aware; I simply forgot. It has been a long time since I have dealt with your kind." He says "your kind" as if it tastes bad in his mouth.

The skinhound nudges my arm with his head, insistent, pushing himself against me. I go with him and wrap my arm around his neck. He's shaking. So am I.

The coat hums against my body, unfurling from beneath me. Tendrils of it crawl their way up and over and around the vivisected dog, pulling him close. Comfort suffuses me as the skinhound lays his head against my sternum. I hold my skinless dog and we both take comfort in that. My insides still feel like they are twitching, but it's subsiding.

Marty frowns.

"What?" I ask.

"You have to realize where you are."

"In a white room with no curtains near the station?"

He looks down at me and frowns. "I have known you for no time and I can tell you will vex me."

"I can be a pain in the ass. Most of the time, it's not intentional."

"The rest of the time?"

"Absolutely intentional." I pat the skinhound's sides and rise to my feet. He chuffs through his nasal bone and stands as well, moving out of the coat's covering. The coat makes a mournful sound in my skull and tendrils of it trail off the skinhound.

Are you missing him?

The noise the coat makes in my head is easy to translate as: *Shut the fuck up.*

I look to Marty. "Thanks for the rescue."

Marty looks almost pained when he speaks. "You need to forget your concept of reality. It does not apply here."

"Hey, I know enough about this elder god magick stuff to know what's real and what's not."

I mean who does he think he's talking to?

"None of this is *real*!" He shakes his hands in frustration. "Not like you know real. Your reality does not apply here. Your physics do not apply here. Your *rules* do not apply here. All that you see and experience right now is your feeble rodent mind trying to comprehend this dimension. You are off the deep end and you cannot swim."

"You're saying things aren't as they appear?"

"I am saying things are not as you perceive," he says. "This place is nothing like your human existence. You are seeing things and experiencing things, but they are not *real*. They are just your mind trying to understand them and interpret them. If you did not have that Mark and your magick, you would be a gibbering flesh sack with an obliterated mind."

Maybe this is why everything feels off. My brain is on overload.

"Okay," I say, "what's the trick?"

"Trick?"

"The technique, the spell." I snap my fingers. "The mojo." I snap them again. "Whatever word you want to use. How do I tune in to this channel?"

"You stay here in this breech box and meditate until your magick puts you in tune with the disharmonious frequency of here."

"How long will that take?"

"No time." He waves his hand. "Just a few decades."

So now I know that not only is Marty *not* human, but he also is extremely long-lived, if not immortal.

I shake my head. "I don't have time to learn your new perception, so what I have will have to do."

"It will not hold. Right now your perception is a cardboard box you are using to move a Chaugnar Faugn."

"A what?"

He reaches out for me, not to grab me but to touch me, his webbed fingers aiming at my forehead.

I slide back and my hand slips into the coat, which lifts its lapel for me. My fingers close on the hard stock of the magick shotgun inside.

Me and the skinhound growl at the same time.

Marty stops. "I mean you no harm. I was merely going to show you what a Chaugnar Faugn is so you have reference."

I shake my head, "Try again, pal."

"A . . ." His fingers stroke the air in front of him and I can feel him literally pulling the word to him. It's like spiderwebs are attached from my face to his fingers and they so lightly, so slightly, tug like filament-thin silk threads attached to my skin. "An elephant." He nods, agreeing with himself that the word is what he wants. "Your perception is a cardboard box you are using to move an elephant."

I shrug. I don't have a choice. "It works for now."

"Soon—"

I raise my hand, cutting him off.

"I don't have time. Take me to Azathoth."

I will deal with my perception when the elephant hits the floor.

"I will not be taking you to Azathoth." He shakes his head.

"Then get out of my way; I will find it myself."

"Did you not learn anything just now? You cannot wander around this place. You will be destroyed."

"Then what should I do?" I spread my hands but keep my Mark pointed down, not threatening. "Just hang out here in this place? Doesn't look very fun."

"Go back the way you came."

I shake my head. "Not an option."

I don't have anywhere near the magick left to wish myself back. I'm not spent but I'm low, and to get here took all I could spare and all I could drain from the soul gem of the King in Yellow. He was a bastard, and I am not, *not*, going to feel bad for killing him and taking his power.

But I don't have enough to get back.

Marty shrugs. "Seems like a quandary."

This guy.

"Marty, I have to do this. I want your help, but if you won't then I will go it alone."

"You will die. Or worse."

"What are you, a cheap novel?"

"I am a keeper."

"Not if you can't help me you aren't."

"What are you talking about?"

I shake my head. I feel my hair brush my ears and brow. It's getting long. "I'm just letting my frustration get the best of me. It makes me a smartass."

"You are the most frustrated woman in the world then."

"You have no idea, Marty," I say. "No idea at all."

He just looks at me, as if he doesn't know what to say.

The coat rustles and babbles along the back of my brain.

"So," I say. "Azathoth?"

He sighs, pulls out the keys again, and says, "Follow me. And stay close this time."

6

THE HALLWAY WE are in is strange.

Like really strange.

Marty opened the door and the skinhound and I stepped right in after him. No shifting away this time.

The hallway is vaguely tubular; is "tubular" a word? I know there's the theme song to *The Exorcist*, "Tubular Bells." (Dad did love that record, yes, record, not a CD but the actual record he had from years before I was ever born. He used to play it, over and over again, especially at Halloween . . . and now it's in my head, rattling around; the creepy theme song to a terrifying movie when I was exposed to it far too young is crawling its way through my mind as I walk through a creepy tunnel in elder god prison on the other side of the universe.) So I guess "tubular" is a word; it just sounds off the way words sometimes can, like they are made up.

The floor and the walls and the ceiling all have a curvature to them. It's uneven, slightly rolling up and down as we walk. There's a spring in my step; the floor has a firm sponginess under my boots. I look down and see the coat has drawn its hem up to the middle of my shins. Normally it drags its tattered edge along whatever I walk across, almost as if it enjoys the sensation. The coat is alive. It talks in my head—well, "talks" is not the right word; it makes noise and gives impressions in my brain. I feel it there as much as I hear it there. The singsong babbling it does feels like a language, just not one made with a mouth, a throat, and a tongue.

It's singing something along with the *Exorcist* theme in my brain.

Stop it.

The song trails off.

Thanks.

The coat peeps in my brain.

The floor shifts under me. It's slight, barely felt, but I'm not imagining it.

Moves, spongy, damp . . . "Marty?" I say.

He stops and turns slightly, just enough that he can look over his shoulder at me, which, to be honest, seems harder to do than it should be due to the squat nature of his neck, but also easier than it should be due to the width of his face.

Did that make as much sense out loud as it did in my head?

He waits, expectant.

"Are we in something's throat or intestine or something?"

He looks at me sideways, wide eyebrows creased together over his near-flat nose. "No, why do you ask?"

Well, that's comforting.

"No reason."

Because I can absolutely imagine a space prison for elder gods made from a big, bloated dead thing.

I consider what Marty said earlier about my perception not being reality. Did I make this look the way it does because I have imagined being in the corpse of some gigantic galactic monstrosity, some celestial or titan or even some enormous star whale cruising around the edge of the universe on autopilot?

Maybe I read too much science fiction.

"Anything else?" he asks.

I shake my head. He turns back and lifts his foot.

"Marty?"

He sighs and puts his foot back down.

"Where is the light coming from?"

"Light?"

"Yeah, the light," I say. "It's ambient, but I don't see a source."

The light around us is dim, but it's there. I can just see a short distance; around any curve in this hallway in front or in back of us the light falls off into darkness, and nearby things aren't high-definition, but I can see, nonetheless.

Marty shrugs. "This is how it always looks in this part."

"You never wonder why?"

"If I wondered about everything there was to wonder about in this place I would never get anything done. Now, do you mind if we keep walking?"

I wave him on.

I don't like this place. Not the way the light falls off in front of and behind me as if we are being guided and stalked by darkness. My senses are wide open and screaming. The skinhound touches my leg, pressing his vivisected body against me. The coat caresses it and I look down. He is looking back, on guard with his one eye, trusting me if anything happens on the front end.

As we walk, we pass doors of various kinds. They are incongruous, don't make any sense, and have no real pattern.

One is a simple wooden door with a dead bolt. It looks a lot like the door to the town home I live in. Did live in. I have no idea if I live there anymore. I called my roommates weeks ago and told

Shasta to just use my debit card to cover my part of the rent if I didn't get back from my "unexpected internship in New York" that I told her I was going on. I have enough money in the bank to cover a month's rent and bills; the best thing about living with a handful of people is how cheap that is. I've been using my account to eat and sleep in hotels when I need to. It's not often anymore. As long as my magick stays at a relatively stable level then I don't get tired or hungry. It happens, but not regularly like it did before. I spent weeks looking for the Man in Black after he put Daniel in the hospital, tracking any trace of him, and if I hadn't just had to kill some supernatural thing to find out the clue then I'd have been good to go, just surviving on magick.

My cell is in the coat's pocket. I'd have been reach in and brush it with my fingertips. I don't pull it out. I'm sure my plan's coverage doesn't reach to this place.

I will call once I'm done with all this shit.

I take my hand out of the coat.

The next door we come to is solid, thick metal that looks like brass but has a bluish tinge to it instead of the dirty butter color of brass. The lock on it is a flat beam of metal laid across two angled brackets that puncture the wall beside the door like staples. There is a symbol written on it in what looks like chalk. It's a series of hatch marks that overlap into a secondary pattern that makes my eyes want to roam over them. Doing this for even a few seconds makes my optic nerve itch far back behind my eyeball, far farther back than I could ever scratch.

Unless.

I could pry my finger in from the outside, over the lid and under the globe of the eyeball itself. I could skim around the sclera, digging, digging, digging, through the socket, over the fascial sheath all tough and sleek until I reach the nerve, which I could then rake with my ragged nail, letting the hard keratin scrape, scrape, scrape, the itch out of it.

My finger is skimming, halfway up my cheekbone, before I stop it.

We keep walking.

Down the spongy hallway we come to an opening.

It isn't very wide. I would have to turn sideways to fit through it.

It doesn't have a door.

A red lightbulb hangs on the lintel, bathing the opening in crimson light.

"Marty."

He stops.

"Where's this go to?"

"Go to?" he asks.

"It doesn't have a door."

"Yes, it does."

"No, it just has this light."

He tilts his head. "Like I said."

"The light is the door?"

He nods.

"Can I see what is inside?"

"They are your eyes, not mine; how would I know?"

"I'm supposed to be the smartass here."

"I am not arguing against that."

I turn toward the red light, dismissing the conversation. I want to see what's in this cell. Like just what kinds of things are kept here? I try to not be curious about things, but sometimes it just happens.

My right hand curls in on itself and I scrape my Mark with my fingernails. It tingles and the magick inside me stirs, slithering through me. I let my eyes slip out of focus, preparing to See.

The coat tightens around me.

"I agree," Marty says. "That would be a bad idea."

"I was just going to take a peek."

"No, you were going to open your third eye."

"Is that what I do when I See?"

He nods. "Do you remember our conversation about the . . . elephant in the cardboard box?"

"Yeah."

"You see the elephant and your cardboard box will disintegrate."

My magick hums in my head, not my brain, but in the bones of my skull, specifically the fine bones of my face just under my eyes.

My Sight is all-or-nothing. If I let my magick kick in and open my . . . *third eye . . . Jesus, what the hell am I doing . . .* then I would see everything as it is, not how I have been perceiving it. All glamour and artifice and illusion stripped bare by my magick.

It might be too much for my human mind.

"It would be," Marty says.

"Don't read my mind."

"You said that out loud."

Am I talking when I think I am thinking?

Is this what going mad is? Do you feel it when your mind slips into madness?

"Usually," he says. "It is, by all accounts, fairly terrible."

"Am I speaking thoughts out loud?"

He nods. "Do not worry; it is less a sign of madness and more a sign of having companions you speak to who cannot respond."

The skinhound chuffs, wet and sticky in his muzzle, at the same time the coat spills out a stream of protestation.

Marty looks at the skinhound and my chest, not at my breasts but at the coat. "You both know it is not the same; do not comport it to be so." His wide seal eyes flick up to my face. "From what I have observed, madness from the Outer Gods is sudden, as if your mind has been snapped like a bit of cold rubber stretched too far, a clean break from sanity, where you know you are out of sync with reality, but you cannot fathom why. Madness from the elder gods, on the other hand, is—"

"Wait," I interrupt. "There's elder gods *and* Outer Gods?"

"And Great Old Ones. And all manner of things, beings, and assorted creatures."

"What's the difference?"

He takes a deep breath.

"Wait." I don't want to stand here for whatever explanation that much inhale requires. "Let me rephrase. To a human like me is there any real difference between an elder god, an Outer God, or a Great Old One?"

"A human worshiper?"

"I ain't worshiping shit, Marty."

"Then no, there is no discernible difference to you. You are the blade of grass; they are the inferno."

Very comforting.

"So, which of them is behind this red light?"

He peers at the red light for a long moment. "That is just a Star Vampire, a baby Shambler from the Stars." He chuckles. "Not pleasant, but nothing close to any of the gods."

I want to see this. I don't know why, but the urge to look upon this thing is intensified by Marty's dismissal.

Besides, a Star Vampire? Images of Bowie in full glam getup are invoked with those words.

I know how to do this.

The coat feels slightly oily under my fingertips as I pull on the lapels, bringing the collar up over my head. As I pull, it understands what I want and the material of it surges forward to first become a hood, then continues on to form a cowl over my face. It moves up over my head without pulling or tugging on any part of the coat that hangs from my body. It morphs as it moves and I feel no change. Even as it forms to the shape I have in my mind, it feels like the lightest cotton, but I know it's not. It's the flayed skin of an archangel, cut off its original host by the Man in Black at some point. The outside feels mostly like thin leather; the inside feels like outer space, a dark void with no weight but still a presence. It has covered my head and face when I use the torc around my neck to teleport, but I've never paid attention to how it feels, too distracted by the teleporting and the magicking.

I am in complete darkness.

Okay.

The pitch black opens in twin pinpricks in front of my eyes, slowly widening like the aperture on a camera, allowing more vision. When I can see clearly but with a limited field of vision I nudge the coat to stop.

I can see the red light and the opening, but everything else is cut off.

My eyes slip out of focus and the magick in my face bones crawls forward. The red light leeches away, revealing the thing in the cell.

This is not Bowie.

The thing in the cell, the . . . Star Vampire, is a throbbing mass, placental in nature, spongy and malformed. The front of it is covered in pulpy tubes that wave; they are narrow where they connect to the body of this thing and widen at their mouths, which suckle at nothing as they sway back and forth as if this thing were underwater. The top of it hunches forward and there is a conglomeration of sacs, none of them matching in size or shape other than being roughly oval and all of them of a thick, veinous skin swollen smooth with whatever foulness they hold. At the top and bottom of the body of the Star Vampire are long, spindly arms that curve and end in scaly raptor-clawed digits. As I look at them all I can see is how they are designed to latch on to something and pull it against the mouthing tubes. It hangs there and I *feel* it watching me, urging me silently to step into the red light, to part the door of its confinement and allow it to feed on me. I can save it from the gnawing starvation it always feels if only I take two steps forward.

Not today, pal.

I step back and blink away the magick, letting it slid back down inside me, clearing my vision back to normal.

Okay, we're done now, I think to the coat.

The cowl the coat has formed falls away and I am back to seeing the red light and the opening. Residual traces of magick leave the Star Vampire a ghost image in the light, a mere tracery of what I saw.

I shrug. "That wasn't as bad as I thought it would be."

"I find them to be lovely," Marty says.

"I wouldn't go that far."

"Some find dangerous things appealing."

I consider that. It's true. The most poisonous plants in the world oftentimes are the prettiest. Poison dart frogs are adorable.

The Man in Black, in his human guise, is handsome at a certain angle and in a certain light.

And I've seen his true form, which is grotesque and horrific.

Damn, I have to stop letting this place distract me. The Man in Black. That's why I'm here.

"Let's go," I say.

Marty turns back to walking in the lead.

The skinhound nudges my leg and we follow. The coat keeps furling and unfurling on my right side, just curling up and lapping back down.

Stroking the side of the skinhound.

Looking down, I watch the dark tendrils of its ragged edge as they slip over the gristle and muscle and subcutaneous membrane of the skinhound. Winnie's whipcord tail of vertebrae bones swishes back and forth, cutting the air like a razor-whip in the hands of an epileptic sadist.

I feel the hitch when the coat realizes I am watching what it's doing.

The tendrils pause mid-stroke and flutter in the current of our passing.

Go on, if it makes you feel better. He likes it.

The coat rubs the back of my neck and gives a little trill and goes back to petting the skinhound.

I'm so distracted I don't see the puddle in the middle of the hallway until I fall hip deep in it.

7

THERE'S THIS THING about falling down.

You don't realize you're doing it until you hit the ground.

One second I am looking down at the coat caressing the skinhound, then I notice the ground is wet, glistening wet, and then . . .

I'm hip deep in water with one leg, the other splayed out behind me on the ground I was walking on in an awkward split.

I manage to catch myself with my hands, but not before my chin cracks against the ground. My teeth click together and pain shoots from the joint of my jaw all the way around the back of my skull in a white wrap of disorienting hurt.

The water I'm sunk in is cold, ice cold, so cold my muscles cramp immediately, locking into long knots of agony, and a hatchet-sharp ache settles into my knee joint. The skin under my pants tingles, then stings, then becomes a million pinpricks of pain all between having my breath slammed out of me and sucking it back in. The coat flaps around me like bat wings. It lifts me up and down, making the water around my pelvis splash up my back.

"Stop!" I yell.

The coat freezes, hovering above me and around me, and I *feel* it's unsure what to do.

Marty stands above me. "Be very, very careful."

The skinhound whines, jerking to and fro in a hitching, worried pace around me.

Before I can ask Marty what he means I feel it.

Something slithers up the inside of my calf and, even with my nerve endings overloaded from the cold, I feel the ridges of hard-rimmed suckers as this thing curls around. They bite into my thigh and my ankle, flexing and gripping. It constricts with pressure, so much pressure it feels like my leg will burst, just pop like a balloon in the hands of an angry, terrible child at the worst birthday party in the world.

Then it begins to *pull*.

It feels as if my hip will come apart at the joint. The ball will unseat from its socket and the tendons will rupture and the muscles will rip until my leg will tear free and be pulled down into this puddle, to disappear and be gone.

I will not fit into this puddle. I am too big and my other leg, which is splayed out behind me, bangs against the edge of the puddle and I feel the bruise forming on the inside crease of my thigh like a secondary thought. My mind is blank, empty with panic, and I don't know what to do.

I push with my arms, trying to pull myself out of the hole. Whatever has a hold of me shakes me like a toy in a terrier's mouth. I roll my eyes up at Marty and he just stands there looking down at me.

He's not going to help he's not going to help he's not going to help, rolls through my mind on a loop.

Then help yourself.

The pressure on my leg intensifies, getting worse. It feels like my bones will snap any second.

I have to do something! Think!

I lift my hand to my mouth and lick the Mark there.

As my tongue passes over the raised scar tissue, the whorls and swirls of the symbol that was carved into my palm, the magick sparks to life stronger than even before and I hear the Man in Black's words about my Mark and bodily fluids. *When you need your magick, it can be activated by touching your Mark with any bodily fluid. Blood is the strongest, followed by sexual issue, but any secretion will spark it to life.*

The Mark glows magenta and the magick wants to run down my arm, but I hold it, stop it, and keep it in my fist. Whatever has me in the puddle pulls to the side and I lean with it, pushing *hard* to make a space, just a narrow opening around me. There is a space large enough to slip my hand into the water.

The pressure on my spine is intense and my hip screams pain at me. I push it all away, ignore as much as I can, and reach into the water. My fingers scrabble along my leg until I touch the end of what feels like a hard rubber tongue that has lashed around my leg. I dig, my fingers already going numb from the cold, and I try to find a way to grip the thing, but it is too slick and too hard and my hand just slipslides over it.

So I dig ragged nails into it as much as I can and I let the magick fly.

I feel the primal energy leave my hand in a raw tearing-out from my Mark. As it passes from me to the thing, I know, I feel, I sense, the enormity of the creature ahold of me and the fact, the undeniable truth, that my magick is *nothing* compared to it.

I could not hurt this thing any real way.

Not if I were trying to hurt the whole thing.

I'm just trying to get loose and so I dump my magick as fast and as hard as I can into the thing that holds my leg captive. I make it *hot*, I make it *sharp*, and I make it *hurt* like a *motherfucker*.

The thing lets me go so fast I don't even feel it, not for a second. My leg is nothing but a dead pain. I bob up just a bit and realize I'm free, but only if I can get out of this hole, because that thing will be coming back and it will be coming back mad as hell. I think about the help I need as I push off the ground, pull myself out, and the coat flaps down and pushes me free in one long *squelch*. I lie on the ground, a quarter of my body soaking wet.

A long tentacle thing slithers up from the water, seeking me. The suckers on its soft pink underside pulse with anger or hunger.

Hangry.

Winnie lunges forward, sinking teeth deep in the tip of it.

The tentacle jerks away and slips back into the salty water.

I sit up, my leg aching as it warms.

It's not the only thing heated.

"What the fuck, Marty?" I don't attempt to keep the anger out of my voice. "What the fuck was that?"

I'm up and on my feet. My leg hurts, but it's all the way on the other end of my body, almost dissociated from the rest of me by my spitting rage at Marty's nonanswer. My right hand crackles, the magick in my Mark hard and crystallized.

Marty looks at me, not blinking. "Why did you come here if you are just going to try to go back to your planet?"

"What the hell does that even mean?"

He motions to the puddle with a spade-shaped hand. "The pathway back to R'lyeh is right there. Did you not try to fit inside it?"

"You didn't warn me. I didn't see the damn puddle."

"I stepped around it. Are you saying you *fell* in?"

My rage has switched to embarrassment. Still hot along my cheeks and the back of my neck, but now I feel sheepish, curled inward. I nod to answer his question and ask, "Where does that go again?"

"R'lyeh."

"Why is that familiar?"

"You have never been?" The tone of his voice lilts. "It is on your Earth." The statement sounds like you would say it about Disneyland instead of a dead city under the sea.

"How is it there *and* here?"

He sighs, "It is not here. It is on your planet. That is just the doorway to it."

"Where is it on Earth?"

"It is anchored at 48 degrees 52 minutes 36 seconds South by 123 degrees 23 minutes 36 seconds West, but it fluctuates on a cycle of sinusoidal frequency that moves it from 47 degrees 9 seconds South by 126 degrees 43 seconds West to 49 degrees 51 seconds South by 128 degrees 34 seconds West."

"I don't know what that means." I feel like I say that a lot. Damn dealing with alien otherworldly creatures.

"'Fluctuates' means 'to vary between'—"

I put my hand up. Marty stops talking.

"That's not the important part," I say. "Let's go back to why I would know what a R'lyeh is."

"You do not act as if you know what it is."

"Marty, I swear I am trying to be patient here."

Ph'nglui mglw'nafh Cthulhu R'lyeh wgah'nagl fhtagn," his voice intones like a bell in the steeple of a desecrated church. The notes and sounds he speaks come from the back of his thick throat and undulate, rubbing against one another like lewd dancers covered in sweet summer sweat.

Before I can ask what his words mean they spark something in my magick and the words become more than words; they turn into snatches of memory, things I cannot know. They slam into me with physical force, causing me to stumble as they drop into my mind like iron plates thrown into a well. They roll into one another in a fluid blending even though I can taste how they are all separate and unique.

The pull of non-Euclidean geometry on my eyeball, tugging the corners of my round sight orb down and up, forward and back, into the fifth orthoplex until my vision is a cubed tangle of nonpartisan physics. The puckering feel of salt water along the marrow of my bones. The slip of green algae over my ovipositor as I hug the wall of the vault hoping, praying to anyone but him, that Dread Cthulhu won't crack an eye and see me there next to him in the sodden corpse city he dreams in.

The memories solidify from sensation and thought into words that scream neon bright across the synapse of my brain.

In his house in R'lyeh, Dread Cthulhu waits dreaming.

Whoa.

My eyes are burning and as I blink it away I find tears spilling down my cheeks. The skinhound sits in front of me. A short, thin whine leaks from between bone-cracking teeth as he looks up at me, head tilted, using his one good eye. The coat rustles around me, anxious because of my reaction.

"I'm okay." I don't know if I am saying it to Winnie, the coat, or myself. Probably a combination of the three.

Cthulhu.

I met him in a jar in a cave under a restaurant in a city that might have or might not have been New York. I carried his soul gem in my coat for a while.

I traded that soul gem to the Man in Black for Daniel's life. He is going to use it, along with the other two he's gathered, to free his father, the Mad God Azathoth.

I look back at the puddle. Somewhere on the other end of that pool of salt water was the real Cthulhu, the whole elder god, sleeping in his prison under the sea. What I had experienced were avatars, representations, of him. They were the real deal but *not* the real deal at the same time. If—no, *when*—I stop the Man in Black I will bring Cthulhu's soul gem back here and drop it down to him. He has always been nice to me. And he has kind eyes.

"Now that you almost fell all the way to R'lyeh do you understand that this is a dangerous place full of dangerous things?" Marty asks.

I nod.

The coat trills in my skull and I feel it shift. Something hard under it bumps against my chest and I know it's the pistol grip on the shotgun stored inside the coat's inter-dimensional folds. It spits gouts of hellfire.

I nod at the reminder from the coat, but maybe Marty thinks it is in response to his words.

I am one of the dangerous things in this prison.

And I have a job to do.

"Let's walk."

8

We walk.

And we keep walking.

And it sucks because my leg feels like wood except for the hard, aching line of bruise in the crease of my thigh meeting my pelvis. My lower back pinches with each step and on top of all that my pants are soaked and chafing.

It takes a lot of concentration to ignore it all and put one foot in front of the other.

The hallway stays pretty much the same throughout. We pass more doors and door-esque things. Rarely are they repeated. Some are familiar, the things I see every day. One a glass door with a small girl pressed against it as if she were watching her parents drive away and leave her as they head to the most magical place on Earth.

But she has no face.

Just a gaping maw under a shock of blond curls tied back with a blue satin ribbon. Brow to chin is a mouth all pink and glistening, spittle hanging from the cracked points of jutting rows of canines, gums swollen around the roots of carnassial teeth as if her last meal left behind residue that has gone to rot and left the gums painful, swollen, and inflamed. Her tongue hangs, lying behind and off to the side of the fangful canines, lolling over the crushing points of the molars. Her throat is a raw red hole that shunts down her neck and into her tiny, prepubescent body in its apron-festooned blue dress.

My mind rolls back to the nurse-like guardians of the cancer god with their flip-top heads full of swirling, grinding molars, and I wonder if they and this are somehow related. Like if they had a family reunion would they see each other there over the fried chicken and noodle salad?

Just a wee, ittle-bittle Alice in Murderland. Move along, folks, nothing to see here.

I see a minuscule gilded cage set into the wall, its bars simple thin golden wires, delicate as spun sugar, that holds a smudge, an amorphous impression of something I can't see behind those bars; it isn't a color or a shape or even a shadow. No shimmer, nothing. But it's there. I perceive it with that sixth sense, the dangling participator from a time when large things with sharp teeth hunted us for food.

This one Marty takes out his ring of keys for. He holds them in front of his face, studying them before flicking through a few dozen keys of various shapes and sizes, selecting one that looks like a fleck of gold dust. He very carefully inserts the end into a minuscule lock and gingerly twists it left, then right. Satisfied it is indeed locked, he drops the keys back to his belt.

"Why check that one?"

"You ask many questions."

"I do," I say. "But why that one in particular? Surely a small bit

of nothing isn't as dangerous as the fang-faced homi-child-al maniac you have back there."

"You should know that things that are small and delicate are
not necessarily safe." He rubs his jowls, looking at me. "You, for
instance, are not very big."

Marty is wider than me, broader in every aspect, but we stand
eye to eye.

"You aren't either."

He tilts his head in assent. "This body is a fruiting body."

"I don't know what that means."

"I serve Satet. I am hers."

"Who is Satet?"

"You shall see soon."

"Well, that's not ominous or anything." I put my hand out.
"Where are you taking me, Marty?"

"To see Satet."

"You say that as if I am just supposed to accept it."

"You do not have a choice."

"Oh, I *always* have a choice, Marty." My voice is deep and rough,
textured with threat.

"Do you not want to kill Nyarlathotep?"

"I want to stop him."

The ridges over his teardrop-shaped eyes crease in the center of
his wide forehead. "That is not the answer I expected."

I shrug. It's not the answer I expected to give and it makes my
brain whirl around on itself like an animal chasing its own tail. I
have to stop the Man in Black; all the existence of my whole world
depends on it. I have done too much, gone through too much, to
not stop him.

But kill him? I will. I have threatened it many times. I am capable of it, if I am capable of it. I have the will, but my means may
fall short.

This may all be for nothing.

And my knees nearly buckle under the weight of that thought, that I may be inadequate to save my world. Why should I be able to? Me. Charlotte Tristan Moore, nobody from nowhere.

Marty studies me. "Have you lost your heart?"

I don't know how to answer that.

So I don't.

"You said the very reason you came here was to stop the Crawling Chaos from setting free the Maelstrom of Unsanity."

"It is."

"You feel very unsure now."

How do I answer that?

The skinhound growls and the coat tightens around me. The skinhound steps forward, growling deep in his chest; the muscles along his spine are bunched, hackles raised, whipcord tail pulled tight along his haunches.

His skull is lowered and he stares past Marty with his one eye.

The darkness down the corridor *moves*.

A spot of color. Scarlet on velvet.

The wet, crimson gleam of a red right hand.

9

I AM MOVING faster than I should be able to.

Magick rushes like boiling acid through my veins and arteries and the coat whips around me and I leave a streak of etheric energy trailing from the Mark on my hand as magick leaks from it. The magick has disintegrated the pain that has been in my leg since the puddle. The skinhound gallops beside me and I shouldn't be able to keep up with him, but I do, two long strides to every leaping lunge he makes. He moves like a cheetah, forelegs and hind moving like the parts of an efficient machine to drive him forward.

We chase our prey.

Running headlong and without hesitation.

I can see him, just ahead of us, a flicker against the dark.

Nyarlathotep.

The Crawling Chaos.

Dreamwalker.

Nightstalker.

The ever-loving, motherfucking Man in Black.

My heart pounds in my chest, beating, beating, bea-ting, beat-ingbeating*beating* against the inside of my rib cage, and my feet are pounding, pounding, poun-ding, poundingpounding*pounding* against the floor of the corridor. The air over my tongue has the ozone crackle of an adrenaline spike and it burns frost-crystal cold as I drag it into my lungs.

I'm closer than I was, but he is still too far ahead, just around the bend, almost out of sight.

A roar of effort tears out of me as I reach down and dig deep into the magick that lives inside me. I shove it from running *through* my body to being *in* my body and I surge forward, legs moving in a blur. I leave the skinhound behind as I draw close to him, to the Man in Black. I see him clearly now, even through the pulsing in my temples and brow. He pelts down the corridor, not looking back, not turning to see me after him.

He's tall and he is thin, slender form wrapped in a well-fitting suit the color of space between two burnt-out suns. His white cuffs and collar flash as he moves, red right hand swinging in time with his impossibly long stride, leaving a crimson smear along the air he cuts through.

The hallway juts left sharply and he disappears around the corner.

I skid as I reach it, trying to change direction without the loss of any speed. My feet slip on the weird floor and go out from under me. I drop into a crouch to keep from sprawling along the floor, my left hand slapping hard where my face should have hit.

I hold myself up and the coat gathers underneath me, helping me push my way upright. I'm only down for a split second before springing back to my feet.

The Man in Black is there.

He stands in front of a door that looks to be made of some kind of semiprecious material that has been sliced into a translucent sheet that forms a hatch. It swirls behind him, amber browns mixing into honey and saffron with crackles of black, like burnt honeycomb running throughout.

He stands, arms open as if we would ever hug.

"Charlotte Tristan Moore." His voice drips off his lips, each word poisoned syrup. "I should have known you, of all the things in the universe, would have some way of following me."

I stand there, suddenly unsure of what to do. He isn't threatening me, isn't trying to hurt me, just holding his hands out, palms up and extended.

"Cat got your tongue?" he purrs. "Lucky cat."

And like that I am cold and clammy *under* my skin.

"I'm here to stop you."

"I am stopped." He smiles and his mouth is full of shark teeth, triple rowed and jagged with shallow roots. Teeth that will rend and tear and cut but will also embed and stick and stay. "Are you not satisfied?"

"Not until you're stopped. *Or dead.*"

He tsks and it is a wet rasp that I feel along the side of my neck like damp fur dragged over my skin even though nearly ten feet separate us. "Can you truly kill that which cannot die?"

"Ask Hastur; he will tell you," I say. "Oh wait, he won't, because he's missing his head."

"You act as if the news of his passing should upset me."

"I know better than to think you give a shit at all about anyone but yourself."

"I care about you, former Acolyte of Mine."

"Bullshit."

"I do have feelings." His voice takes on that drippy saccharine mock hurt as that damned red right hand lies across his narrow chest. "In this form anyway."

Wait.

Is he closer?

The space between us seems smaller. He appears to be the same distance from the amber door, but it *feels* as if the ground has shifted, moving him closer.

Or me closer to him.

Does he have power over this place?

The thought is a bath in ice water. I know the Man in Black is powerful; he's so tremendously powerful I should fold in on myself so that I never draw his attention to me, but he fucked that up when he showed up on my doorstep.

But I also know, because of my connection to him, even though I broke his hold, that I can hurt him. When I turned on him I jammed a magickal knife into his side. I know that wound has not healed; it may never close. He still suffers from it. I wounded him, so he can be wounded. He can be hurt. For all his power, I may be one of the few things in the universe that can kill him

That's why I'm here.

On the other side of that very universe from my home.

So I can fight him, but if he can manipulate the very environment around me . . .

Shit just got real.

"As a matter of fact I still have many *feelings* toward you, Charlotte Tristan Moore."

He's closer. Not much farther than the length of his arm.

I step back.

He lifts his red right hand and wags a skinless finger at me. "Do not run, not from me, little girl, for I shall catch you."

The words leave his shark-toothed mouth and roll over me, low and dark and seductive, all hurtful delicious promise and sticky-sweet threat, and that thing inside me, that thing I built and made and crafted and *willed* into being through many long, *hard* years of therapy and work, kicks to life and I think, *Little girl?*

The hellfire shotgun fills my hands before I even realize the coat has put it there as I shake off the Man in Black's influence, which slipped in like a scalpel, so sharp I didn't even feel the cut. The shotgun crackles under the Mark on my palm as my magick channels down into it, charging a load with a buzzing in my molars that makes my ears itch.

"I've got your *little girl* right fucking here, you red-handed son of a bitch."

I squeeze the trigger.

A gout of blue balefire belches out of the barrel and two things happen simultaneously.

The skinhound finally catches up with me from my chase, skidding around the corner with the *click-click-click* of razored crescent claws.

And the Man in Black *moves*.

The balefire slams into the amber cell door and runs like water splashed against a sheet of glass, sizzling rivulets of flame dripping onto the cobblestone floor and extinguishing in a hundred small wisps of curling black smoke as if someone blew out a hundred struck match heads.

Nyarlathotep does a quick two-step turn, his suit coat flaring at his narrow hips, and grabs the edge of the door. In a blink, he pulls it open and slips behind it, disappearing inside the cell.

He's getting away.

"No!" Marty yells from behind me, the sound pulling out of his wide throat all sticky and wet like a swamp tree being uprooted.

I lunge as the amber door begins to shut. I hear Marty's voice again, but it's just noise that gets swallowed up as the edge of the door slams shut on my fingertips and pain, sharp and blazing, jolts through my arm across my shoulder and up into my neck. It's so intense it chases the magick that was in my Mark up and out and down into my belly with a splash.

I pull, hard, using all the strength in one arm since I'm still holding the shotgun in the other. The door is open still, crushing against my fingers, but it's not budging.

"Shut that!"

From the corner of my eye, narrowed and blurry from the strain of exertion against this door, I see Marty move toward me, chubby hands out, and I know in the back of my brain he is about to try to pull me away from here to let the door close.

Before I can lash out with the shotgun like a club the skinhound is between us, hackles raised and a threatening growl rolling out of his vivisected chest.

Marty stops moving forward.

I plant my boot on the wall next to the door and thought-whisper, *Help me, dammit.*

The coat sings out and unfurls down my body to splay against the wall in ribbons of inky black. The sleeve over my arm goes liquid, tendrils of it spiraling around my wrist and over my hand.

Pull.

The muscles in my back tighten under the pressure as I push with my leg and pull with my arm, using all my torso in a chain to get some leverage. The coat draws tight around me, adding its strength to mine, bracing my musculature so that I can exert all of my physical strength without my tendons unanchoring and tearing muscle from bone.

The door slips open, just an inch.

One.

Scant.

Inch.

It's enough to shove my hand inside.

I boil the magick inside me back down and jet it from the Mark in my palm, the etheric energy singing from the raised lines and whorls of scar there, like a forceful stream of water.

The door creaks open just a bit more.

And then it gives, flinging open.

I have one moment to hang suspended in the air with nothing to hold on to before I feel the pull, inexorable as a whirlpool. I am sucked into the open prison cell.

10

I'M TUMBLING, ROLLING, elbows and knees *whack-a-thack-thacking* along a hard surface I assume is some kind of ground. It feels down, as down as anything can feel when you're flipping around like a toy thrown by a tempestuous child. Each time a part of me strikes the surface it's a bright flare of pain that flashes bright and immediately dulls to a mushy bone-bruise ache that I know will hurt for a long time.

I come to a stop on my side.

Goddamn, that hurts.

Blossoms of pain in all my joints and protuberances. The aching agony of my leg comes roaring back now that I'm not dumping magick into it.

The Man in Black is out here, somewhere. I can't just lie here till the hurt stops. Get up. I have to get up.

I open my eyes to a dim grayness; the air is thick as paint and breathes into my lungs about as easily. Pushing off the ground, I stand, turning as I do, looking for the Man in Black. He might have kept going; he's on the run, on a mission, trying to keep me from catching him. He also has things to do. He has three of his fellow gods' soul gems, enough to break his father out of jail. I don't know if soul gems expire or go bad; he could be on crunch time.

I'm not in a room.

I'm in a rocky field; under my feet and stretching out from where I stand are wide pieces of dark slate, rippled with fracture lines and murky, stringy strips of discoloration. It's like I imagine a stone beach in Maine would look, but flat and not against the ocean.

I've never been to Maine, so it probably doesn't look anything like this. Maybe it looks more like the ground after a volcano erupts and the lava cools into black volcanic glass.

But not like that.

Rock with no water and just the chalky, gritty trace.

This place is bare and barren, exfoliated, stripped of anything soft and gentle. The rock is scored with hatch marks, thin to thick grooves dug into the stone's surface. They variate, some short, some longer, and always in tandem. The in and out of it plays tricks with my depth perception in the weird gray light, making the surface appear to ripple, to undulate, and I want to steady myself as if I am on a boat in the middle of a large ocean . . .

Back to work. Where is the Man in Black?

I find him talking to a cloud that looks like ink dropped in a glass of water, all swirling tendrils and wisps that swing and sway drunkenly back and forth.

I see him, too far away to make out clearly. If it weren't for his red hand that he waves as he talks, I wouldn't have spotted him in his ebon suit, raven-wing hair, and light-eating skin.

My legs feel like wood as I take my first step toward him.

He extends that skinless scarlet appendage toward me.

The cloud turns.

My brain clenches at the concept of something without a face turning, but it's not the physicality of it; there is no change in the appearance of the inky cloud, but its intent is now focused on me.

It swells as it comes closer and my ears fill with a clickety, chattering sound.

As it expands I see the Man in Black give me a shark-toothed smile and a two-finger salute with his red right hand before disappearing out of sight.

The cloud is coming toward me. Expanding as it does, a storm over the plains, moving inexorably and unstoppable, all destruction and devastation.

The locust chattering is loud and getting louder.

The coat pulls against me, tugging and jerking, babbling in my brain, the pitch of its voice growing sharper the closer the cloud comes. The collar flares up, brushing my cheeks.

I lift the shotgun that is still in my hand and send as much magick down into it as I can. My head swirls. I've been pulling magick like crazy and I feel the gnawing emptiness of being depleted. I am running low.

The slate under my feet vibrates, the primordial, elemental immenseness of the thing coming toward me radiating against my body like a pressurized front. I don't know what I can do against something so big, so amorphous, so overwhelming, and it rolls over me just how tiny I am, not much over five feet tall and standing before this thing. The rabbit impulse fills my brain and I want to run and hide and burrow and tuck myself deep underground to save my hide.

But I am *not* prey. Not anymore.

It doesn't matter how I feel. It matters what I do.

The coat slithers down over my hands and I feel it creep up over the back of my head as the collar becomes a hood again. It tightens around my legs, preparing to protect me.

I open my stance, planting my feet, lowering my center of gravity, and brace myself. I've stood before things more powerful than this. I've faced down gods and creatures and things not from my reality.

It's close enough now that I can see the inky darkness of it is filled with hundreds of hooked beaks that snip and snap, and their striking against one another is the chattering I hear. Like a swarm of starving cuttlefish suspended in some viscous pigment.

I take a deep breath as the coat slithers its hood over my face.

My fingers tighten on the shotgun.

From the outer darkness to the utter deep, I hunger.

The voice is thunder against my bones.

And then the Hungry Dark is upon me.

11

THERE IS A razor-thin slit across my eyes, just enough to see through . . . if there were any light. If the world hadn't descended into darkness.

It sits there, around me, surrounding me, enveloping me, like I have been dropped to the depths of the ocean. But it's just darkness.

And it's not just darkness.

The clicking has subsided into a noise that is gritty in my ears, a grinding like a millstone over grain. The sound of molar against molar, keratin rubbing keratin, the coarse shush of chewing on nothing. The Hungry Dark swirls around me slowly, a shark circling through the chum to find the source of the bleeding.

And then the coat screams as the first bite is taken.

The sound of it cuts across my cerebral meninges like a rusty razor blade, slicing and snagging at the same time, all the way through the three layers and getting into the soft center of my brain. My finger convulses and the dark is lit with blue as the shotgun kicks in my hands, spitting a gout of hellfire. It is only a flash before the Hungry Dark swallows it up.

My right hand goes ice cold, the Mark etched into my palm pressed to the shotgun's grip and the back covered by the extended coat, and my magick just keeps dumping into the mystical firearm I hold. My magick runs hot usually, but it's cycling into the weapon as I rack the slide and fire into the darkness, and the shunting away of that etheric energy drains the heat from my hand, my bones aching and the muscles sore without it. My tendons feel brittle from my wrist down to my fingertips and with every squeeze of the trigger they feel like they will just snap and shatter and burst into a hundred fractured pieces.

The cold creeps up my arm in a brittle, grinding ache.

My left hand is hot from the backlash of the hellfire spitting from the barrel, which is smoking from being fired over and over and over again.

The Hungry Dark pulls back, maybe because the gouts of bluish hellfire I'm launching into it sling light like it's liquid, even though the fireballs just get extinguished in its inky depths. Maybe because through the slit in the coat's hood I see the shots plow through cuttle mouths, the tendrils they are attached to melting, beaked razor mouths disintegrating like the ash at the end of an insomniac's cigarette.

The Hungry Dark gathers itself. I feel it pull away like the sucking of a receding tide, dozens of beaked tendrils hovering and swaying as they part and move.

I have a bad fucking feeling about this.

The coat quivers along my skin and it's gone silent.

Silent is *not* good.

I shake my head to open the slit a little more so I can see what's going on.

The coat shushes me.

My left hand comes off the magick shotgun, moving toward my face.

The coat growls in the basement of my brain, but it opens wide enough for me to see clearly, "clearly" being a relative term given that I'm staring into a mass of inky darkness.

Something is happening in the center of the Hungry Dark.

The darkness there boils, bubbling around itself, roiling and churning like the ocean set ablaze from underneath by a volcano that has decided to spew itself out from the mantle of the Earth and into the belly of the ocean.

What comes forth isn't an eruption.

No, it doesn't exit the Hungry Dark in a rush, not in a spurt, but in a hideous slither made even worse by the very languidness of its birthing.

It's a mouth, a beak, large enough to cut me in two.

As it slips from the inky blackness of the Hungry Dark it parts into two great hooks of glistening keratin, to let loll out a long, mottled radula the color of a corpse drowned three days ago and gone bluish pale and gleaming white, the brightness of it shocking as it swirls around the upper hook of the beak, its hard toothy surface rasping along the slick razored edges.

I watch it, unmoving, frozen, stuck. I am the rabbit caught by the python in the field. Where can I go? Nowhere. I will be cut down.

The giant beak drops as its parturition finally completes, the bottom edge of it scraping on the rock underfoot with a keening that sets my teeth to grinding. It rises, not unlike the python in my mind, swaying as a living, sighted thing and moving toward me.

The cold is only in my fingers now, my magick settled into the shotgun. I slip my finger of ice against the trigger.

I'm going to die. That's okay. I don't want to, but I can't see stopping this much, and truthfully the concept of death is something

I made friends with long ago in the dark times after what happened to me.

But I'm going to make this thing choke on every bite it gets.

The two halves part, opening. The chitinous ribbon of its tongue coils and writhes in the pocket of the bottom jaw, whipping around, the minutely toothed surface glittering even in the low gray light. The coat babbles along the back of my brain and I know it is saying that thing will shred it like wet tissue under a belt sander.

The jaws get wide enough and I pull the trigger.

The shotgun bucks and spits out a gout of blue hellfire that scorches across the distance.

The Hungry Dark's mouth snaps closed quick as a thought.

The hellfire ball splashes against the front curve of the beak, splitting in two and dissipating as it rolls down the sides. The etheric energy of the blast just trickles and drips to the stone beneath the mouth.

Fuck.

The Hungry Dark shakes like a cat who just got a faceful of water and I feel what I can only describe as rage fill the space it has made around me. It's not rage, not a human emotion, some small spiff or flare of puny anger that humans have, that *mortals* have, in them, but something as all-consuming as the hunger that it embodies in its liquid silk darkness filled with cutting hookbills.

The space between us thickens, the energy roiling out of the Hungry Dark congealing into something firm, something solid.

It's coming.

The thought crosses the synapses of my brain in a bioelectric jolt and the Hungry Dark lunges toward me. The mollusk mouth yaws open, the hard keratin slick like the inside of an oyster shell. It rises over my head and tilts down, as if to dive, ramming me down its gullet to be cut off at the waist when it snaps closed. The micro-toothed tongue curls my way, long strings of ichor hanging from its edges, and my brain, my terrible, foreseeing brain, shows me that it will lap me up, wrap me in its sharp embrace so that I can't fight, can't get away, can only be pulled into the mulching, scissoring hookbill mouth and masticated until I am pulp.

The coat hardens around me and I watch certain bifurcation come.

The radula scrapes across the part of the coat that has become a hood, dropping down so it can constrict around me.

I raise the shotgun, planning to shove the damn thing as far as I can down that throat.

A strangled growl followed by a gleam of pale light that catches the corner of my eye like a stray fishhook that digs in deep and drags my vision to the left.

The gleam goes from a small sliver to a blast of striated muscle and prickled tendon as the skinhound crashes into the Hungry Dark with enough force it knocks me back a step. Crescent razor claws scrabble on hard chitin, clicking and clacking and scratching to find purchase, to hang on, to rend and tear. The skinhound darts his head between the two sides of the beak, and long yellowed fangs clamp onto the radula. The mouth jerks and the skinhound slings sideways, hauling the sharp-toothed ribbon out as he falls to the stone. The skinhound hits the ground at my feet *hard*, curved vertebrae clacking on the stone. The radula stretches thin, then contracts, lifting the skinhound back into the air, even with my waist. The Hungry Dark snaps the beak shut, severing the radula in a spurt of blue liquid that I feel slap across my chest through the coat. The enormous mouth flies backward, winnowing like an injured shark, sinking into the black depths of the Hungry Dark.

It's gone before the skinhound strikes the stone again.

The skinhound rolls, coming up to his feet, the end of the radula glittering in his jaws. The skinhound shakes the thing and drops it, quivering, to the ground. He looks up at me with a tilted head to see me with his one good eye.

He looks pleased with himself for a long second.

Then the Hungry Dark roars around us like a tsunami of ink and swallows us into its depths.

12

ALL IS DARKNESS and I cannot see.

I am pushed down, down, down, to my knees, then to all fours, by the pressure that envelops me. I am submerged, wrapped inside the coat that lies over me like a blanket. It has stopped wailing and now just grunts along the inside of my skull as it is pummeled from the outside.

My chest is so tight it feels like I'm being throttled and my traitorous brain keeps running, spinning, trying to sling me off into the abyss of a panic attack, and I *clench*, I *clamp*, down on that furious sharp-toothed rodent that lives in my cranium always waiting for a moment to scrabble free, to scritch and scratch its way to making me mindless.

Can't panic, won't panic, can't panic, won't, panic, can't panic, won't, can't, swirling and whirling and twirling until the thoughts become a loop that *is* the panic I am trying so hard to avoid.

My lips hurt with the rough abrasion across their thin skin as I part them. An earthy murk of mineral rushes in over the flavor of my blood. The etheric energy of the magick curls into my mouth like the steam off a cup of hot soup, giving me a ghosted taste of what it could be, all potential and taunt and no substance stronger than enough to make my own magick clench like an empty stomach.

The skinhound whines, so low and pitiful I'm not sure I even heard it.

Come on.

I try to pull the magick from the ground like a drowning man trying to pull oxygen from a blocked air tank.

The coat groans and I feel the sharp bite of a small hooked mouth as it breaks through, slicing into the skin of my back.

I press harder against the stone and I *pull* like I'm trying to lift the goddamn thing. Every muscle I have is contracted, drawn tight to the point of spasm in my squeezing, and I tremor all over, like a seizure or a convulsion is rippling through me.

It feels like every inch of connective tissue in my torso is tearing free of its anchors.

Give me the fucking magick!

The mouth in my back bites again, snipping, sinking through skin to muscle, and the pain blooms across my back and through into my chest and all I can do is draw in air to scream.

The magick rushes into me like a crashing river.

Oh.

My.

God.

I am a cup.

Pressed down.

Shaken together.

And running the fuck over.

13

I'M BURNING UP.

I'm a candlewick in a forest fire.

I cannot hold what I have grabbed. This magick is going to incinerate me from the inside out if I don't Get. It. Out.

The cuttlefish mouth snips at my back again.

And I pour all of this magick into it.

I am not a reservoir. I am a channel.

My mind expands, reaching outside of my body, and I am riding the current of primal etheric energy I am pulling from the stone and shoving into the Hungry Dark.

The coat goes liquid, melting off me into a puddle of darkness.

Without it pressing me down, I rise to my feet. I feel it pooling around my legs, but I can't see where it ends and the Hungry Dark begins. The magick I am siphoning *thrums* off me in pulses that the Hungry Dark presses against. I can feel it, snapping at the magick, trying to consume and overwhelm what I am doing, but it is futile. It can't. In that way of understanding without knowing that happens with this magick shit sometimes I know that the Hungry Dark will not overcome this. I am using the very same magick that has kept it imprisoned. It is primal, near primordial, and has a weight to it that is more than anything mass would give. It feels . . . inevitable, as if this magick will always prevail against whatever it is applied to.

It's overwhelming.

My magick is quick and hot; it ebbs and flows with vitality, springing from me or taken from other things. Before, when I used other magick as a source, it became my magick. Not that I owned it; it transformed, transmogrified, into my magick, the magick that lives in me.

This is *not* that.

This—"magick" doesn't even feel like the right word—*energy* doesn't give a fuck about my magick. It would be like dumping the ocean into a glass of tap water and expecting the water in the glass to desalinate its contents.

I think all of this on one track of my brain while a separate one chases the stone's magick as it races through the Hungry Dark. I'm holding on to the tendril that ate its way to my back, using it as an anchor, a connection to the thing that is the Hungry Dark to shunt this magick into. As it flows it changes the very substance of the Hungry Dark and the tendrils it passes through solidify, becoming hard, brittle things that break with the slightest contraction or movement. I watch them quiver, then snap with a high, glass-on-glass shrill. They fall in a weird rain, shattering as if they were glass when they hit the stone.

The Hungry Dark is on the run.

A savage, malicious glee rises in my belly as I pull more magick and push it into this personification of starvation that tried to devour me and mine.

I feel the coat swish in and out of my legs like some weird cattish creature, its voice a faint murmur in my brain.

The inky darkness of the Hungry Dark roils back away from me, the ground between us littered with shards of it, some small cuttle mouths still opening and closing as they lie. It finally gets far enough away to reveal the skinhound, lying in a heap, curled in on himself. Even from here I can see his wounds.

The thought that he could be dead flickers against the rage in my belly.

I take a deep breath, gathering the magick from below, to burn away every iota of the Hungry Dark. It took what was mine and I will obliterate it from existence. I will abolish it from even memory or thought, no atom of it left to cling to another.

Mine enemy shall suffer annihilation at my hands.

The Hungry Dark runs, crossing the distance as it withdraws.

It parts to reveal a pale figure moving toward me.

Marty closes the distance, moving faster than he appears to be. "You have to stop."

Stop?

The concept is as foreign as shards of glass in my mind.

"Listen to me!" he snaps. "Stop it or you are going to kill us all!"

I cannot comprehend the meaning of his words. They're just sounds, noise, nothing more.

He pulls something out of his coveralls. It looks not unlike a shark tooth the size of his own face. It's wide at the top, curving down into a wicked point like a short, stunted blade. His mouth moves, but I hear no sound through the rushing of my own blood in my ears. Dropping to one knee, he lifts the tooth over his head and drives it down, slamming it into the rock.

I feel it reverberate as if he hit me across the shins with a hammer. It shudders in my bones. The magick I'm drawing in and moving through me ripples.

Marty raises the tooth again and slams it down once more.

I feel it pierce the stone deep in my core.

I am cut off from the magick so suddenly it feels as if I have been eviscerated, split in two and spilled onto the stone. I fold in half, sucking in air, trying to push aside the aching emptiness that is now me.

The coat swirls up my legs, holding me up from falling.

I don't know how long I stand there just trying to pull myself together. Time has no meaning. It could be one minute or a hundred years. Everything is wibbly wobbly, and timey wimey. Slowly, glacially slow, I manage to even out my breathing, to let go of enough hollowness to lift myself upright.

Marty is staring at me.

"I told you to stop," he says.

"I couldn't."

"That is why I had to stymie you."

"I don't think you're using that word right."

He points at my head. "Human brain," he says, then points at his mouth, "not human language."

I look down at the tooth he shoved into the rock. It doesn't look like a tooth anymore. Now it looks like a rapidly sprouting plant. Greenish vines curl off it, tumbling to the rock, where they slowly but steadily crawl out from it. Every inch or so a small offshoot unfurls and latches onto the rock, burrowing in to hold it fast. Above each of them another thing unfurls that looks quite a bit like a leaf shaped like an asymmetrical heart.

I'm making it look like the closest familiar thing I can with my perception. Just like I did with Marty. Just like I've done with this entire place.

"It will spread as the Hungry Dark recovers from what you did to it. You have weakened the walls to the point that it could escape if it tried. Luckily, it is a simple, single-minded thing. Once it gathers its strength it will be drawn here. It will come and find this." He sweeps his hand down to the steadily growing thing he has planted. "Being the Hungry Dark, it will devour the entirety of it and as it does this will return the vitality you robbed back into the walls of this cell, restoring it to full strength."

"That's actually ingenious." I mean the compliment.

He grunts. "It is as if it were designed to work as such."

Apparently, Marty can't take a compliment.

The coat slips down my legs. I feel steady. Not 100 percent, but I don't need the bracing. It furls up, slapping at the vines that come too close. I look over at the skinhound.

The moment I do, the coat leaves me.

My skin prickles into gooseflesh as I feel the fact that I am uncovered for the first time.

I still have on my clothes, but the coat is not touching me.

My mind is silent and I am cold without its constant contact.

It slithers across the stone, moving rapidly toward the fallen skinhound.

I go after it.

14

I KNEEL BESIDE what is left of my pet. Friend.

Winnie sprawls on the stone. I've gotten used to his appearance. You know how you have a person in your life and as the time passes their looks just become them? They just look like your friend. It's like that with the skinhound. The lines of striated muscle in all their groups and bunches, running the spectrum of reds, from pink like cooked salmon to the deepest red of rare venison; they have become soothing to me. I don't get squicked out by the way his tendons, tough pearly bands and ropes of connective tissue, contract and elongate as he moves. The glimpses of organs moving under the sheath of subcutaneous membrane that holds them in place don't make my head swim. Whether I look into his lidless egg yolk of an eye or the dark socket where I once gouged out the other one I can read him.

He has been destroyed.

The Hungry Dark has done so much damage.

One of his back legs and his whipcord tail are just gone; the places they used to be attached are gnarled, chewed. They look as if they were hacked off by a dull axe, the bone has a ragged choppy texture, and bits of bonemeal stick to the mangled muscle around it. Dozens of holes gape along Winnie's body, small ones the size of pencil erasers and larger ones I could sink my fist into. They hold a liquid, some fluid from inside him that shimmers in their depths as if they were all communion cups full of wine. Strips of membrane wad together along a two-foot tear from the center of his breastbone down along his torso and under the crease of his flank. From it spills out a rope of intestine like a lavender-blushed sausage.

The coat moves around him in a swirl of darkness. It touches him in many places, skimming his injuries, worrying over him. It's not in my head anymore, but this close I can feel the anxiety radiating off it as if we are still, if not connected, then in tune.

"Oh, Winnie, I'm so sorry."

He suffered this saving me.

At my voice he moves, lifting his head slightly. A small mewl threads its way out of his throat. His blind socket is toward me, he cannot see me, and he doesn't have the strength to rise, but he tries, he struggles to move toward me, and the effort makes his wounds open and his essence leak out onto the stone until he collapses back into a quivering thing.

Fuck, fuck, fuck.

I can fix this. I've fixed people before. I fixed Daniel. I've fixed myself. I'm magick.

My right hand, the Marked hand, is moving toward the skinhound as I call up the magick that lives inside me.

It doesn't want to come forth.

I'm low. My reserves at an ebb. None of what I took from this place stayed with me. My magick normally sits in my belly and moves through my blood. All that is gone. I still have it, but it's farther down, burned to the roots of my magick, the parts of it that live in my bones, soaked into the marrow of me, in the deep tissue pockets and small organs you can't squeeze. In my gallbladder, my spleen, my pineal gland. Intrinsic but tucked away in my nooks and crannies.

But for the skinhound, for what he did to save me . . .

I *force* the magick to do what I want. I drive it out and compel it into my Mark.

I feel it uproot, tear free from its mooring inside me as it goes, and my head swims, crackly white blitzes on the edge of my vision, and my mouth goes so dry my tongue has become a piece of dehydrated meat that sticks to the roof of my mouth, sealing it shut.

I don't care. I keep pushing.

My head pounds.

I shut my eyes against it and keep reaching out, holding the etheric energy of my magick in the bones of my hand. I will release it when I touch the skinhound.

Something grabs my wrist and jerks, slamming my hand down. Pain flares across my knuckles as they *whack!* against the stone and my concentration breaks and there is a surge of nausea as the bits of magick I had forced into my Mark flee back to their hidey-holes in my corpus.

I clench my jaw against the surge from my stomach, squeezing hard to keep from throwing up.

After a few minutes the jerking cramps pass and I can breathe, sort of, if sucking in short jerks of air and shoving them back out to hyperventilate into having oxygen again counts.

Finally, I can open my eyes. The coat slithers off my arm.

"He is right, you know." Marty is standing close, looking down at us. "You cannot use all your stamina or you will be useless. In fact, knowing how stubborn you seem, you might even will yourself into death."

"I can fix him."

The coat slides up, a part of it forming a rounded shape that hovers up by my head, almost as though it has risen up to talk to me.

It shakes back and forth, very clearly disagreeing with my assessment.

Little shit.

"He is too far gone," Marty says. "And if you expend what little vitality you have left trying, then you will be too far gone as well."

"If you're about to suggest we leave him you can go to hell."

"The Hungry Dark will—"

I'm on my feet without thinking. My head spins so hard I nearly fall back down, but I still growl out, "Go. To. Hell."

Marty shakes his head. "We cannot stay here."

"I'm not leaving him."

The coat flutters against my leg and I know what it's thinking without hearing it. *We're not leaving him.*

"I thought you were here to stop the Crawling Chaos."

"Don't." The word comes from my mouth like an axe chop, short and sharp and hard. "I'll get to him. This problem is the one we are dealing with right now."

"The Hungry Dark will return. You will not be able to shunt it aside again."

He's right. I can hear the chitinous clickety-clack of the Hungry Dark like a faraway plague of locusts. We have to do something.

"You have tricks." I step closer to Marty. "You fixed this place. Fix him."

He shakes his head. "I cannot."

"Then take me to someone or something that can." An idea forms like a whirlpool in the ocean, spinning lazily until it begins to churn. "You were taking us to your boss. Take us there quicker."

He stares at me for a long moment.

"I'm not giving you a choice on this," I say.

He sighs and shakes his head.

"I am not carrying him."

15

THERE'S PRESSURE ACROSS my chest making it hard to take in a deep breath that matches the pressure in my lower back, which feels like my spine has fused to my pelvic bone in one hard mass. I'm walking and each step becomes a repetition of the one before it, a plodding exercise of zen mindfulness that is literally putting one foot in front of the other as I follow Marty's shuffling gait down the hallway again.

The coat wraps across me in a wide strap, over my left collarbone, between my breasts, and tight across my ribs on the right. Other parts of it have lashed across my hips, attaching to my jeans in a crisscross web. I lean forward to balance out the weight of the skinhound, who hangs off my back in a hammock sling the coat has become. I can feel the coat's voice barely skimming the edge of my mind. It's a soft, melodic babble like a river's lullaby. It's not talking to me; I'm just getting feedback by proximity.

I think it's singing to the skinhound.

That doesn't feel right.

I ignore the small pain that is setting up along the side of my knee and pay attention to the coat, tuning in closer to the frequency of it.

It's not singing. There's a focus to its melodic, alien voice, an intent.

It's . . . praying? I think it's praying.

What in the world would the skin of an archangel pray to? God? After all the crazy elder god shit I've seen I don't know what to believe about actual God, like the Judaeo-Christian-It's-Sunday-Morning-*God* God. I guess he could maybe be another elder god. The town I grew up in is like most small towns; it's big on church. It's ingrained in almost every aspect of social life.

I was raised to believe in God and Jesus and all of that. I believed that God loved me, had a purpose for me. I believed that his son had died on a cross to save me from my sins. I loved being saved. The concept of being redeemed made me feel special and protected.

And then, when I was fourteen, Tyler and his three friends pulled me into his room at the first high school party I had ever been to and they . . . no.

I'm not going to go into all they did. They hurt me. Put me in the hospital. Shattered my innocence. Turned my whole life inside out.

I left my belief in God on the floor of Tyler Wood's room. Why didn't God stop that from happening to me? He can't exist, because if he does and he allows all of that, then fuck him. I just can't hold belief in something so cruel.

But leaving God behind doesn't mean I could avoid the church.

Not in my town. I never returned to the church I grew up in after that night, but my parents did and their friends did. The amount of *praying* for me that people claimed they were doing . . .

well, it was a lot. I know a fair amount about some of the Bible, mostly from those childhood sermons and Sunday school.

I never told my parents, but the God of the Old Testament always seemed a bit of a dick, even when I was young. Like the story of the birds.

You never heard about the birds?

Quails, I think they were. Yeah, quails.

My memory is a bit shit on this, so bear with me. The Israelites were in the desert and God fed them bread every day. After months of wandering around they were tired of it and complained, wanting meat. God got pissed, offended that his original providing wasn't good enough, and rained down so many quails that their corpses were heaped waist high on the ground and as far around the Israelites' camp as a day's walk.

Think about that.

You ask for a little meat from this otherworldly being, this god who demands worship and has taken to providing you everything, and he makes you walk over a carpet of dead birds for a full day. Each step, if you're in the front, is a crunch of tiny hollow bones under your sandals, little feathers stuck to your feet and up to your shins with bird blood and gore.

If you're in the middle then those birds had been stepped on by hundreds of people. They were paste, a mud of liquefied bird and sand. Imagine slogging through miles of *that*.

I don't even want to think about what it was like for anyone at the back of the march.

That's some fucked-up, repugnant shit.

And spiteful. Spiteful as fuck.

Who knows? Maybe Yahweh *is* an elder god. He'd fit in with the Man in Black pretty well. Maybe Jehovah is in this prison somewhere. Maybe his cell is just full of rotting quail corpses.

The thrill I get from that thought makes me feel conflicted, somehow guilty for it even though I don't believe and haven't for years. There is a worm of doubt that burrows through my doubt, a thin, niggling thing that squirms after all of the crazy elder god shit I've seen, and that Yahweh-as-an-elder-god concept isn't just me being a smartass but something that some part of my mind thinks may just be true, and that part rubs that concept up against a childhood of being instilled with the belief that God *does* exist and, more, to even question that or anything about that means you are a bad person deserving of eternal punishment. The same eternal punishment made for God's enemy, the Devil.

It's running on a background track as I walk, my brain doing this as my body is engaged in a function that doesn't demand much bandwidth. Idle brains are the Devil's workshop or some such thing. The conflict of the thoughts manifests as a little stabby pain in my temple and a fist-tight tension deep in my chest up under my heart.

Why does my brain do this?

Trust me, after a decade of therapy and introspection I have come to the conclusion that brains are assholes.

Marty stops and turns.

I stop.

He has a look on his face.

"What is it, Marty?"

"We are taking too long."

I shift, adjusting the coat to move the skinhound's weight to the side. The coat grips me tighter.

Relax; I'm not putting him down.

Something—I don't know if it's my own sweat or some fluid from the skinhound—has soaked into my jeans to the point that it trickles slowly down the back of my leg.

"I don't have the magick to teleport us anywhere."

He tilts his head.

Oh, Marty doesn't know all I can do.

I reach up and touch the torc that circles my throat, lying loose across my collarbones. The metal of it is cool and chimes slightly as my fingernails strike its slick surface. "This lets me wish to places. It's how I got here."

"Then use it to get us to Satet."

I shake my head; the torc slides around my throat. "No."

"You refuse or you cannot?"

"I've only ever used it to go somewhere I could pinpoint by magick. This place feels really off to me. I don't trust it to not put me someplace really dangerous."

"Where did you get your jewelry?"

"Ashtoreth." The name is bitter.

"You know Ashtoreth?"

"Know her?" I laugh. "I threatened to kill her if I ever see her again."

"Then you *do* know her."

There's a familiarity in his voice and I get the impression he knows her as well. I can't be surprised; she *is* the goddess of whores, seems like everybody I meet knows her.

"Did she give you that when you threatened her life?"

I shake my head and the torc slides back and forth slightly. "The Man in Black made her give it to me."

"You allowed the Crawling Chaos to collar you with the choker of Ashtoreth? That is a brave move, human."

"When you put it that way it seems like a bad idea."

He shrugs.

The torc hasn't been a problem. It has done what I was told it would, allowing my magick to track elder gods and wish myself and others there. It also just kind of grants wishes if I make them too casually. It is a thing of treachery and chaos with a danger to wearing it, but I've got this.

The sling on my back is heavier. Now that we've stopped walking there is an ache in my spine that feels like vertebrae grinding on each other, as if all the soft stuff between them has worn away and now it's bone on bone and it's a rough, grinding, unlubricated ache that locks and ratchets in my lower back.

And whatever it is that's trickling is trickling its way down my calf, making a run for my shoe.

I adjust the coat and skinhound sack, moving it to the side so it hangs differently. "So what do we do? I can't walk any faster."

"We cut the obtuse angle off the quadrilateral."

"I don't know what that means."

"I was speaking hyperbolically."

"Don't condescend to me, Marty. I won't respond well to it."

He sighs and shakes the keys. "You would call it 'taking a shortcut.'"

"Why didn't you just say that?"

"I did."

This guy is infuriating. I tilt my head because I am just tired of talking around things.

Marty stands there holding the keys.

"This thing"—I shrug, lifting the coat/sling higher up across my back—"is surprisingly heavy. Will this shortcut get us where we are going quicker?"

He nods and the skin around his neck creases into folds, all loose and bunched up. "Is that not the nature of shortcuts? To bleed out the time in the travel?"

"Then ramblers, let's get ramblin'."

He turns and we walk down to the next door. It's a gate, impressive in a Gothic manner. I can smell the iron of it, taste it on the back of my throat. The bars run top to bottom, stout and thick and not enough space between them for me to stick my arm through. Around the bars swirls what looks like razor wire, the distinctive Z pattern to the blades flowing along its length like a liquid buzz saw. Along the top and bottom are scalloped plates of iron giving it decoration while also reinforcing that this is a gate meant for function.

Marty touches the lock with his right hand, fingers stroking the metal, tracing the keyhole. There is a crackle of crimson that passes as he pulls his chubby fingers away and reaches for the ring of keys in his other hand. His fingers wave, stroking the air just inches from the keys. After a few seconds he snaps his fingers and another crackle of energy zaps over to the key ring. They chime as they jostle against one another and then one key slides free, swinging around like a needle on a lodestone to stick up, vibrating slightly. Marty plucks it, letting the ring and the other keys fall and hang beneath his hand. He inserts the key into the lock. It gives a rough scrape as he turns it, as if the tumblers inside had rusted together.

Hand on the gate, he looks at me.

My back is aching more and more every second from carrying the skinhound in the coat/sling and Marty's looking and not moving incites me to snap, "What?"

"I am deciding if warning you that we want to pass through this cell without drawing attention to ourselves is worth doing."

"You doubting my stealth mode abilities?"

"I did just see you with the Hungry Dark. So far you have been less than unobtrusive."

"That was just me doing what I had to do."

"It was not subtle."

"I don't do subtle very well."

"The thing in this cell will be something we do not want to draw attention from."

"Then why are we going in?"

"It is the shortcut."

I wave his concerns away. "I will be quiet like a bunny."

He frowns at me.

The gate creaks on unoiled hinges as he swings it open.

16

EVERYTHING GOES *WOOBLY* as I step through the gate.

Yes, that's the word I fucking meant to use.

"Woobly."

Not "wobbly," not "uneven," "tottering," or "unbalanced."

More rattletrap than that. A sound and a sensation. The air pulsates and changes viscosity, like an estuary where light, clean fresh water spills into heavier, brackish salt water. It feels almost oily as we pass through an invisible membrane of some kind and my perception fluctuates like a loose drumhead under a striker, all thuddy and throbby and *woobly*.

The next step, I am clear of it and standing on a wide path that leads across a rolling field of flowers that look like roses. There is light from somewhere, but it is dim, like pre-dusk twilight. Marty steps up beside me.

"Do not touch the flowers."

"Why not?" I wasn't going to, but with the warning I am suddenly curious as hell. It's a fault in my personality; I can't help it.

"It is . . . not advised."

"That is not helpful."

I move to the edge of the path where the flowers stand, drooping inward. Looking down at them, I simply see delicate petals that curl into one another and roll away from their center, very much like a rose. These may be roses, some kind I just don't recognize. I'm not a botanist. Carefully, moving slowly so that the weight across my back doesn't pitch me forward, I crouch. The skinhound doesn't move except to breathe as he has been.

"You should heed my warning."

I wave him off. I'm not going to touch the damn flowers.

But still.

There is something . . . intriguing about them. They glisten along their edges, each petal a varying shade of red, thin and delicate.

It niggles at the back of my brain; they remind me of something.

I lean closer, just a touch, not even an inch.

The flowers rustle, bobbing slightly, and a trace of light runs along the edges of the petals on the one I am studying like a microbead of quicksilver.

Razors.

The petals are razors.

The thought is no sooner in my mind than the flower takes a swipe at me.

It lunges on its stalk like a cobra striking. I jerk back and tumble onto my ass, stopped from sprawling by the mass of the coat/sling cocoon on my back. The coat hisses and I can't tell if I hear it in my mind or in my ears.

As I think apologies and push myself up to stand, the flowers begin shaking, rubbing against one another with a shushed chattering not unlike the rattle of a venomous snake. It carries out over the field of them like a stiff breeze. Even from here I can feel their thirst.

Marty says, "I warned you."

"I didn't touch them!"

He shrugs. "Let us walk. Maybe we can pass through before they arrive."

"They?" I ask as we begin moving. "Isn't this a prison for the flowers?"

"No, why would you think that?"

"So, something in here needs those things?"

"'Needs' may be the wrong word," he says. "'Desires' would be much closer."

What kind of creature could desire bloodthirsty roses?

I don't want to find out.

Knowing my luck, though . . .

17

THE RUSTLE OF the razor roses becomes white noise as we keep walking.

The path under my feet is identical to the floor of the hallway, spongy and undulating. Not dirt or soil of any kind, much more like flesh.

I'm not thinking about that.

The path maintains its width, more than wide enough for Marty and me to walk side by side. Every so often, on one side or the other, the path will branch off, curving away to disappear among the bloodthirsty flowers. Marty doesn't take any of these, doesn't even seem to notice them, so I just keep walking. As we pass, the razor roses keep waving from the edges, as if trying to seduce us closer.

"They are persistent."

Marty grunts. "They thirst. I have been thirsty. It can be maddening."

"Don't you water them?"

"Only enough to sustain them. This is not a place of comfort."

"Are you trying to make me feel bad for them?"

"If you allowed them to drink it would be blissful for you. Their bite flows with a narcotic that leaves their consorts filled with pleasure."

"No thanks. Almost fell for that once; you don't get a second chance." I hike the sling up on my shoulders. The skinhound is heavy on my back. I want to put him down. I want to abandon him, just leave him, because everything has become one leaden sensation. It doesn't even hurt anymore; maybe it does, it's hard to tell, but it is the repetitive one-foot-in-front-of-the-other slog that consumes me.

"On some planes of existence they are very sought out."

"Are you trying to be a pusher, Marty?" I snap. "I think it best to keep my fucking wits about me in a place like this, so don't ask again."

He falls silent.

We keep walking.

I don't know how long we are at it. Each step compresses me down into that place, working on me. My spine is bent and I am watching my feet lift, then fall, then lift again, and that is my whole world. My steps, the weight that bends my back, my own breath, and the whisper-rustle of flowers that want to drink my blood.

I keep walking until Marty says, "Oh no."

I let the weight of the coat-wrapped skinhound pull me upright. The motion makes my back twinge and the skinhound inside whine just a bit.

Three women stand down the road from us. At this distance, they look like tall, slender spikes driven into the path. I can't even see that they are women, but they *feel* feminine.

"Know them?" I ask.

"Too well," Marty says. "I hoped we would not gain their attention."

The last offshoot path was long ago. Now there is the road behind and the road in front and plains of razor roses to each side. Going that way is not an option; we'd be bled out in seconds.

I say what Sensei Laura used to say.

"If you can't go around, you go through."

18

THEY ARE FUCKING beautiful.

They stand, so similar and yet distinctive from one another, as if they were carved from the same block of anthracite coal by the same sculptor. They are three-in-one, a trinity, a triptych of cruel elegance complete as one yet whole on their own. Their skin is so black it glistens blue, the color of hematite with cobalt gleamings. They are not human, but human*esque,* so much *esque,* and it feels like when a predator mimics its prey to get close enough to strike. Long of limb and wide of shoulder, they stand with the easy grace of something that slinks through the night, something that prowls, something that chews its food in the dark. Up close, they are definitely feminine, small breasts and swelling hips covered in bands of a metal that looks mostly like copper, which sweep up and out along their torsos as corsetry. It bites deep into their skin, cutting to maintain its place, and I can see the crust of some form of fluid along the top edges of where it meets their wet charcoal skin.

Their faces are carved with a cenobite comeliness that all of man should be drawn to them.

Scalpel-thin upper lips lying atop overfull bottom ones. Their cheekbones are harsh, slashed into their faces under eyes that stare, unblinking, with large black pupils. A delicate brow, almost completely smooth, travels up to hair that hangs long in tight braids fitted with smaller bands of copper metal, draping over their shoulders.

In each left hand they hold something. The one on the left has what looks like a coil of stiff rope, the right one what appears to be a wide, flat club, and the center one holds something that looks not unlike a mop of her own hair.

For a long moment I am unsure if they are anything more than a sculpture, they are so still.

Then one of them, the center one, opens her mouth and speaks Marty's name.

Not "Marty" but the string of syllables that is his real name.

Marty tilts his head in a semi-bow. "We are not here to concern you, Sisters of Mercy."

Her hand sweeps to the left, indicating an offshoot of the path that drops almost immediately in a slope, invisible if you aren't even with it. "Did you bring us something better than this pale lump of gristle to play with?"

At the bottom of the slope is a short, gnarled tree, its trunk wide and thick and looking not unlike it has been chewed upon. Stubby branches twist around the top of it like a crown, jutting and winding around one another like some gnarled crown.

Tied to it is something vaguely human shaped. There are too many limbs to it and they bend and crook the wrong way on too many joints, but it's close enough that I feel sorry for whatever it is.

It doesn't move, just hangs there. Flaps droop from its back to hang round about its waist in almost a skirt, but even from here I can tell it has been flayed.

I look back over and find that all three sisters are paying attention to me. By "attention" I mean they are watching me as a cobra watches a mouse, as if I am a meal to slide down their gullets.

My hands go up. "No."

"You deny our need?" the center one asks, while looking at me as if I were a piece of candy she wanted from the case.

"Lady, I don't know your need. I just know I am not here to be anyone's plaything."

"You may . . . *enjoy* our attention." She steps closer to me. "Many do, especially when they have been marked by trauma."

I take a step back, the weight of the skinhound in the coat twinging my back hard enough that I can't keep it off my face.

Her right hand lifts, the very form of gracefulness. "If your burden hurts your back then you should absolutely allow us to work out your kinks."

Her words undulate as she speaks, flowing with a cadence that is almost hypnotic, as if I could sway along with the rhythm they hold, and I feel the *pull* low in my body.

"Sorry, lady, I don't play like that with people I don't even know their names."

Eyebrows slash up, giving her a sly look. "So you do play with those whose names you know?"

"It was an expression," I say, putting as much decisiveness as I can into my voice. "Not a statement of intent."

I don't play that way at all. Never have. That got stolen from me so long ago and I was just, possibly, starting to maybe find it again when the Man in Black showed up and now here I am.

The thought of what could have been if he had just *not* arrived on my doorstep, if none of this were real, flashes through my mind. If things had just stayed normal, if I hadn't been singled out by the Crawling Chaos for his . . . *machinations* . . . yes, that's a great word, his machinations, then Daniel would have come over and he would have apologized and explained and we would have worked it out and, oh holy fuck, by this point I could have been involved in my first serious romantic relationship. It would have been messy, there are minefields inside me that I am sure would have surfaced as we grew closer, but Daniel is a good man and he would have been patient and we would have worked through things because we *both* wanted to, because we were *both* committed, and—

Fuck the Man in Black for stealing all of that from me.

My mouth tastes bitter. The ashes of what could have been.

I look up at the woman.

The exaggerated disappointment that fills her face almost makes me laugh.

"Who are you?"

"We are the Sweetest Sisters, the Infernae, the Kindly Ones."

I've heard those words before.

They trip through my mind, kicking things loose, and my eyes sweep over her, seeing things I didn't before.

The blue tone that traces her form isn't some reflection of the deadpan lighting of this place; it is a change in the texture of what she wears as skin. I can pick out patterns amid the seeming randomness, hatch mark slashes along her shoulders that blend into wide flat spots, long curving lines that rise above the normal skin around them like ribbons, teardrop marks that rain upward along her clavicles, and a mix of it all that wraps her thighs beneath the copper winding she wears.

It's scar tissue.

Her skin has been wounded, split, cut, gouged open, and then healed over to leave keloid marks and cicatrice patterns. They are heavier on her right side.

Someone is left-handed.

I look to her sisters. Their left hands. The one on the left isn't holding a coil of rope. It is a whip, long and wicked. The one on the right isn't holding a club; it's a paddle, wide and flat, the edges scalloped in a toothlike pattern. A truncheon.

It's beautiful.

And also wicked.

The Sister before me isn't holding a mop of braids. It's a flogger, a cat-o'-nine-tails, a scourge.

And now I know why the double entendre of "working out my kinks" struck a nerve in me.

"You are the Furies."

She nods. "Your kind used that name for us when we roamed your plane of existence."

Marty speaks, "You know them?"

I nod and intone the words that press against my lips.

> "*Such things as these are done by younger gods*
> *with power wholly beyond justice*
> *at the throne dripping with murder*
> *all round its foot, all round its head.*
> *I can see before me the earth's navel,*
> *which has taken bloodshed on itself,*
> *a ghastly defilement to have.*'"

The Fury smiles at my quote, lips not quite parting. "Ah, sweet Aeschylus. Do you know him?"

Know him? "He's been dead for a long time. Centuries."

Her face sharpens, drawing into a blade ready to cut. "Did you kill him?"

"No. He was killed by a turtle."

"A tortoise?"

"Well, by an eagle technically. The story goes, the eagle had a turtle in its claws and dropped it on Aeschylus's head from on high thinking his baldness was a stone large enough to crack open the shell."

She steps back. "That's absurd."

I shrug, which reminds me again of the weight on my back because I can only do it slightly. "That's the story as I was told it."

The Sister with the whip is the first to laugh, just a small snigger, almost a snort.

There is one second of silence until we all begin to laugh, even Marty. Even me. It rolls out of us, and even though I keep mine tightly controlled it feels good. Goddamn, I have been so *grim* for so long. The skinhound isn't the only thing that has been weighing on me. The entire hunt for the Man in Black has been a grind. It feels like I have done nothing but chase him since I learned he wasn't humanity's malevolent protector. The sacrifices I've made along the way.

Daniel.

The laughter turns from wine to vinegar in my mouth.

I can't think about Daniel. I have been studiously *not* thinking about Daniel despite the monotonous walking when my brain just wanted to wander back to him, to the image of his face as he turned, knowing I was about to leave him behind. Green eyes rimmed with tears, unashamed, full bottom lip pulled down by sadness, and his voice, ah fuck, his voice as he said the last two words to me.

Don't go.

In those two words were oceans of hurt I could drown in. I had to abandon him. I had to. I didn't want to.

I had to.

Because of the goddamned Man in Black.

And now I stand here with the skinhound hanging off my back like an albatross, wounded, dying, because I brought him with me to this place.

He doesn't deserve this.

The Man in Black is the one who deserves to be wounded and dying.

Rage sparks in my belly and becomes a roaring gutfire that heats me from the inside. I am sweating. My muscles tighten and my blood sings at the thought that the Man in Black needs to pay.

The fire that thought brings to my blood is quelled by the still, small voice inside that says when I find him I won't be enough to stop him.

All this suffering will be for naught.

The Fury lets her laughter dribble away and tilts her head, looking at me. The motion makes her braids sweep around her shoulder in a clicking of small copper rings striking one another.

"Why so sad, Marked of Ashtoreth?"

The mention of her name draws me short.

"Why would you say that?"

"You wear her jewelry."

I feel the torc, heavy against my collarbones.

"How do you know Ashtoreth?"

"She is our sister."

"You're related?"

"Are we not all related?"

"Do you mean, all you gods are related? Or all us women are related?"

"Mother, maiden, crone." She waves her empty hand around. "We are one and all daughters of the night."

"I hate that your kind never give a straight answer."

She shrugs and it is so elegant it makes my teeth hurt.

"So, which one are you?" I can't remember the names of the Furies. I only remembered that bit of verse because I thought it was cool when it came along in Lit class and the parts about the younger gods and the throne dripping murder and the earth's navel that has taken on bloodshed really worked for me.

I had a long time there where it was all dark in my head.

And because of the story about the turtle, which is absurd.

"I am Megaera." She indicates her sisters, left, then right. "This is Alekto and Tilphousia. And you are?"

"Charlie."

"Char-*li-a*." She repeats it weird and the intonation of it, a back-throated chop on the first syllable and a soft drawing out of the second, makes the hair on the back of my neck stand up.

"Meg . . ." I can *feel* her in front of me, swelling larger than the space she consumes, like the ozone crackle of an oncoming storm.

"You are from the humans. Your kind sent us to this gray, flavorless place."

"That wasn't me."

"You are all the same."

"I thought we were all the same, you and I. Not me and those assholes from way back then."

"We have been here forever."

Her words hang between us and I feel they mean what they say and as she speaks them I can sense that time is moving differently around me. I can't explain it; it's the same as the difference between the time on a cooped-up rainy day and the time spent running in the sun. The time passes disparately. It is different here. It feels unmoored, slipshod and ramshackle, tenuously tied to the time I hold inside my own body.

My magick kicks, nudging through my belly, nosing up under my spleen, nuzzling along my gallbladder as awareness grows and I can *feel* my cells; they are all microscopic timepieces designed to last until they fail, to hold out against time for only so long, and they die and regenerate and it all is little bursts of time. I am tiny bursts of time that keep me existing, nanoseconds encapsulated in the molecules of my body, bits and scraps of continuance that only matter as they connect to the other ones inside me and that, as the cell walls that keep them encaged break down, scutter away to join the stream of time that rules us all.

Wibbly. Wobbly (not "woobly"). Time is a slippery little fuck.

They *could* have been here forever.

It's all illusion and folly and vanity of vanities.

Marty clears his throat.

Megaera and I both turn and look at him, and from the corner of my eye I see that her face is as flinty as mine feels.

"What?" I ask.

He shuffles, looking downward. "Speaking of time, we should—"

"You are not going to pass by without partaking of our hospitality."

Megaera says it as a statement, not a question.

Marty swings his wide palm in my direction. "She has to keep a schedule."

Meg gives me the same flinty look.

"I *am* on a time crunch," I say. A mild scrabble of panic starts buzzing at the top of my spine, the fact that I have no idea what the Man in Black is doing at this moment the seed of it, trying to blossom into mind kudzu, unfurling burrowing tendrils of itself through my brain to take it over.

No, thank you.

I clamp it down. I can only do what I can do and I can't do any more.

"Where do you go?"

"Marty is taking me to meet the boss."

"Serket?" she asks.

"No, someone else." I turn to Marty. "Who are we going to see?"

"Satet," he says. "They are one and the same."

"Not to us," Megaera says.

"You do not acknowledge both names?"

She doesn't answer.

I step to the left to draw her attention back to me. "Secret, Satin, whatever her name is, that's who we're going to see."

Her brow furrows as she looks at me.

One of the Sisters, the one with the whip, speaks up. "If she is to audience with Serket, perhaps we should let—"

Meg snaps her fingers, silencing her sister, and draws herself up, stretching to her full height, spine straight, shoulders back, long, slender neck extended as she looks down imperiously at me. Queen of Pain, Empress of Agony, Sister of Mercy. "This may be a cell, but it is *our* cell. Tribute must be paid to pass."

"I thought you liked me," I mutter.

"The sky is gray," she responds.

"What does that have to do with anything?"

"Exactly."

Okay, that was good. She got me there. The Furies come equipped with a streak of smartass. So noted. I'll let that one slide.

I ask, "What counts as tribute?"

Marty moves slightly, rocking forward, then back, then forward again in an uncertain motion. "You should not. This will not go well."

I wave his words away. Meg seems reasonable. For an other-worldly entity she seems downright fucking amicable.

And we can always go to a fight.

I don't want to fight. Not three against two. Marty handled the Hungry Dark, but he seems almost . . . *cowed* here. Not inspiring confidence. And I have the weight of the skinhound on my back. He's out of the fight and if I get dropped he's dead. That's just the facts.

If a fight broke out right now would you fight with me or stay with him?

The coat is silent in response.

So, the skinhound would win. Something surges inside me and I'm not mad at that.

Protect him, I think.

Meg turns, moving down the slope without looking back or speaking.

Before I can ask Marty if we should follow, the other two Sisters gesture, arms moving in unison, indicating that we should.

So we do.

And the razor roses serenade us with a low chiming of scalpel petal against scalpel petal as they sway to track our movement.

19

THE TREE IS bigger than I thought from up the slight hill. The trunk is at least ten feet tall and the broken, gnarl-ended limbs stretch another fifteen in some cases. The roots snake down into the sandy circle we find ourselves in, burrowing thickly in an abstract sculpture of stability.

The bark of it is a dull silver and dark gunmetal gray that twine together, stained with something that looks like sap but I feel is probably blood or a reasonable facsimile of.

Speaking of reasonable facsimile

Tied to the tree is a lump of something that looks vaguely humanoid. Mostly the right proportions, some extra bits and bobs, like a third grader's clay sculpture of a person. Yeah, it's close, but it's all weird lumps and deep thumb impressions and strange creases in strange places on its near-albino pale . . . flesh?

The back of it has been shredded.

It doesn't move. Isn't breathing.

"Um," I say. "What is that?"

"That," Meg says, "is *not good enough*." The glare she gives Marty would shatter glass.

He shrugs. "Be thankful that much is provided."

Meg whirls, braids whipping around in a hissing, warning chatter, like a snake's rattle. "You instruct me to be *thankful*?"

The rage coming off her is palpable, radiating like a heat shield. Her features have gone feral sharp, pulled tight against the bones of her face.

I wish I had a weapon in my hand.

The Mark on my palm tingles. I shake it out.

She steps toward Marty; the scourge in her hand swings back.

The coat tightens around me and I know it is pulling tight over the skinhound, wrapping him up to protect him. The skinhound whimpers, just slightly, and I feel it against my kidneys.

"Meg!" I spit her name sharply, forcing it to be a chop of a word, something to get attention.

It pulls her short.

"What's the problem?" I ask.

She stares at me and I watch the conflict in her mind. She's deciding if I warrant an answer or if she should strike me down. The flogger bobs in her hand as it clenches and unclenches, the falls drawing my eye as they shake.

I wish I had a weapon in my hand.

The torc jerks tight, slipping up off my collarbones and cinching down across my throat in a hard line, and it goes ice cold as it does what it does and grants my wish.

Oh fuck.

Meg's scourge is in my left hand.

20

THE AIR FEELS solid, all of us frozen in one long moment.

The thing in my hand clicks and vibrates and I get the feeling it is not happy to be held by me. The handle is thick in my palm and feels like wood. There are knobs on each end, the pommel and guard, that look rough-hewn. I can see splinters jutting from it looking to stick and snag soft flesh. The handle belly, though, is smooth against my skin, as if polished. Some form of leather thongs, a dozen or more, fall away from the guard, spilling out to hang toward the ground. They are almost as long as my arm. Every few inches there are knots, some of which hold pieces of what looks like metal and bone.

The thing jumps in my hand.

Capping the ends of each fall are a length of glistening onyx beads that flex, flinch, and curl, bumping one another as they do. I lift the scourge up so I can see better.

One of the lengths curls out, revealing a long, curved hypodermic barb, a sharp-pointed stinger with a drop of venom the color of rotting honey quivering at its point.

My mind turns immediately to scuttling things. Many-legged creatures that protect their soft insides with a hard shell and a way to deliver poison to anything that might crack them open and suck them empty.

The scourge is tipped with scorpion tails.

The tail that points at me jerks, flicking. The drop on its point flings off and, before I can blink, strikes me on the cheek.

For a long second it doesn't burn.

Then that second is over.

It feels like someone put a cigarette out.

On my face.

There is a worm of *firepainagony* burrowing to the bone under the skin. I swipe at it using my right hand.

My Marked hand.

The thick, viscous fluid smears across my palm, mixed with my plasma and my blood. I feel the map of scar tissue on my palm swell as it drinks in the combination.

Oh hell—

It's all I have time to think before my magick curls from my hand, slithers up my arm, roaring to life inside me, and I can't think anymore.

The whole world goes green and all my brain translates is weird shapes and the impression of shapes. Things unseen swarm in my vision and the world has become a water-filled kaleidoscope. Sounds beat against my eardrums, but there is no room for them to enter and become anything recognizable and it's all murk and congealing sonic leftovers. I slam my eyes shut, the ones in my skull, but my third eye tears open and I look down as my brain unhooks itself from the acid burn pain that chases through the veins in my arm. The pain floats off from me, lifting away, now only in my body and where a small part of my mind can pay attention to it, turn it over and over, studying it, dissecting it into smaller and smaller pieces so that it can be absorbed and frittered away.

Dissociation. It's a wonderful thing.

The rest of my mind works overtime to prepare for the onslaught of images that are going to invade it through that third eye, the soft spot, like a calloused finger through the soft spot in an infant's skull, one hard push and it's through. The poison-tainted magick screams up along my neck and flares out along my jawline.

And it stops.

Just . . .

stops.

I feel it, tight in my throat, my glands swollen, my epiglottis saturated and heavy and threatening to shut off my windpipe. But my vision doesn't go sideways into nightmare-o-rama. I swallow and it's a handful of fire ants being shoved down my esophagus, little pellets of fire stitching down into my belly.

But it eases the constriction in my throat, the inflammation of my jaw and soft palate.

Someone says something. I can't understand their words or recognize their voice; it's all still sound crashing like waves against my ears, but I can tell it's someone speaking to me.

Shaking my head, I swallow more of the venom magick down. It breaks up like congestion, compacted and mucus-like, falling from my throat like ice shearing off a glacier. It tumbles down my gullet, sticking here and there as it does.

My vision backs down with each swallow until there is just dull darkness behind my lids.

I open them.

Everyone is watching me.

Meg isn't seething anymore.

No, the look on her face can only be called one of wonder.

"Sister?" she asks.

The word hits me with a physical force . . . no, that's not right. The word *lies* on me with a weight, a burden of import, a mantle placed across my shoulders. It indicates a kinship, being a section of a whole, a part of a totality, the same but not the same, a union, an affinity, and an aggregate.

Tribe.

Clan.

Kith.

Kin.

Sister, and all that it could possibly mean.

"Meg—" And I don't know what to say after that.

The conflict grinds inside me, emotional tectonic plates shifting against one another. I am drawn to the claiming of sisterhood with these glorious creatures who stand around me and am, at the same time, repulsed by the nature of them.

But why?

My still-dissociated brain picks at it with the speed of thought now that the venom magick is in my belly (and lower) and sits simmering inside me, not a distraction but a sensation not unpleasant at all.

Why would the thought of being kin with these . . . *magnificent* engines of retribution, these vessels of wrath, make me turn aside? "Vengeance is mine," saith the Lord; well, to Hades with that; vengeance is *theirs.* I know wrath; it's in my DNA and has been most of my life now. I've delivered revenge and retribution. I have the body count to prove it. All I have been through has forged me into what I am, fated me to be here in this moment. If I stand before the original avenging angels and they want me then why would I say no to that?

Meg stands close to me.

I didn't see her move.

"You swallowed the poison."

"I did," I reply.

"Only a *sister* can do that."

The Fury with the paddle speaks up, "Or *her*."

I look from one to the other. "Her? You mean me?"

"She is not her!" Meg snaps at her sister, and shakes her head. "She speaks of Serket," she says to me.

"Serket." I roll the name around in my mind. I'm used to gods having more than one name, but it's usually multi-word titles that are descriptive. This two-names-only-a-few-letters-off-each-other bit is really going to be hard to keep up with. "She's who we're traveling to see, the warden of this place."

Meg nods.

"She is not a sister?" I ask.

"No." The word is harsh and definitive from her.

"Care to elaborate on that?"

Marty clears his throat. "She is—"

I snap my fingers and hold up my hand. "Marty." He takes the tone in my voice as the command to *shut the fuck up* it was meant to be.

I look up at Meg. "What is she if not a sister?"

"She is Other. Different. Not of the fold nor the cut of our cloth."

"But she could swallow the venom?"

"She Who Tightens the Throat could indeed swallow any poison. She is of that nature."

She Who Tightens the Throat? I've heard some pretty ominous names, but that one sends chills all the way down to the backs of my knees. I have a feeling I'm not going to enjoy meeting her when I do.

The thought quickens me and I feel the weight of the skinhound upon me. Strange how I had forgotten him for a moment. He is still hanging inside the coat across my back, but for a moment there I had shunted the feel of that pressure to the side of my mind and had stopped thinking about it.

"You know I am not like you." I say it softly, attempting to not offend, and the words make a hollow longing in their wake as they leave my mouth. *Fuck, what is this? What the fuck is wrong with me?*

"The results do not lie," Meg says simply.

"Okay," I say. "If I am a sister then let me pass through."

Meg's full bottom lip rolls out and down into a frown. "You would leave us?"

"I have to." It takes all I have to clamp down on the urgency that rushes to fill my voice. I don't want to hurt Meg and her, my, sisters. "I have a thing I have to do."

"You will return to us?" the Sister with the whip speaks up.

"If I am able. I will."

Meg nods, her braids clicking against each other in an insect chatter. "Then you have our blessing."

I watch her, unsure if she is being sincere. It appears she is. Her face is serene, a blank slate of granite. I smile and nod myself, for lack of a better way to acknowledge this. I hold out the scourge. "Here you go."

She shakes her head. "It is in your hand, sister."

"It's yours."

"I will grow another."

"Okay."

I've just gotten myself turned away to begin following the road again when she speaks.

"Tribute must still be paid, sister."

21

THE OTHER TWO Furies lead Meg to the tree and the razor roses chime as they do, blooms leaning and turning like small heads of scalpel edges.

The skinhound lies a few feet to my left, next to Marty. The coat has completely cocooned Winnie and it feels weird to stand tall without the weight of them hanging from my shoulders or the comfort of the coat touching me. My head is so quiet it feels almost hollow, as if my own thoughts are rattling around inside, echoing off the walls and the hardwood floors.

Yes, my mind apparently has hardwood floors.

The scourge hangs in my left hand. A small spot of warm pain has set into the top of my forearm as I keep my wrist tilted up so that the falls don't touch the ground. I don't know why it feels important to keep them up, but it does, so I go with it.

The Sister on the right, Alekto of the Lash, curls her fingers into the metal that curls along Meg's ribs, digging under the edge and pulling it away. It comes free, but it doesn't want to, pulling away slowly, her coal-colored skin sticking to it and peeling off reluctantly. Meg leans backward, pulling away with a groan that sounds like pain.

And sounds like the exact opposite of pain.

On the other side of Meg the other sister, Tilphousia of the Cudgel, digs in.

Meg's groan climbs to a moan that thrums against the poison-tainted magick that still sits low and heavy and sloshy in my belly. It makes me want to squirm, but I stand still and suffer through it. I try to never fucking squirm. Not ever.

It takes minutes that feel like hours for them to remove all the wrappings on Meg.

Now she stands before me, naked and, well, frankly, *glorious,* like a cobalt memorial to female pain and suffering and the power that comes because of it. Lines follow her form where the copperish bands once lay and thin trickles of some shiny substance that may or may not be blood run in zigzaggy rivulets along her sides and across her curves.

It doesn't lessen her; it magnifies her, displaying her strength of form. She is a godsdamned woman in all her glory.

My chest feels heavy, choked with emotion.

Pride.

Clotted with pride.

Tilphousia gestures for Meg to move toward the tree and she does, carefully taking each step as if it were the most important step she could ever take, as if the measurement of all of time and space and fate rest and rely on that gentle placing of her arched foot.

Reaching the tree, she leans forward, pressing her chest against it, lifting her arms to drape casually over the lower limbs. It is a move of grace and delicacy but not weakness. She turns her face to the side and presses it against the tree as her sisters move to each side. They use the bands of her former clothing to wrap and bind her wrists to the branches.

They are not gentle about it.

They pull and twist, knotting the bands tightly, their long fingers moving in precise, graceful movements, and it brings to mind the chanoyu, the Japanese tea ceremony, and its embodiment of grace and precision, every movement deliberate, a physical expression of something spiritual. Hypnotic and zen, a perfect distillation of intent. They move with no waste, not one increment of overreach.

My brain reaches out, sorting through the bit of Japanese I've picked up through the years of martial arts. The words for this are there, somewhere, tucked in a cranny, stuffed into a nook. I dig and scrabble.

Kinbaku: tight binding.

No, not quite.

I dig more as I watch the grace of the two Sisters and the elegant suffering of Meg.

Kinbaku-bi: the *beauty* of tight binding.

Marty makes a noise that sounds similar to clearing his throat.

It pulls me from the moment with a flare of annoyance that I let ride into my voice as I hiss, "What?"

"We should consider leaving."

"We can't."

"They are occupied. If you do not insist on carrying this"—his hand sweeps to indicate the coat cocoon—"then we can be outside of this place before—"

"No."

The shock on his face at my tone is almost comical.

"No? Care to explain?"

"No."

It takes him a long second to respond. "You are infuriating."

"Yeah, so I've been told." By the Man in Black. "Look, Marty,

I'm not leaving them without honoring my word. No way." I can't explain to him the connection I feel to the Sisters, but it is there. A bond. Meg needs this, whatever this turns out to be.

I need this, whatever this turns out to be.

After all that has happened to get here I feel . . . unmoored. Disconnected. I know the coat being gone has a big part to play, I can feel the emptiness on the inside of my skull from its absence, but it's more than that.

I don't feel like myself.

I don't feel truly human.

It's not just the magick; it's all I have done to find the Man in Black, all the truly terrible things that have led me to here, right here in a field of razor roses, watching two embodiments of revenge bind another embodiment of the same vengeance. My chest is full of darkness, crackling, sticky, jagged darkness like the brittle broken bits of bottle on the bottom of a riverbed, the kind that cut you from heel to ball, slicing your arch to bleed free in the cold running water, and I need something, some kind of release, or I am going to lose it.

I cannot lose it.

I have many more miles to go and many more fucking evil shit chaos gods bent on destroying everything in my world to kill before I sleep.

Well, just the one, just the Man in Black, but you get my point.

This darkness has to go somewhere, has to be lessened, or passed on like a cup of sour wine and an unsweet cake passed over a casket laden with someone who has been freshly corpse-ified, all the sorrow and misery and everything wrapped in that not-so-holy communion, and someone has to eat it, swallow it right down their gullet, to pull it out of this world, out of me.

As I stand here with her instrument of pain, it feels like Meg wants to take it.

Take it all.

My own personal sin-eater.

Can she do it?

Can I do it?

The scourge twitches in my hand as the Sisters step from Meg, their work done to completion.

Meg's voice comes to my ears, muffled by the tree her face presses against. "I can, sister, I can, and I will." And something in it, some tone or modulation or urgency, sinks in like a red-hot hook that curls through my chest and draws me forward to her.

Four strides and I am there, close enough to truly study her.

There is a fire in my belly, maybe it's the poison-tainted magick, maybe it's just that old familiar belly beast mix of pain and anger and fucked up that I've had inside me for the last decade, but this close to her it boils and threatens to spill over and I have to put this somewhere and I need to know, I. Need. To. Know she is the one who can take it.

The iris of her eye, the one turned to me, flares wide, then narrows, and the avidity that rolls off me like gas fumes envelops her and there is a near-audible *click* in my ears as my question is answered and she turns her face to the tree and her muscles tense, then relax in long, lithe lines, prepared to absorb all that I need to unleash.

I step back and the weighted end of the scourge swings around, pulling my arm behind me, building in violent potential. It hangs there as the moment tightens, narrows, constricts until there is just me, just my darkness, just Meg, just her submission, and just the space between us.

I take my first swing.

22

THE FALLS HIT her across her right shoulder, splaying wide as they do.

They don't bite. They don't snag.

They bounce away, the slickened scar tissue that decorates her rejecting my blow.

It reverberates in me, the frustration of the failed strike howling in my guts.

I shake out the scourge and lean back to swing again.

Wait.

This is . . . *off.* I don't have any power.

Not nearly enough to properly use the tool in my left hand.

Left hand . . .

I switch it to my right, to my dominant hand, which is fitting.

The wood lies across my Mark as my fingers close tight around it.

The magick in my belly roils up, all liquidy-shimmering and splashing as if I am hollow, and spills down my arm. The flail comes alive and I am connected to it, to the bits and bobs of it, to the tips and tails of it; from my fingers to its stingers we are now one piece of thing sculpted from the same substance and intent. It becomes an extension of my own arm, the instrument of my will.

I don't swing it as much as I let it roll backward, the weight of the scorpion tail tips pulling on me, stretching my muscles, the elongation of them creating a chain reaction, building energy in them, the kinetic potential and the magick mixing as my breath draws in.

At the end of the languorous sweep of the scourge I *clench*, pulling my arm forward like a streak of lightning. The long leather lashes whip past my face with a forceful whispered sound. Some dark thrill races from the sweetmeat where my jaw becomes my throat all the way down to the intimate bottom of my pelvis.

The scourge strikes Meg's back with a cracking *smack!* that jolts me like high-voltage electricity and my head goes swimmy. The lashes spread across her back like a spread hand, reaching up and around her torso. The scorpion tails sink, hooking on with their barbed stingers, latching on to her anthracite flesh. I feel them pumping their venom through my connection, the slick, twitchy throb of injection.

Meg arches against the tree, her body contracted to escape the pain. A guttural noise rises from her throat that carries back to me and my head goes swimmy again. She hurts because I hurt her. She is taking this, suffering this, because *I choose it*. She is bent to my will, submissive to my intent. She is my playground, my toy, my receptacle for all the darkness I have accumulated along the way here.

I yank the scourge, jerking the stingers free in a harsh movement. Some slip out in a spurt of rotten honey-colored venom; some hang and tear, pulling stripes through Meg's skin.

Blood, or what Meg has for blood, begins to flow even as I let the scourge's momentum pull it around into another swing.

With even more purpose I whip the scourge back against her skin.

The angle is different; this time the scourge wraps around her, where her ribs should be, the falls lying along the narrow valleys of her rib cage, as if my aim were good enough to place them there where the skin is thin and the meat is tender, where the stingers can really sink and dump their venom, my venom, deep into her body. Meg gives a howl as I rip them free. Through the connection I feel the barbs sing off the bones of her, chiming out as a submelody to her scream of pain.

She turns her face and there are tears streaming from her closed eyes.

Tears running into the folds of her smile.

I don't know why, it doesn't make me angry, doesn't feel like an insult, it simply feels like confirmation that Meg wants this, but that small smile sets me to work.

I set to, throwing the scourge against her with vigor, striking again and again and again and again, each blow in a new patch of exposed skin. The scorpion tails sting, the pieces of bone and steel bite deep, and I become a machine, a thing, an object that only exists in this moment to inflict as much pain as I can on this creature who calls me sister.

There is wetness on my face.

It's salty enough as it enters my mouth that I don't know if it's Meg's blood or if I'm crying.

Each blow Meg jerks and howls.

Each blow her blood runs like it's escaping.

Each blow my darkness dissipates, laid across Meg's back and sides and arms and hips and legs. Anywhere I can hit I do hit, kissing her violently with my lash, with my darkness, with myself.

I create patterns and as they appear, a half-dozen lines at a time, I see that I am carving into her something thaumaturgical, something alchemical, some form of some symbol and pattern that is laden with magick. My magick. I don't know what it is, this Mark I cut into her, but it is something that means something, a rune, a ward, a glyph of some kind.

My will, and her submission to it, along with the application of blood and violence, and I am turning Meg into my fetish, my totem, my talisman. It's all instinctive, I don't know high magick, I only know how to use my own power, but this is something different, something sacred and holy and hallowed unto us.

From the corner of my eye something moves.

I turn my gaze just a micro-movement.

Marty.

Marty is reaching toward the cocooned skinhound.

There is no thought as I pivot and lash out, the scourge striking along the back of his hand. The scorpion tails flex, digging into the flesh there. I pull them free before they can begin to pump poison, but Marty's hand still flares, angry red coals glowing in the pockmarks left by the stingers that penetrated. He jumps back, pulling his hand into his coveralls. His eyes bore into me, glittering black with anger, but I don't care; *stay the fuck away from my friend*.

I don't miss a beat in whipping the scourge back around and applying it to Meg's back.

She has stopped making noises.

No moans or groans, no whimpers, no howls, just deep shuffling breaths between blows and we are synced up, heart and heartbeat. Heat suffuses my upper back, the muscles worked into a state of lactic burn. My flexors are steel cables. My spine a rod attached to the ball socket joint of my pelvis.

Tears flow down my cheeks, hot and oily along my jawline,

mingling with the layer of sweat that coats me. Meg also streams, also coated, but not with sweat, with her blood. The blood of sacrifice, the blood of consecration, the blood of saining, washing away my dark, soaking up the residue of all the things I have had to do to lead me to this place of atonement.

By her stripes I am healed.

I lay one vicious blow across her sacrum, the entire bloody length of the scourge cutting across the seat of her spine in an underscore to the Mark I have laid upon her, and my knees buckle, dropping me to the ground.

Meg slumps against the tree.

I kneel there, pain blossoming slowly through my knees from the hard ground. My arms shake, micro-tremors chasing one another through my muscles like rats through tubes.

I stare at the symbol cut into the flesh of this embodiment of vengeance and the lines blur together in my sight, painted over with the gore of Megaera, one-third of the trinity of punishment. Her skin puckers in dozens of puncture wounds from the stingers of my scourge, and the slashes that yawn open like mouths bleed blue-black, and the poison I have instilled in her traces varicosely in a wobbly map behind it all, swelling and thickening her flesh until it gleams like overripe fruit, something thin-skinned that you could push your finger in to the third knuckle and it would hang loose and mushy around it like undercooked pie filling.

I think the Mark is mine.

And I feel it, running between us like webbing, a thousand little connections between my magick and her essence.

Meg is mine.

Everything is silent, the world around me one big *whomp* of nothingness, and I can't tell if it's real or if I cannot hear because my head is full of rushing blood.

And then, through the nothing, murmuring noise I hear softly, ever so softly, Meg say, "Thank you."

My bones go liquid at the words and I slide sideways to the ground clutching the bloody scourge to my chest as the exhausted and empty scorpion stingers flex weakly against my skin but do not pierce me.

23

I WALK TALLER, my spine straighter, feeling lighter inside despite the burden of the skinhound strapped across my back.

The coat has wrapped him completely, securing him against anything. I tried to probe the cocoon with my magick, to get a sense of what was happening inside, but the coat is too dense for that to work. It either thickened or is using some form of mojo to keep me out. It did make part of itself into a strap for me to use as a sling, but it is not in my head at all. The coat's alien babbling voice is completely absent, allowing my own mind to stretch and ramble, trying to fill in the empty.

I feel changed by what happened with Meg, like I dumped out a whole slew of psychic mess. My anger and pain and, yes, I will admit it, fear are all still here, still in a sticky ball behind my breastbone. It's all stamped into my DNA and I'm going to need it to push me through finishing what I've started, to drive me to keep hunting the Man in Black.

But letting my darkness go was squeezing pus out of a wound, or sucking poison out of a snakebite, or some other gross way of removing poison. It cleared out all the dank psychic material I had gathered in my hunt for the Man in Black. All the killing and the fighting, not to mention the betrayal and deception, that got me here had built up like sediment, like loam, becoming chains weighing me down. My head was muddy, my spirit bound up.

Now I am clear.

Focused.

Intent.

The Man in Black is going to pay.

The scourge clicks and clacks with every stride. It hangs from my belt, the handle tucked in tight at an angle where I can pull it free with only a moment passing. The stingers hit across my thigh with every forward step, scritching along the surface of my jeans but not biting me. I can feel the magick inside me spooling thin and slow into the lash, tracing along the leather and the knots, slowly drip-filling the stingers that begin fermenting it into more poison.

Soon it will be fully ready to use.

Meg insisted I take it and I did. I didn't want to leave her behind, but I couldn't take her from that cell, Marty made that clear, even though I felt, still feel, tied to her. I'm swearing this right now, if I live through this thing I am doing I will be returning for her and my other two sisters.

"You should have left that thing behind."

I glance over at Marty. He is walking beside me, matching my stride. His right hand is shoved deep somewhere inside his coveralls. He isn't looking at me, just looking ahead down the undulating cobblestone hallway we walk.

He's mad.

I can hear it in his voice.

He's pissed because I laid open his hand.

He'll be fine.

"It was a gift from Meg," I say in response to his comment. "Besides, it's not like I can have too many weapons in a place like this."

"I was not speaking of Megaera's Kiss."

"If you mention me leaving the skinhound again we are going to have a problem, Marty."

"We have more danger to pass through and that burden will slow you down. The time you spent with the Sisters moved our goal."

"I don't understand."

Marty sighs but doesn't answer.

"Explain how our goal moved," I say.

"This is not just a prison of walls. It is not stable or stationary; if it were then it would never be able to hold its occupants. It shifts and evolves; it is wheels within wheels within wheels, interlocking and overlapping and intertwining. Things move in this place to maintain the stability of it."

"Like a gyroscope."

"Nothing like a gyroscope."

"Like a gyroscope made in cosmic hell."

"Nothing like a gyroscope," he reasserts. "But now the chamber of Satet has moved and we have further to go and will have to pass through an extremely dangerous place."

"Didn't we just pass through a dangerous place?" The cocoon on my back shifts and I remember the Hungry Dark. "Two dangerous places?"

He shakes his head and keeps walking.

I reach down and stroke the scourge; magick crackles between my fingers and its still-damp surface. "It's a good thing I kept this, since I'm not letting go of Winnie."

"Winnie?"

I shrug. The cocoon is heavy, so it's just a small one. "The skin-hound."

"Why do you call him that? He does not have skin."

"Same reason I call you Marty."

"Because you cannot pronounce the proper word?"

Smartass. "Because I'm a pain-in-the-neck-type girl who does whatever she feels like doing."

He turns those droopy eyes my way. "I do not believe that to be true at all. You seem to be one who is doing nothing she feels like doing."

His words run over me, washing me in sadness, and he's staring at me a little too closely.

"Don't get insightful now, Marty. You'll ruin your reputation."

"You do not understand how difficult you have made this simple task of traveling."

I'm not answering that. He's right that I don't understand, but then again, I wouldn't know even if I hadn't done anything. I don't think any of this would be easy, regardless of what I did or did not do. Nothing in my life has been easy since Nyarlathotep, the Crawling Chaos himself, came through my door and took a big chaotic shit on my life.

I feel what little bit of peace I have from scourging Meg slip away in a terrible trickle, just leaking out of my limbs and dribbling away to nothing. I'm still better, but any little bit of light there was a moment ago has been snuffed out. Why am I feeling this way? Why has this nagging drain been a part of me since before I wished my way to this place?

Yes, I know there's weirdness galore. Yes, I had to do, and am still having to do, terrible things to stick to my mission.

I know that my mission is important. If I don't stop the Man in Black then all the world is forfeit.

That is, all outside elements.

In therapy somewhere I learned that the outside elements, even bizarro ones that belong in some horror movie, are not the main factor in my emotional makeup. I might react to them, and so far it has felt like I've been doing almost nothing but reacting to them, but they are not me. What I am going through is not who I am.

So what is this drain on my spirit?

It's not fear.

I do have that. A fair amount. I am in a scary fucking place and dealing with things that could kill me or worse.

And I fear that I will fail this. That Daniel and my family and anyone I care about will become nothing but food and playthings for the evil locked away here. It's on me to stop the Man in Black, I didn't choose to be that one, but here I am, responsible for so much. I cannot be this girl. I am not the responsible one. I'm not too reckless, but I'm not responsible either. And I might not mean to fail, but I may just not be enough, not nearly. I am human, and not a very good one a lot of the time.

And I'm tired.

I won't lie down, but damn I would like this to be done so I could lie on a bed next to Daniel and talk as our arms and legs intertwine, wine on our breath, a little jazz on the stereo, just the right amount of covers on us to be warm but not too hot.

The impulse to just wish myself away, to go back home and grab Daniel up and do that thing, to take what little time we could have and make it perfect before the Man in Black unleashed Azathoth on the Earth and destroyed us all, well, that urge nearly drives me to my knees. I keep walking, head down, eyes forward, but all I want to do is stop and leave.

Why should I save everyone? Why is that *my* fate? Who did this to me, 'cause I sure didn't choose it for myself. Hell, after that night, *the night*, the first time my whole world was shattered and destroyed, I barely have the desire to save myself in any way. All sense of purpose and justice was torn from me as I lay there and I decided that I was just a meatsuit here to move around through meatspace and in the end it wouldn't matter because we all die.

But now . . .

Fuck, I don't even know if death is the end.

So here I am, trudging beside an otherworldly janitor, with a barely living skinless hellhound strapped across my shoulders with the living skin flayed off a wayward archangel

Marty stops. "What are you thinking?"

"Nothing," I say so I won't scream at the frustrating futility of it all.

"Good," he says. "We are here."

24

"This is the next shortcut?"

Marty nods. "It is."

It's an opening, not much taller than I, that falls to darkness just a foot or so beyond its threshold. No gate, no door, nothing to bar passage.

"It is kept shut by secrecy."

Did Marty just answer the question I hadn't asked yet?

"Don't read my mind, Marty."

He half-shrugs with his right shoulder, the hand still covered deep in the pocket of his coveralls.

"So what does that mean, 'shut by secrecy'?"

"It is hidden on the inside of the cell; none of the occupants there can locate it."

"But if they did . . ."

"They cannot."

"But if they—"

"They will never discover this entrance to and from their cell."

It's my turn to shrug and the motion shifts the skinhound co-coon, pulling it heavy across my shoulders. "It's your party; you can cry if you want to."

"What does that mean?"

"It means, not my circus, not my monkeys. You run this how you want to. I just want to find the Man in Black. You say I have to see this Sakesh—"

"*Serket*," he corrects, emphasizing the two syllables as *sir* and *ket* with hard consonants.

"Fine. Serket. You say I have to see her to make this happen, so lead on, but get on with it, because I am tired."

"Then let us stop prattling here like hens before the distance between us and your goal moves again."

"After you." I indicate the opening.

Marty nods. "Stay close. I cannot find you if you become lost here."

I pop a salute to him and follow as he enters the opening.

But I stay close, because despite my smartass attitude I have a feeling I don't want to get lost anywhere in this place.

25

THE AIR CHANGES, becomes damp and chill. The clean scent of wet, rotting vegetation climbs into my nostrils and curls up in the upper portion of the back of my throat until it is not only all I smell but all I feel. It's the air of fall, deep fall, just before Father Winter reaches out and breaks it with a hard frost or sleet.

The darkness only lasts a dozen or so steps before it begins to break up into varying shades and hues, deep purple velvet, pure except where spoiled by a sweet spill of indigo ink. Each step defines shapes more and more until I know we are in a forest of sorts. The trees are wide set; there is more than enough room for Marty and me to walk without any danger of touching them. That's good. After the razor roses from the last place we crossed I would hate to see what trees would do. I can tell they are bare limbed and they look like normal trees. Oak, perhaps ash or even hawthorn, something deciduous.

Even though we walk on bare dirt.

No leaf crunches underfoot.

There is no rustling, no dry rattlesnake whisper of waxy cuticle against desiccated epidermis, thin slivers of dead chlorophyll stacked like newspaper.

I look at the bare limbs of the trees and wonder if they are trees at all.

"Calm down."

I start at the sound of Marty's voice and flare angry at my reaction. I hate feeling like a typical girl.

"I'm calm." My voice lashes like the scourge against my hip. I can hear it in my own ears.

He points at my waist level.

I look down and my right hand is glowing, little bits of magenta etheric energy dribbling off my fingers. They tumble off the ends of my blunt nails and sputter downward, dissipating before they can hit the ground.

I clench the hand into a fist, the raised scar tissue there hot against my fingers.

Maybe I'm a little more stressed over this than I thought.

Deep breaths.

In through the nose, out through the mouth, tip of my tongue pressed against the roof of my mouth just behind my teeth, where the governing and the conception vessels in acupuncture meet. I breathe through it, trying to turn the upward-flowing energy from my yang meridians into downward-flowing energy through my yin meridians the way I was taught in Qigong class.

Normally, at home, this is effective in four or five breaths.

So what if it takes two dozen?

I'm fine.

Marty nods when my Mark stops dripping with magick. "We must be very careful here."

"I've heard that before."

"Listen better this time."

I resist the urge to flip him off.

We keep walking and I keep waiting for the branches over our head to come alive and reach down toward us.

They never do.

The trees thin and we come to their edge. The branches recede, leaving me to stare up at a canopy of stars. They scatter across the underside of the night sky like diamond dust tossed onto a funeral shroud. They blink and glitter in an odd timing.

In the center a yellow moon hangs, its edges rough, as if hewn from some soft stone by an unsure hand. It reminds me of the skin-hound's one remaining eye. This moon glares down balefully, but it feels empty, blind, unseeing—more akin to a yellow marble than an eye.

I shake off its hold and look in front of us.

The land lies at an angle.

The downhill slopes in rises and dips but always heads lower. The path carries on for a bit before losing itself in the curves of the land. Deep in the valley nestles a cluster of lights that appears to be some form of village.

The other path is more straightforward, heading from us to a peak.

On that peak a tall, thin stone juts into the night, piercing the air around it. Even from here I can feel it as if it were radiating heat that reached into my bones, pulling me toward it, toward this . . . Witchstone that has put a spell upon me.

Marty turns to me. "Which path?"

Is this a trick? I'm not the guide here; he is.

"Both will lead to where we are going," he says.

"But which one is the quicker way?"

"That is your decision."

"Don't you know?"

He shrugs with such casualness I truly don't know how to interpret the movement. Turning from him, I look back at the scene in front of us.

Thick lemongrass sways in a slight night breeze that I can feel across my cheeks. The paths remain open, free from vegetation and undulating up and down the hill in a manner that reminds me of a slithering snake. I glance down at the village. I can't make out anything but the lights; however, it *feels* as if it is inhabited, everyone tucked away inside against the horrors of the night, and I wonder if they are like the razor roses from the Sisters' cell. Are they comfort for the thing kept here? Food? Worse?

I pull my brain from the thought of being worse than food to something that needs this elaborate of a cell.

This reminds me more of a zoo and less of a prison, although a zoo is actually a prison for animals, but the creation of habitats for the things held here is more zoo-like. Perhaps these habitats keep the things here—the elder gods and the Great Old Ones and whatever other kinds of things might wind up here; maybe these habitats keep them docile.

I bite back the desire to ask Marty that. I'm getting distracted.

My eyes turn and travel to where they have wanted to go since I stepped out from under the broken stick canopy of the trees.

To the Witchstone.

It is not a jumble of lights. Not a vague impression of a town. It stands on the hilltop and thrusts proudly and defiantly toward the moon. One long, dark finger that lies out across the night sky, it gleams, the sallow moonlight running over its edges, cutting its ebon shape from the darkness.

Deep inside me there is a vibration, a humming, some chattering little buzz that feels like ants have made a home in the honeycomb tunnels of my pelvic bone; the resonance of their nesting sends a delicious thrill up my spine that clenches my jaw and grinds my molars. I am a tuning fork set to the frequency of that tall, black splinter and it calls to me, calls to the marrow part of me.

I don't speak because I am unsure if I can form words or if I will just moan out the timbre and the harmonic of the Witchstone's song echoing inside me. I raise my hand and I point and even that simple act, just moving my arm closer to the monolith, reverberates through me.

Marty sighs and turns toward the upward path. "I suppose it is the more direct route."

26

THE WITCHSTONE LOOMS above us as Marty and I stand at the base, stretching much farther than it appeared to from the edge of the trees. From there it looked to be maybe twenty feet tall.

It juts into the sky, a gray so deep it may as well be black. The surface is smoothly wavy, like a slab of shale, except where it has deep grooves that flow from the base up until I cannot see them anymore. The grooves are slick and smooth, as if they were cut by some form of heat, rather than jagged or rough like chisel work. Thin cracks chase the surface, but they don't give any indication of weakness. This stone is immortal.

As I stand here, looking up the length of it, the monolith stretches on forever, as if it never ends, forever racing away in Euclidean lines. This close the humming call of the stone has become a full-body experience and I feel it itching under my skin like grit slipping in the subcutaneous membrane. I feel hot, feverish, damp under my clothes as my magick rages in my body like a virus.

My hands are fists by my sides.

I want to touch it.

I don't want to touch it.

I want to touch it.

Take a step back, one small step, a half step, just take a step back, goddamn it why can't I just take a step back?

It is ancient. No, it is primordial, very much like the rock that held the Hungry Dark. The secrets of all time locked in its shale surface, which has borne witness to history. But this rock, this . . . stone . . . Witchstone has not been a bystander. It has been involved in disasters and cataclysms across time and realities. Somehow I know, in the part of me that just knows things, that this stone exists in many places and many times. It exists on Earth, my Earth, and on planets and in realms I have never dreamed of, couldn't conceive of.

It is a splinter lodged in the skin of existence.

The part of the coat that acts as a sling across my chest ripples, and I'm so consumed with all the feelings racing *inside* my body that a sensation *outside* my body startles me.

From the corner of my eye I see a tendril, thin and liquidy like cuttlefish ink spilled in zero gravity, rise from the coat where it crosses my shoulder. The tendril suspends there for a long moment, pulling my attention from the monolith. Water begins to run from the corner of my left eye from the strain of looking over the curve of my own cheekbone. The tendril dips out of sight and I blink rapidly to dissipate the pain from the orbital muscles that control the axis of my eye.

The sensation of cool liquid running over the skin of my throat sends a shiver through me that contradicts the sticky prickly heat of my magick fever.

The back of my brain bursts with a babble of music that is the voice of the coat. It fills my mind like a perfume and I smile because of it, despite everything.

I have missed you.

The coat chatters away and it reassures me even though I don't understand, but its presence in my mind gives me the break I need to take that step back.

The magick fever from the black stone's call doesn't lessen, but I expand with the small bit of autonomy and settle myself back into myself.

Thank you.

The coat murmurs.

How is he doing?

The coat is silent for a long second and then it whispers like silk along the folds of my brain and I understand without understanding. Does that mean I comprehend?

It's bad. Not desperate yet, but real, real bad, Ringo.

I will take care of this, of him.

The trust in the coat's response puts the steel back in my spine. I have to do this. So much relies on me.

And the dark buzzy cloud of doubt boils up on the edge and I shut it down. I cannot think about failure, about how weak I am, how human, how much I just want to be done with all the crazy shit of late.

How much I just want to lie down.

Nope. Work to do.

I turn on Marty. He's also looking at the Witchstone and rubbing the back of his right hand; the pressure of his fingertips makes the loose skin there fold and bunch and then pull smooth. The red marks from where I nailed him with the scourge are gone, slicked over as if his skin were Silly Putty.

"What now?" I ask.

He doesn't look at me as he answers, "Now we find the door out of here."

"You don't know where it is?"

"Did you miss the part where I mentioned that the doors here were locked with secrecy? The knowledge of where the exit lies is not easy to come by."

"Well, you need to come by it."

He points up. "There is the key."

"The Witchstone?"

"I've never heard it called that, but yes."

"It's the door?"

"The key." He turns to look at me, big seal eyes harsher than you would think they could be. "Are you not listening to me?"

Anger flares and the magick fever in my body spikes as it crackles through me. "Who do you think you're talking to?"

"Someone who knows nothing about anything."

"Isn't my job to know anything about this place," the words snarl out of my mouth like tangled barbed wire, "unlike some people here."

"You expect expertise on a place designed to confound and keep captive creatures and concepts of vast and varied abilities?" He chuckles, but it sounds bitter and mean. "You humans want the world and do not know what to do with it."

My hands curl back into fists, the ragged nails of my right hand digging into the raised lines of the Mark there.

The coat babbles in my ear, the rapid flow of sounds encouraging me to action.

I push words through gritted teeth: "Stop insulting my species and point me to the goddamned door."

He turns so fast his skin pulls and drags on the air, fluttering along his face and neck. His mouth yawns open too wide and his teeth have gone too sharp, dripping with spittle. His voice rides breath gone all carrion, meaty and stinking of iron, as he barks at me, "I cannot point you to something if I do not know where it exists!" His finger stabs toward the monolith. "That is the only thing here that can show you the door."

The blood that trickles from the cut of my nails through scar tissue fills the cup of my palm, all sticky and metallic as it drips between the gaps in my knuckles.

I scream in his face and lunge forward, swinging.

Marty moves fast, faster than I thought he could, and my fist cuts through the space his head just occupied. I'm fully committed, swinging with all I have, swooping the blow from deep inside me.

I can't stop before I hit the side of the Witchstone. I can only open my hand so I don't crush my knuckles on the unforgiving stone of it.

My bloody Mark slaps the black stone of the monolith and everything implodes.

27

THE SHOCK WAVE throws me back and I twist away from the brunt of it, the weight of the skinhound in the coat slinging me around to one knee that strikes the rocky soil. Pain flares up my femur and my teeth clack together, pinching the edges of my tongue. My mouth goes all hot and soupy with the taste of iron nails. The coat screams in my brain like a high-pitched steam whistle and I squinge my thoughts to get it to shut the fuck up because while it screeches I can't see because my eyelids are fluttering like butterflies set on fire.

I snatch the tendril of it off my neck. It comes free in a tear of pain as if it had been sewn in place and I am ripping out the stitches.

The coat's voice stops like a switch has been flipped.

My vision clears and I am looking down the hill. I see the shock wave rippling away from us as it displaces the lemongrass. The air fills with the sticky-sweet fragrance of citrus as the saw edges of the blades rub against one another and release the oil trapped in them.

From the corner of my eye I see Marty roll up to his knees. His hands move around his body, pulling and tugging at his skin as if it were clothing that had gotten twisted. He's grumbling and spitting some language that beats a tattoo on the drum inside my ear, all rattling and bouncing like pebbles on a stretched skin. The air around his mouth is actually tinged blue with his alien cursing.

But I am watching the shock wave.

It rolls down the hill, looking like it is gathering speed, but I know that is probably an optical illusion.

It strikes the village in the nestled folds of the valley, far at the bottom of the hill, and all the lights go out.

A few seconds later, over Marty's muttering I hear the tinkle of broken glass and the sound of splintering wood.

There is one long moment of silence so complete it is almost an empty void. It surrounds us before sparks begin to pop down the hill, tiny flickering lights moving around where the village was. The din of movement and the voices of many people begin to roll up the hill toward us.

I don't look over at him as I ask, "Marty, what's happening?"

"The second-worst thing that could." His voice sounds heavy with dread. "You have woken the inhabitants of Stregovicar."

The flickering lights keep multiplying and moving, converging until, at this distance, they appear to be one giant flare of light. They begin snaking up the hill in our direction, a string of flickering flames that are obviously torches.

"Marty?"

"Yes?"

"What else?"

"Explain."

"You said this was the second worst. What's the first?"

Before he can answer the night sky above us *groans* and the moon spins on its axis like a marble, rolling back on itself until it reveals a design, a round scarlet spot that looks familiar even though it is completely alien and foreign. My brain struggles, as if it has become some sodden and mushy cereal concoction, to make sense of it, to place it somewhere. Recognition runs and trips through my brain like a lost child in the forest fleeing from the wolf that has huffed its breath between sharp fangs to make the back of her neck wet.

My brain cannot decipher what the moon is doing.

What it is becoming.

Until it blinks.

28

THE NIGHT SKY does more than just loom above us; it hangs with sinister intent as the unblinking orb roams, peering down upon us, and I don't know what to do with this idea, this concept, this knowledge. The size of it, the width and breadth of it, are immense, dwarfing me and Marty as if we were inconsequential. I can only gape up at it, the night air drying the back of my throat and turning the saliva on the backs of my teeth into shellac. The Hungry Dark was large, even huge, but this?

This is a whole other scale.

I feel tiny, like a speck, a little piece of flotsam that has no value beyond being a nuisance at best.

The roaming orb blinks and it is like an eclipse where a crescent razor slices away the moon for a long dragged-out moment, just excising it from the vast darkness of the sky that isn't even the face of the thing I am under but the slope of its cheek, nay, the dip and crater of its eye socket, before the lid, whatever the lid is, springs back to the edge of the moon orb revealing that blood spot like a bad omen, a superstition, a portent of stillbirth and doom.

I don't think it can see us.

We are too small, too insignificant.

But if we move . . .

"Marty, what happens when *it* realizes we are here?"

He points down the hill. "You should worry more about *that*."

It takes a grinding wrench to pull my eyes off the moon that stares down at us to look where he points.

There is a swarm of crooked, broken humanity climbing the hill in our direction.

Every heartbeat they get closer and closer.

They stump along on misshapen limbs that angle oddly from torsos twisted as if their spines have been used for knot practice.

Not all of them are crippled. At the forefront of the mob stride a dozen tall, well-muscled figures. Their limbs swing loose by their sides as they lope up the hill with an animalistic ease. Behind them the mob devolves in capability and it appears that they are dragging their lesser-abled with a series of ropes or cords of some kind.

"Should we try to stop them?"

Marty looks at me. "How would you propose to stop them? Will you kill them? *Can* you kill them?"

I look down the hill. They've gotten closer, close enough for me to see faces clearly. To pick out individuals. It appears some of them are children. Many of them look pitiful, starved, and even abused.

I have killed.

I have killed a lot. More than I ever thought I would be capable of. After what happened to me I've had homicidal thoughts, fantasies of murdering the people who did that thing to me. I never thought they would come true. And I never, ever thought they would come true the way that they did.

I don't want to go any farther down that road right now.

And I've killed things, things that look human and things that did not.

I used a shotgun to take the head of the King in Yellow and his servant.

I am a killer.

I. Am. A. Murderer.

My eyes spot a girl in the crowd. She's small and looks to be about ten years old. She struggles coming up the hill and stumbles. When she does, the ropes that are around her waist yank her back to her feet and she stumbles on, carried along with the crowd. She has big eyes. I can't see their color from here, but they look dark and she has dark hair that swirls around little birdlike shoulders and the thin stalk of her neck. She's so undernourished that her little knees are bigger than her little thighs and her little elbows are bigger than her little arms. She wears a ragged sackcloth of a dress. I watch her being dragged up the hill.

"I don't think I can."

Marty shakes his head. "You disappoint in your choice of timing in growing a conscience."

"Sorry if it's inconvenient. Why don't you figure out where the door is and we'll just get out of here before anyone has to die."

"If the people of Stregovicar overtake us then we will be the ones to die."

"I won't let that happen."

"How will you stop it?"

"I don't know." I begin moving toward the oncoming crowd, who are almost upon us. I can still *feel* the eye in the sky staring down on us like a lead weight in my chest. There's a clock ticking on all of this and I don't know how much time is left on it. We need to get out of this place.

"Find the door," I say over my shoulder. "That's your job. I will buy you some time."

Speak with confidence even if you don't feel it.

Marty mutters something under his breath, but I do not stop to find out what it is.

As I walk the few steps down the trail I shift the cocoon lying across my lower back until it is as comfortable as it's going to get.

"Secure yourself so you don't move around and throw off my balance," I say to the coat. "But if I have to fight you have to get off me or I will have no chance."

The strap across my chest shrinks in response, widening so it does not swing or sway. Thin ropes of the coat wrap my hips and under my other arm, and the cocoon is secure. It is still heavy across my back and I'm still off-balance, but now the weight should stay in one place and I should be able to move without worrying about it slinging me off my feet.

Shoulda woulda coulda. Here's hoping anyway.

I pull the scourge off my belt. The falls of it rub against one another in a clickety-clackety manner. It shakes slightly in my hand as the scorpion tails flex, the stingers preparing their venom. I put it in my left hand, widen my stance so that I am stable, and shake a little bit of magick down into my right hand. The Mark in my palm begins to glow and crackle. I raise it in front of me and it casts a bloodred highlight onto the swaying grass before me. The mob is close, almost too close.

I take a deep breath and from low in my belly, with all the power I can muster. I command:

"Stop."

And, surprise surprise, they do.

29

THE LINE OF men in front of me stand in a staggered phalanx. I say they're men because they're only wearing loincloths made of the same ragged material as the girl's dress. Their chests move like bellows, but not like they've been exerting themselves, more like the way large predators keep their blood hyper-oxygenated so they're always ready for the stalk, and the hunt, and the kill.

The metaphor that comes to mind is not a stretch from the reality of their appearance.

They look like brothers or some sort of close kith and quick kin. All of them with wide, sloped shoulders and curved, flexed spines. Muscle stacks into cords and slabs on their frames, but it lies oddly. They are as hyper-muscular as a gym freak body builder, but their muscles wrap their bodies like ropes twisting around their torsos and limbs, making them look alien despite their humanoid bodies. Their faces are heavy, the shapes on them thick, with brows that jut like cliff overhangs and cheeks that sit high up by small, close-set eyes so that their mouths have as much room in their heads as possible. Heavy jaws hang low, full of thick, jagged teeth, above wide throats.

Their mouths appear to be made for one thing, and that is eating large chunks of meat.

"You understood the word 'stop.' Do you understand the words that are coming out of my mouth?"

From behind the front line of predator brothers a figure moves, coming between them. This person is slender and feminine, with long limbs and a narrow torso that is covered in another sackcloth dress. Her hair hangs limply by her face, not moving or swinging or bouncing, just lank against her collarbones. As she moves, the loops of rope that connect her to everyone else are slung over her arms at the elbows like a purse so that they do not tangle about her feet. She tilts her head and looks at me, her eyes much larger than those on the men she stands among.

It *feels* like she's studying me.

I can see her studying me, but I can also feel it up against my skin as if she's probing me with some sense that is not one of the five that normally come standard issue in humans.

I don't like that.

I pull my mind in the way that I learned to do so long ago in therapy. Shutting myself away while still being present and functional. Putting up mental shields and locking down emotional hatches so that I am not vulnerable. As I do this, visualizing my mental and emotional doors slamming shut and locking, I feel that shutting away that is so familiar from so many years of it being the only way I could cope with the world.

There is a new component.

Magick.

My magick forms a seal between me and whatever she's trying to do. I feel it slip over me like a force field. And it's new, but it feels like I've done it a hundred times before. As I've gone through this journey of crazy shit since the Man in Black came into my life, the more I've used my magick the more intuitive it has become. It is a part of me, sewn into my DNA, intrinsic and immersive.

But this is the first time my magick has done something new that I didn't have to think about and make happen.

I can tell by the expression on her face that the woman in front of me does not appreciate it.

My eyes slide sideways to the little girl and I am surprised to see the same expression on her face as on the woman's face.

A quick glance shows the expression is on all of their faces.

Behind me comes a noise that sounds like someone clanging a bell underwater. Seconds later a ruffle of magick brushes past the back of my neck. Marty has done something and it doesn't seem to have worked. It takes all of my discipline to not turn and see what he's doing, but I'd be an idiot to take my eyes off the thing in front of me.

And I try very, very hard to not be an idiot.

My brain slips sideways into a micro-memory.

Knuckles strike my cheekbone hard enough to scrape open the skin and bruise the bone. I hit the mat like I've been dropped from a great height and I have no air in my lungs because of the impact. I had only turned my head for one moment because Sensei Ken triggered an air horn on the other side of the dojo. My left eye began to swell immediately and leak like a broken faucet. Sensei Laura was a blur as I looked up at her.

"Never be distracted," she said. "Distraction will kill you in the street. Eyes always on the immediate threat. One slip you are dead, or worse."

Sensei Laura was right. And in this case I do not want to find out what the "or worse" is.

So, eyes front and Marty can take care of his own damn self.

Finally, the woman speaks; her voice is flat, no intonation to any syllable or vowel, as if they were all of the same consequence.

"We do not comprehend you."

"You don't comprehend what I say or you don't comprehend what I am?"

"We do not comprehend you."

"Is this a situation where the only words you say are 'we do not comprehend you' and that's all I can understand because I'm human, but you're actually saying everything? Are you Groot?"

"Normally when they bring things like you they are not like you."

"Nobody brought me."

And the minute the words leave my mouth I realize that Marty brought me here. Marty is the keeper. Marty is in charge of these cells, is in charge of these prisoners and their care.

Their care includes feeding.

And as I look at the hulking men with their oversized mouths and their rending, tearing teeth a cold sensation comes over me. This woman thinks that I have been delivered like a pizza. That I am her food.

As confirmation she points over my head, and I know she's pointing at Marty above the hill from me.

I shake my right hand in a "no" motion, waving my finger. Magick drips from the Mark as I do and sizzles on the grass at my feet. The pleasant scent of lemongrass and sage rises to fill my nose and it's warm and comforting and reminds me of Nana Bobo's house and her always-burning candles and pots of potpourri in liquid warming on windowsills.

"Do not mistake me for helpless."

She smiles and her teeth are miniature versions of the men around her. "We would never mistake you for helpless. Carrion is helpless; live prey never is."

The men around her shift. They don't move forward or take a step, but their intention is even more focused in my direction than it was a moment ago.

The smell of lemongrass and sage is even stronger.

I shift the scourge to my right hand and, as my fingers close around the handle, the falls began to frenzy, as if they have been electrified. Magick rolls from my palm into the scourge; a circuit has been connected and it makes my head swim for a second. From the scourge I feel the desire to lay into flesh, to hook into skin, to penetrate muscle, and to pump my poison into veins so that it may dissolve meat and tendon and bone.

That's not *my* thought. I did not know the scourge had thoughts. But now I do. And, even though I am not a tool of punishment, the scourge has it right and I want to hurt things.

My eyes move to the little girl again, to her big dark eyes and her sallow little face.

Her mouth is open. Even smaller versions of the meat grinder teeth fill it.

Looking at her sparks a maternal instinct that I didn't even know that I had. That thing that's inside of me that may only be maternal because I am a woman. It could be the same instinct that a man would have but wouldn't be called maternal. I wonder, is there any way that I can cut her free from the bonds that tie her to the rest of the group? Can I take her with me? Can I save her?

"You cannot."

The voice beside me is close enough that I feel the syllables lightly tap against the skin of my arm.

Marty is there beside me.

Looking at him, at his dumpy frame and his oval shape, I don't know how he came upon me without me sensing it at all. He looks so normal, so very, very ordinary, that I forget he is a supernatural creature.

"What did you say to me?"

"You cannot save her; you cannot separate her."

"I don't like when things read my mind, Marty."

"I have discovered the portal out of here," he says, turning slightly to the left to look back over his shoulder at the monolith.

"I don't think they're going to let us just go."

He shakes his head. "No, they will not. You will have to devise some way to extricate us from this situation that you have put us in."

"Hey, I'm not the only one here with power. You could do something too."

"I found the exit. And you did summon them here."

The anger flares inside of me and it's all I can do to not wheel on him and unleash my wrath. I'm heated, emotionally and magickally. I feel the etheric energy drip from my right hand and the smell of lemongrass and sage is strong in my nose, strong enough to distract me from my wrath, strong enough that I can just say from the side of my mouth, "I'm not going to back-and-forth here with you, Marty." My eyes still watch the group of people in front of us, their faces taking on the open-mouth pant of hunger that reminds me of a starving pack of wolves. And I find her face again and even though she has the same feral appetite raw in her little features I still want to save her.

Marty's voice is so close it is inside my ear canal.

"Look closer at the ties that bind them."

I do and, oh God, I wish I had not.

It's not ropes that string between each of these people but rather a twisted tube of flesh that hangs and droops coming from the waist of one into the waist of another until they are a loosely strung net of snarling people. The ropy flesh is lumpy and shiny and looks very much like an unstuffed sausage. Blue veins trace along the surface, running into one another, and branching off big arteries covered in an opaque thin sheathing, and the blue of them is not a solid color. It's not the same blue that I can see in the veins that run underneath my wrist. Not the blue of blood in humans before it is exposed to oxygen but rather the dirty blue of a filth-painted ocean. The blue that has the greens and even the yellows as a part of it. The blue that looks like decomposition. The blue of a steak aged even just one day too long to be edible, where meat and sustenance spoil into poison and corruption. The blue that makes your stomach turn.

My brain feels as if it has been stuffed with cotton and there is a connection that is trying to be made and is trying at the same time not to be made, where my own mind seeks to protect me from the horror that I am seeing and my body knows before my brain lets me know, and acid fills the back of my throat in a sour, bitter burning. I swallow it back down and it goes with a coating of the sticky-sweet must of the burning lemongrass at my feet and my stomach wants to revolt.

The cells in this prison are custom-made to hold their occupants. The Hungry Dark has nothing to eat to keep it weak. The Furies have a world of incisions and pain with their blood roses. Cthulhu sleeps in his city under the sea.

And then I realize what I am seeing.

Intestines.

The horde of people in front of me are all connected by intestines.

They are not the inhabitants.

They are not prisoners.

They are not people at all.

They are the stomach of the thing that hangs above, that looks down upon us with the moon for an eye.

"Are you colluding with the meal you have delivered?"

The woman between the large men is speaking, but not to me.

"You have made a mistake. Return to your hovels," Marty says.

The woman tilts her head and from the edge of my vision I see the little girl mimic her. This looks like a cluster of people connected by their intestines, but they may be one organism. One thing with many moving parts.

I have to remember I am seeing things imperfectly.

The woman speaks to Marty again. "What is wrong with you?"

"You are the one who has mistaken their schedule. This is not a feeding."

"You are not right."

"I am correct."

It takes her a long time to respond to that and when she speaks every mouth in the horde speaks at once in a boom of sonic noise so loud I feel it on the skin of my face.

"You are food."

30

I'M REACTING BEFORE the first part of them can step forward.

I'm tempted to pull magick from the earth (is it earth? Is it the flesh of whatever we are inside? Is the occupant of this cell the cell as well? Say that three times fast.), but I learned my lesson on that with the Hungry Dark.

It is *my* magick I unleash.

Calling to it makes it rise inside me, the bubbling, boiling etheric energy that lives in me as if it were a separate thing entire but somehow intimately connected to the very fiber of my being. I feel it in my blood and more, in my cells, in the bits and bobs that make my cells. The shock wave from striking the Witchstone actually gave me a little boost of magick, but it's still low, and it takes a little effort to get it to comply to my will. I push, clenching inside, and shove it raw and hot from my

Mark. It stops dripping and begins streaming, not like a beam or a ray, but more like water from a spout or a spigot.

A sweep of my arm in front of me and the lemongrass between me and the horde combusts and flares into a tall curl of licking bluish flame and thick gray smoke. I breathe in and choke and cough.

All I can taste is the astringent, sticky-slick coating of lemongrass and sage on the inside of my mouth and down my gullet and it has the sour drawing up of pine needles and the sooty, citrus bite of burnt lemons and my mouth puckers and my tongue feels like icy metal against the roof of it.

The stomach horde people fall back in unison and scream the same way.

It takes an effort to stop the stream of my magick.

It just wants to keep going and pouring and flowing and it feels good and I just want to let it, but I know, in that crying mewling little part of my lizard brain, that if I do so I will be spent and helpless and so, teeth grinding together as I do, I stopper my magick. The Mark on my palm is on fire, and the magick has gone from magenta, wine-colored spears of fire to blue-black tongues of flame of the size you would find atop birthday cake candles. They trace the squiggles and the wiggles and the swirls and the whorls of the Mark on my hand. I bat them out against my jeans, leaving behind little singe marks on the denim.

Damn, that hurts.

And the stoppered magick makes my wrist and the bones in my forearm ache.

The fire races away from me as it eats the grass. It's a narrow wavy band with flames about waist-high. I can feel the heat backwashing toward me; the soil or whatever the grass is growing from is a black smoldering band like a moat between me and the horde. But the wall of flames is thin, only a few inches wide, and I can see it beginning to break as it continues its march pushing back the stomach people.

I turn to Marty and say, "We've got to go. Where is this portal?"

He jerks his head and begins trudging up the hill toward the Witchstone, moving faster than it looks like he would be able to. I shoulder the coat cocoon, but it does not move. It is securely lashed to my body, so I lean forward and run as fast as I can toward that tall splinter of ebon stone that juts into the night air.

By the time I reach it I am out of breath and my thighs are on fire and all I want is to lay down. I glance over my shoulder and see that the horde have broken through the wall of fire and are stumbling their way toward us.

I suck in air. "Where's this damn portal?"

Marty lifts his hand and points a chubby finger in the air to the top of the Witchstone.

"I don't see anything."

Marty reaches over, faster than I can move back, and taps me on the forehead with his finger.

My eyes blur and then jerk back into focus. Now I can see a wavy area, like water on a windy day, hovering above the tip of the Witchstone.

Great. That's perfect.

"With their configuration," Marty says, "they cannot climb and thus they cannot escape."

That makes sense. I don't like that it seems like he read my mind, but I don't have time to make a point of it.

I study the Witchstone and my chest feels tight. I can see where the carvings are deep enough to fit fingers and toes and they should be fairly easy to hold on to, almost as easy as the footholds and handholds on the rock-climbing wall at the gym. But that's only down here where I can see. I don't know if the grooves will stay as deep at the top. The stone is wide and flat, cut into a hexagon, so the surface is even for the most part except for some cracks and gouges and the symbols carved into it.

The noise from the horde fills my ears like a drumming, getting louder as it gets closer.

I don't know if I can do this.

My thighs are trembling from running up the hill, my right hand still feels like it was stuck in a pot of boiling water, and I feel the lack of my magick from where I poured it out deep in my stomach, as if my sugar has dropped and everything inside me is loose and jiggly.

But the horde is coming.

"Can we go back the way we came?"

Marty shakes his head.

"Why not? Is it because we can't let them loose in the rest of this place? Because I don't care about that."

"The way we came is no longer there," Marty says. "The entrance moves and changes and, once used, disappears to someplace else. Again, as I said, hidden in secrecy." He points up. "That is the only way we leave this place."

"Can you climb this?"

"Do you refuse to use your collar and take us straight there?"

My fingers touch the torc around my neck without me even thinking about it.

Marty leans closer. "You said that it could let you take us places. Let it take us *out* of this place."

"That's not how this works. I have to know where I am going."

"We would be going there." He's pointing again.

"You want me to teleport us to the point of the Witchstone? I'm not Nightcrawler."

"And yet you expect us to crawl up the side of this stone." He snorts in disgust. "Absurd."

And for some reason Marty is smiling.

I take a deep breath, drawing it into my lungs all the way to the bottom, and I hold it there, letting the oxygen leech into my bloodstream. I take a few more deep breaths to clear my head. The horde is almost here, very nearly upon us, and I feel the threat of them like pressure against my back.

I tuck the scourge into my belt and the scorpion tails scratch at my jeans as it swings back and forth.

I move closer to the Witchstone. As I raise my right hand toward the highest rune cutting I can reach, my brain flips through several things in a fast, dizzying sequence.

Does this hand have the strength to hold me to this rock?

Is my Mark going to react to the Witchstone the way it did before?

Where is the point of no return in this? Where will I have to make the decision to either slide back down and try to fight or keep going because anything past that and the fall will kill me or at least break me and make me an easy meal for the horde?

What if Marty falls? Do I let him go and keep climbing or do I climb back down and try to save him?

I know the answer to that last one. If Marty falls he's on his own.

I trust the same applies to me.

The dark stone is cool under my hand as my fingers slip into the groove of the rune. It's deep enough that my fingers fit all the way to the second knuckle. The tiny ledge is rough, covered with loose pebbles not much bigger than sand. Lifting my right foot, I wedge the toe of my shoe into a rune that sits about mid-thigh on me.

My eyes have already found the next place I'm going to grab and with a deep breath I exert. I *pull* and haul myself up to it.

My fingers slap into that ridge and it feels exactly the same: dusty dirty and deep enough for me to be secure. My foot slips on the surface as it tries to find a place. It only takes a second for me to find it.

I stay there, barely three feet off the ground.

The skin on the fingers of my right hand feels as if it is tearing, like it is thin and fragile, and the stress of pulling myself up has made my wrist begin to throb already. The weight of the coat cocoon along my back pulls on me, threatening to drag me off this rock. The muscle chain on each side of my spine sets to burning like my quads as I push down and pull up at the same time and lift myself another two feet up the side of the Witchstone.

I don't want to go on. I want to stop.

But I can't stop.

My fingers dig into the next set of ridges and I jam my toes into the crevice and I scramble, my body moving independently of my brain because everything that I do makes it catalog the hurt that comes with it. As I haul and pull and tug and shove with my legs I wish so desperately that I could teleport to the top of the stone.

The wish forms in my brain. I squelch it down and crush it into nothing before the torc around my neck decides to take me up on it and I wind up trying to balance on what may be a pinprick of stone.

Or I wind up hanging in the middle of space and falling from there to the ground, broken and helpless and at the mercy of the horde.

Or I wind up half in the stone and half out of the stone just hanging out into space dead and embedded in an ancient, magick rock.

I pull and haul and tug and shove and another thought sweeps across my brain over the developing net of pain that my body is becoming and I wonder: *Exactly what part of the creature in prison here am I climbing?*

And I don't want to know, so I destroy that thought before it can take root and blossom into something I so do *not* want to know about.

I hear Marty grunt near me and I see the edge of him on the other plane of the Witchstone. He seems to be keeping pace with me, which can't be that difficult because I feel like I am snail-crawling up the side of this rock.

The rough stone inside the ridges rips the skin across the underside of the fingers on my right hand. I feel it shred in thin lines that feel like a mix between a cut and a split, and the pebbly little sand embeds itself in the soft meat under my calluses.

And then something grabs my bottom foot.

It just has the toe of my boot, but it latches on tight and the pressure from the bottom and the top feels like it is crushing the bones where my toes meet the pad of my foot. The sound of the horde moaning and groaning and crying out rises up around me, punctuated by the moist clacking and gnashing of teeth.

I don't look down.

If I look down I will fall.

I clench every muscle that I can and try to sink into the stone I'm pressed against.

The thing that holds my foot yanks down and I slip. My other foot stays locked in the crevice that it's in and my fingers don't maintain their hold, sliding back until I'm barely holding on by only the first set of pads on both hands.

I pull and I kick with the foot that is being held and I push with the foot that is shoved in the crevice and I use every bit of physical strength that I own to tear my foot out of whatever is holding it.

The pressure ceases with a snap and my body surges up the stone so fast that the momentum of it bounces my pelvis off the Witchstone and I nearly fall back, undone by the very salvation that I created, but I manage to stay attached and scramble up to give myself a buffer and margin of safety.

I stop and rest, shallow breathing, sipping air while trying to regain my strength, and I know from my classes that I cannot stay here. Staying here is depleting my strength. Staying here is going to stick me here and sticking me here is going to make me fall . . . but I have to look.

I can't not look.

At the base of the Witchstone the horde have gathered in a circle and they press tightly, stomach to back, arms raised, mouths open, and the noise that comes out of their open throats undulates and wavers its way up from beneath me.

The tallest male of the horde is right beneath me, his hands and fingers slapping the stone in a futile gesture only about ten inches below the bottom of my lowest foot.

They don't appear to have the ability to jump.

I need to move either way, though. I cannot stay here. Staying here is an impossibility.

Turning my face back to the top, I see that Marty has drawn ahead of me and now hangs with surprising grace for his bulk. His body hangs out in space as his feet and hands dig into the runes and symbols and sigils carved into the basalt stone.

My nose and mouth are inches, and by "inches" I mean two, away from a set of hatch mark grooves bisected with a swirl and a squiggle and something that I'm unsure is even a shape. The air that I sip dislodges the grit in the grooves of that symbol and it flies into my mouth and into my nose and down into the top of my throat, where it scratches and digs and immediately makes everything want to close up and for me to begin coughing it free and it's all I can do to keep my lungs under control because if I begin coughing I will not be staying on this rock.

"You should cut that thing free."

My eyes are watering and I'm struggling to not give in to the coughing fit that wants to take me over.

And so all I can do is look up at Marty in response to what he just said.

"It is weighing you down and is going to keep you from getting out of this place," he says. "I do not know why you insist on hauling it with you anyway."

The jerky pressure inside my chest eases up and the scratchy sensation in the back of my throat becomes a trickle that could erupt anytime back into a coughing fit, but, for now, I can live with it.

But I still can't reply to Marty. So I ignore him and begin to climb again. One hand over the other, one foot above the next, and I slowly lizard crawl my way up the stone. The farther up I go the more cracks and fissures there are in the stone. None of the faults looks deep enough for the stone to split and fall in two, but they are rough against my skin, scraping up my forearms and my chest even through my shirt, snagging on my clothes, and just making this harder.

Every foot I climb feels like a mile.

My foot slips as I push up, cracking my chin on the stone.

White static flares into the backs of my eyelids as my teeth slam into one another and my mouth fills with the warm copper-salt taste of my own blood. My immediate instinct is to spit it out, but I clamp down on that, swallowing it, and I keep swallowing it as long as it keeps flowing into my mouth from the hole I've just incised on the inside of my cheek.

The reverberation of my magick striking the stone and waking up the horde gathered beneath me was enough of a warning that there is no fucking way I'm going to spit a mouthful of my blood on its surface.

Keep moving.

I continue pulling and struggling as my brain slips sideways into a weird image of me doing that: a mouthful of hot red liquid splattering across the stone in front of me, going deep into the runes and symbols cut here, flowing into their depth and running along from this point, spreading out. The symbols begin to glow as it does, radiating magick, sorcery, and necromancy like some kind of tainted, evil lighthouse designed to draw to itself some elder god manner of fuckery that I do not ever want to deal with.

My mind clears as I draw even with Marty.

Swallowing blood has made me thirsty. My throat feels nearly welded shut.

This high up, and we are really, really high, the horde below look much more like what they are, a lumpy string of shapes, like a stomach and intestines. The stone has narrowed to the point that I can reach around it to a certain extent and lock myself in place by grabbing one of the grooves on one side and one on the other so I can relax just slightly.

But not too much.

Marty and I both hang on to the side of the Witchstone only a few feet from the very top.

My body hurts so much that my brain feels like it is suspended in thick, chunky oatmeal or congealed pudding.

If you don't eat your meat, you can't have any pudding.

Marty's not even breathing hard.

Fucking Marty.

In that moment I hate him. A lot.

It takes a lot of effort to choke out the words, "What do we do now?"

He doesn't reply, doesn't say anything at all; he just lifts his right hand and points at the portal that I can see shimmering like a heat-wave oasis about a meter above us. The portal wavers and roils and distorts the moon that lies behind it.

I don't *hear* Marty chanting, but I damn sure *feel* it. It makes the Witchstone under me vibrate and thrum like a tuning fork.

I clamp on with all that I have in me, draping my body and using the friction of the stone's rough surface to help keep me from slipping off it.

The coat is still silent and still heavy on my back, completely withdrawn around the skinhound cocooned within it.

My teeth chatter and I can't tell what is the vibration of the Witchstone and what is the trembling of every muscle inside my body. Pain just moves around in flashes, jumping from my left knee to my right hand to the small of my back to my left shoulder to the back of my heel on my right side where I was grabbed and all points in between. It just jumps, twitchy little jumps of pain, which go from sharp stabs with needles to flaring firepain to aches that feel like bones are being ground together.

I roll my eyes and look over my arm as I hang there and I know that I don't have much longer.

I cannot.

Do this.

Anymore.

My face is hot and wet and my eyes are burning and my mouth trembles and I'm crying.

I'm going to fail.

I'm going to fall.

I'm going to die.

I'll take the skinhound with me.

And the coat.

And my whole world.

My parents.

My little brother, Jacks.

Daniel.

Javier and even traitorous, treacherous Ashtoreth.

I am not enough.

Why did I ever think I was?

My tears keep flowing, but my mouth stops trembling and turns into a snarl.

Who the fuck do I think I am?

The hubris, the arrogance, the unmitigated gall, to think that I, little Charlie Moore, little damaged girl from a little town, could stand, no, could *stop* the machinations of gods and creatures like gods.

Of course I am going to fail. I was never *not* going to fail.

I should have stayed behind, should have taken what time I had to find out what me and Daniel are. Even if destruction and apocalypse are coming I would have had that. If I'd chosen not to come I would not have failed, and death is the end of the road either way.

What a fucking laugh.

What a joke.

It won't take anything to be done with this. All I have to do is let go.

Just stop trying so damn hard.

.

.

So easy.

.

.

My hands relax.

I lean back.

It's inevitable.

The front of my shirt tugs, snagging on the rough surface of the stone as I begin to tilt away.

Gravity takes hold of me.

.

.

No.

No.

I latch back onto the Witchstone with a ferocity that bangs my cheekbones into the hard black surface of it.

I might fail, but I will *never* quit.

I have exactly one second to steal a glimpse of pride in my own fortitude before the portal slips over us and everything that I am is slung to another place altogether.

31

I CANNOT SEE.

It's not darkness; it's just nothing, like I've closed my eyes, but I haven't.

I'm pulled away from the Witchstone in what feels like a vaguely up direction, but even as my mind scrambles to understand all that is happening to me I know that the direction only feels up because the portal was above me. I am constricted, sealed tight, as if I've been encased in cellophane. It binds me and I struggle and I feel it pull tight around me as I try to move my arms and legs and, even with all of my strength, I can barely move an inch. It covers my nose and my mouth, sucking in and coating my throat, and there's no air, no oxygen, to be found.

My brain flips, turning into a wild animal.

I can't breathe. I cannot breathe even though I try and I try and I try.

My fingers dig into my cheeks trying to tear it, trying

to open my throat, but there's nothing there. Whatever has sealed me doesn't exist except to stop me from breathing.

Except to choke the life out of me.

Except to smother me.

My eyes, my blind eyes, feel like thumbs are pushing them from behind, trying to pop them from my skull, separate them from their sockets. The pressure in my head is incredibly intense. My left eardrum pops in a spit of pain and goes hot, blood and fluid filling the canal but unable to escape. Knives stab into my lungs as I fight, trying to get anything in them.

I cannot hear myself choke.

The only noise is the black fuzz inside my skull.

The sheath around me tightens and twists, squeezing me until all I can see is red.

Air.

Don't want to . . .

Why?

Breathe.

Breathe.

Air.

No.

No.

Magick.

Stop.

32

THE AIR THAT rushes down my throat feels like ice and makes my lungs hurt as if crystals that grind and creak have formed inside them.

But I drink that precious oxygen in, gasping so violently that I choke.

Am I going to be sick?

I gulp and swallow and fight to keep everything in my stomach even as I keep forcing as much air into my lungs as I can.

My brain makes a quarter turn and I realize I'm helpless.

The spike in adrenaline that thought brings lets me open my eyes and slow down on the air intake.

My face is on the floor.

The uneven surface stretches out and away from me. My cheek hurts, not like it smashed into anything, but like it's lying on a rock.

My shoulder hurts. Like it did smash into something. Like a rock.

A network of pain comes alive in my tangled body. One arm is underneath me, one arm behind me, and my legs are pulled up to my chest in a broken fetal position.

Slowly I roll over, carefully pulling my limbs free from themselves, making note that there isn't any sharp pain, no grinding, so none of them is broken.

I have to sit up because the coat cocoon is still on my back and latched on firmly.

I'm in a corridor that looks very much like the ones that me and Marty have walked through since I got here. Same uneven floor, same even lighting, and I can see places along the walls down the way that look very much like the incongruous doors that I have passed by on my travels in this place.

Marty.

I turn as fast as I can without spiking the pain network in my body, looking for him, and find him behind me, sitting with his back against the wall, his knees up, and his face in his hands.

He's not moving.

Does Marty breathe?

I haven't noticed.

"Marty?"

He still doesn't move.

"Marty, are you okay?"

It all hurts as I push up to sit. The scourge on my belt rattles at me like a serpent about to strike.

Shush.

The top of my femur, where it goes into my hip, feels like it has a soft spot on it, a fist-size spot of hurt I recognize as a bone bruise.

That's going to make walking difficult.

I take a few deep breaths and push the pain down into the general network of ache I already have.

It takes me a few seconds to shift into a position I can sit up in, where it doesn't hurt me too much and I'm not leaning back on the cocoon.

"Marty, come on, man, we have to almost be there."

Marty shudders, just a slight tremble that runs from his feet up into his shoulders. His voice is slightly muffled behind his hands.

"No more shortcuts."

The relief that I feel at the sound of his voice is palpable. It actually eases my pain, not much, nowhere near completely, but some.

"Why was that so rough?" I ask.

With a sigh, he looks up. The skin of his face is droopy; he looks tired. "That particular cell is designed to not let anything escape."

"Then why is there an exit to begin with?"

"You must provide an exit."

"Do you? Because it feels like all of the things we've come across should be locked away forever."

He laughs and it is a harsh bark. "Forever? What a human thing to say; you have no concept of forever."

I try to not take offense, but it isn't easy. "Isn't forever just a concept? I mean really in the end of things? No one has experienced forever yet and thus forever may not even exist. Time may even prove to be a static thing. Unmoving, unbending, never advancing."

"You have interacted with gods and you still doubt eternity?"

"I've met a lot of things that claim to be gods and maybe they are, they're powerful enough, but it's not like just because something has been around forever means it will be around forever. Everything works its way toward the end."

Marty rubs the bridge of his nose, the skin crinkly on his forehead under the wide pads of his fingertips. "She is going to love you."

"Who is? Secret?"

"*Serket*," he corrects me. "Or Satet, definitely Sihuanaba."

"I'm going to find it impossible to remember that name."

"Serket is only two syllables. *Sir* and *ket*."

I shake my head. "Trust me," I say. "I know myself."

"You may call her She Who Tightens the Throat."

"Well, that's a lot of words."

He shakes his head, making the skin on his neck fold in on itself, and his voice has heat when he speaks. "Then simply call her whatever you wish. It is what you have done with me."

"Yeah, if I have trouble remembering her two-syllable name, *surely* you understand why I can't use your"—I stop myself before I say the word "gibberish"—"alien-to-me name."

"You *are* only human."

I don't like his tone.

I say, "I don't like your tone."

"I do not like your species."

"I don't know your species, Marty, but if you're any indication I don't like it any myself."

"Now you are simply being childish."

"So what if I am?"

"It is . . . unbecoming."

"Well, I am becoming tired of being in this discussion." I have to use the wall to stand up and once I get there I can't let it go for a moment because I think my knees are going to fold out from under me.

"I do not know why you find me so infuriating."

I've hurt his feelings. Great. Perfect.

"It's not just you, Marty. I'm tired and I hurt and it feels like I have been here for months. There's a time crunch going. The Man in Black is not waiting around for me to catch up with him and you walking me in circles in this place and taking me into cells where things are not meant to escape from is wasting time. Any minute he could find Aza Croft's cell and set him free."

"*Azathoth.*"

"Get up, Marty. Take me where I need to go. I'm done with this place."

He stares up at me with those big seal eyes for a long moment.

But when that moment ends he pushes up from the floor, stands to his feet, and begins to walk down the corridor, leading the way.

33

"THIS IS WHERE we part ways."

The corridor curves, a bit sharper than it has thus far, enough so that I can't see up around the bend. Another corridor, looking exactly like the one we are in, branches off to the left.

"What do you mean?"

Marty points ahead. "You carry on that direction. When you reach the next door, that is where you will find whom you seek."

I tense, despite the weariness I feel.

"The Man in Black?"

Shaking his head makes the flesh of his face jiggle. "No, ahead you will find the resting place of Satet. She is the one to complete your task. Only she knows where to find what the Son of Azathoth seeks."

"What do you mean you have to go?"

"I must go in this direction," he says.

"If this is some trick just to ditch me . . ."

Marty whirls on me. "In all of this journey at what point have I abandoned you? At what point have I proven to be anything short of helpful?"

I don't trust him. Not completely. And looking back on it, I've not even tried to hide that fact.

"I saved you from your own reckless behavior"—he throws his hands up in the air—"running into the holding place for the all-consuming Eldritch. . . . ." He shakes his head. "I should have left you there, but I did not."

"Hey! You did that to fix the cell you had that thing in."

"Broken by *you*."

"You do have a point."

"I am a most reasonable thing."

"Look," I say. "Just drop me off at the front door."

"You are not the only task I must complete, I have machinations of my own that I must attend to. I have delivered you to the very place you did not even know you needed to find."

"Satchel will show me where Azathoth is?"

"If you convince her she must. I would suggest not calling her the wrong name would be a good place to begin."

"Satet?"

He nods. "Satet, Serket, She Who Tightens the Throat."

"I'm not using the long one."

"Those are the short ones. Simply call her Satet and be done with it."

"Satet. Satet." I repeat it slowly to sink it into my brain, dragging out the first syllable and chopping the last. "*S-aah*—tet."

Marty shakes his head. "Somehow I still feel as if you will get this wrong."

"Oh Marty, your faith in me is astounding."

"I cannot stress any further that you must convince Satet to help you. No one else, *no one,* has the knowledge of where Azathoth is held captive."

"If she is the only one who knows then maybe I should not bother with this at all."

"Nyarlathotep is the Offspring of Azathoth. He will eventually peel enough layers to find his father. They do share a core essence. He is the only one who could track Azathoth with enough effort. Do you believe he would give up his goal just because it proved to be difficult?"

No. I know the Man in Black. I think back over all that has happened, everything orchestrated by the Man in Black from the moment he walked through my door holding a sword. Everything he has done has brought him to this point. Everything he has put me through has brought me to this point.

Neither one of us can turn back now.

"I can see on your face that you understand."

Marty turns and begins moving down the side corridor.

"Are you coming back?" I call after him.

His voice carries along the walls, echoing as it leaves the corridor's opening.

"I am always coming back from somewhere."

And then he is gone, disappeared into the dark, out of sight.

Cryptic son of a bitch.

34

I FIND THE doors.

I can tell they are different from the others I've passed. It's the first set of the double doors I have come across. They are narrow and tall, stretching all the way to the top of the wall, but only wide enough together for one person to pass through. They gleam in the low light as if they have been boiled; the wood of them is light, nearly a honey color. The grain of them looks like coffee swirled into cream, forming abstract, eye-pleasing shapes. Bulky hardware hangs from them. Hinges on the edges and knobs in the middle with strike plates around them, made of what looks to be a patinaed bronze with bright bluish-green oxidization mixed with pearly gray and interrupted with random marks and mars that reveal the bright and shiny metal beneath.

Oh, and there are penguins.

Two of them.

Standing guard.

Stop laughing.

They stand on either side of the door. These are not short, pudgy little seabirds who are about to break into song and do a little tap dance.

They're tall, taller than me, nearing seven feet, and sprouts of greasy white pinfeathers lay tight against a thin membrane of skin the nicotine yellow of the cotton in a used cigarette filter.

Their hips splay around the sag of a belly that hangs like a pendulum between gnarled knobby knees and slopes upward into a narrow chest with a jutting ridge of bone that leads up to a crooked neck that looks as if it has been wrung, the gooseneck of a vulture turned sideways. The feet are massive, scaly things underneath them, splayed in a wide platform of arthritic, knotted joints that end with curved talons, the tips of them broken and jagged. Flipper wings huddle close to their sides the way an elderly woman tucks her folded wrists up under her breasts to hold in escaping body heat. Bumps and knobs of extended phalanges form the tips, looking like the finger flanges in some nightmarish bat wing, the ends of each tipped with more cracked talons. The black keratin of them shot through with ribbons of chunky, cheese-yellow fungi. Each of the joints under the thin membrane of skin looks angry, feverish, as if they ache and hurt.

Both of them are spotted with lesions, running sores that lie raw and open, the skin gone soft and mushy in its putrefaction. The edges are crunchy, with thick slabs of dried fluid that seeps and runs until it dams up against sprouts feathers or is captured in a wrinkle or even another sore. Their tiny heads sit on their crooked necks; they look very much like skulls.

The membrane lies tight, and the hooked beaks that jut from their faces look as if they've been dipped in ink, which makes the rows of jagged teeth that line its edges shine bright. The teeth are long, narrow triangles set close together, teeth that are made to cut flesh into strips so that it can easily slide down those constricted, crooked gullets. The eyes are set deep in sockets that look like black smudges behind the beaks, so far inset that they appear to simply be thin lines of glittering red.

They stare straight ahead, so still that I would think that they were statues if I couldn't see their bodies expand and contract in time to the huffing breathing that creates a fog of noise in this part of the corridor.

They don't appear to see me. They've taken no notice of me yet. But I don't know what they will do when I approach the door.

Damn you, Marty, for running off.

The temptation to turn back and go down that side corridor after him looms large from the back of my brain, but I don't turn and I don't leave. I need to be in that room.

I hope I don't have to fight these things.

Marty's words come back to me, the ones about the elephant in the cardboard box. If this isn't what these things look like then I wonder if my brain is protecting me, and if it is, from what? What do they look like in their true form?

The temptation to open my third eye is almost as strong as the one to turn and go after Marty.

No.

I won't risk that.

Good bet when dealing with elder gods and their bullshit: Always assume it could be worse.

Because it is always, irrevocably and invariably, worse.

I move toward them, taking my time, choosing my steps. Maybe I can slip by unnoticed, be inside that door before they even know I've opened it.

Maybe they're awkward, clumsy, and slow-moving.

Because that's what you always choose when you pick a guard.

My mom watches nature documentaries. Anytime she has control of the television that's what she watches.

That or cooking shows.

I remember a documentary that included penguins. They gave a lot of facts that I don't remember, but some of the footage they showed of penguins darting through the water, capturing fish as if it were nothing—that, I remember. I was struck, impressed with the speed and dexterity they showed. They exploded on their prey, which had no time to do anything except be eaten.

Yes, they were awkward on land, waddling and toddling over the ice floes on flapper feet. But these two would not have to chase me. I'm going to walk right between them. All they have to do is turn and I will be trapped between them and the door.

I stop walking.

The image of them cornering me is so strong in my mind I can *feel* them, their bulk pressing against me, stiff feathers digging into my skin, the hardened trails from their suppurating wounds scratching me as they pin me against the hard door and I cannot escape as they lower their faces and begin using their scissoring beaks to tear the flesh from my face in long, winding strips.

Panic chews at the bottom of my brain.

No, no, no, no no no, no, nonononono—

My mind splits like a lightning strike.

One part descending into a burrowing, animal howl.

The other part not even thinking, just clamping down on my body, forcing my mouth to stay closed and not give voice to what the other brain is screaming, forcing my legs to stay upright, forcing me to not collapse to the floor.

Breathe.

I have to breathe.

Very carefully, I part my lips and let a ribbon of air slip down my throat and into my lungs.

As it leaks back out, I can't keep the quivering murmuring start of a sob from escaping with it.

Did the penguin on the left move?

I blink away the rims of tears so I can see clearly. They squeeze out of the corners of my eyes and run down my cheeks as I focus on the one on my left.

It looks the same as it did before.

But it also doesn't.

I don't know if it really moved or if I'm being paranoid.

I take a step forward.

The penguin doesn't even twitch or acknowledge me at all.

I take another step.

Still nothing.

Maybe I'm crazy.

Speaking of, my mind has shut up. I feel unfractured again.

Way to go, brain, dissociate to protect me from a panic attack, come back together so I can face a real-world threat.

Real-world . . . Giant freak show murder penguins.

This is my real world.

The adrenaline is draining, dumping back into my system to be reabsorbed. I can almost feel it leaving and being replaced by weariness.

I'm running on fumes.

Panic attacks, even small ones, just take it out of me. Couple that with all that I've been through since getting here and carrying the cocooned skinhound.

I don't have any more time to waste.

One foot in front of the other, I move toward the door.

The penguins don't move as I draw near. I keep my movements as smooth as possible, nothing sudden or jerky. My heart feels like it's been wrapped in string that tightens with every step.

I'm using every trick I can to not let my brain slip back into panic mode.

One small track of my brain is counting in twos.

Most of me is watching the penguins.

I step between them.

This close, I can see up into the sockets of their eyes. The dark of the sockets is thick like a scab of hardened, blackened blood. From the edges of them leak more translucent-yellow plasma-like tears. The red eyes that I saw earlier are splits in the deepest parts that reveal raw inner flesh.

Their blindness weighs upon me and I *feel* it against my skin just like I feel the moistness of their huffing breath.

Now between them, I'm close enough to reach out and touch them. Just stretch out my arms and my fingers will graze their hips. My eyes slide to the right and focus on a bundle of tiny feathers in a knot on the side of that penguin, and that little self-destructive urge, the suicidal bastard urge, that lives in me causes my hand to actually begin to move in that direction before I stop it.

Not today, Satan.

Two more steps and I can almost reach the door; a lunge would take me to it, put the handle in my grip.

No sudden movements.

They cannot see me. That doesn't mean they don't know I'm here.

What if the door is locked?

I pushed the thought out of my mind. I cannot entertain that. The door will be unlocked. It has to be unlocked.

I lift my arm as I take another step.

The metal of the handle is cool under my fingers as they slip around it. The handle spins down easily from the weight of my hand.

It reaches the bottom of its arc and the door unlatches with a crisp, sharp *click!*

Oh fuck.

Shadow covers me as the penguins turn in unison. One of them gives a yawping cry that feels like staples in my eardrums. Rushing forward, I use my body to open the door and step over the threshold. I turn to shut the door and fire explodes in my shoulder and I am shoved forward by the blow and then jerked short with a harsh yank.

Looking frantically over my shoulder, I see one of the penguins has hit me with the talons on its flipper wing and now those talons have snagged the coat. The penguin is trying to tear it off me or drag me back out of the door, where I can be eviscerated and my soft insides opened to steam into the air and be devoured by the two of them.

I dig in with my feet and drop, lowering my center of gravity to make it harder to hold on to me. The coat constricts tighter around me trying to hold on. My right foot braces on the right-hand door and I lock my knee and hip as a brace, but I am not strong enough to hold it long, not against a predator as powerful as the penguin.

The scourge on my hip flails about, rattling like a knot of snakes. I can't reach down for it; my hands are locked on the strap of the coat on my back, trying to hold it on to me. It slips in my hands, the fabric of it tearing. My fingers sink into the rips and I can hear the coat screaming in my brain one more time. The penguin throws its head back, beak wide apart, streamers of spittle flapping between sharp cutting teeth. Behind it, its partner gnashes its own beak and hops and flaps its taloned flipper wings.

The penguin that has hold of the coat rears back and the strap breaks across my chest, slithering out of my grip. I latch on with all my strength. The force of it spins me around and slams me into the door that is still closed. I strike it with my chest and the edge of it feels like a machete blow against my sternum.

I hold as tightly as I can even though all the air has been driven from my lungs.

The straps slip another inch from my grasp.

I won't let go.

If the coat gets pulled from me I will be outside this door and fighting. I will not abandon it, having come this far.

I yank down, jerking and pulling on the strap, sawing it back and forth.

The coat's alien voice swirls in the bottom of my brain.

An image of the penguin's talons flashes in my mind. They are only a few inches long and gently curved like a bear claw. The flanges they're attached to have joints, but they're not fingers.

I feel it when the coat understands.

And I watch it morph itself around the snagging talons, push them up, and then part like water.

The coat drops to the floor and the penguin falls backward, knocking into the other one, suddenly off-balance for all of its bottom heaviness, and unable to stop its fall.

They hit the ground in a thud.

I pull frantically to get the coat inside the door.

It's so heavy. How did I carry this thing so far and so long?

The penguin doesn't try to stand. It spins onto its belly, wide scaly feet digging into the floor to push it forward. It rockets toward me, mouth wide enough to clamp onto my thigh. Its teeth would saw through my flesh and bone in seconds, amputating the leg just below my hip.

I barely get the coat inside and slam the door shut.

It shudders as the penguin slams into it, but it stays shut.

They begin to howl and croak outside the door.

My legs give out and I drop to the floor. I don't even feel the impact.

All I can do is lie there as my body trembles from toe to crown and weep with exhaustion.

35

It takes a long time for my body to be still.

Long enough that I start to get cold. Ache crawls into my joints, growing until it's enough to make me get up off the floor. My shoulder is on fire. The skin of it feels stiff and crackly as I move. It breaks open and the unmistakable trickle of blood begins to run under my shirt. I pull on the fabric and find a gaping hole where the penguin's claws shredded it. My fingers are swollen, as if they've been injected with liquid, and I can't really close them. I can only form a painful claw.

The scourge on my hip twists and tangles its falls on the ground around me. The tips of the lashes flex, each of the scorpion stingers glistening with little drops of venom.

It's dark in here.

And it feels big around me. Shadows obscure the walls and the ceiling and there's no echo of any of the sounds I make. Lights pills from the edges of the door that I came through, outlining the lump of the skinhound still cocooned in the coat. The penguins have quieted down, given up on me. I can picture them back at their post unmoving except to fill the air around them with moist, fishy breath.

I scoot across the floor, which is hard and flat with no texture to it. Not slick or glassy like tile but smooth as a river stone.

My knee lands on one of the scorpion tails, pinning it sideways against the floor. It stabs, trying to sting me, trying to inject me with its venom.

The anger inside me from this is a tiny flash, a minuscule flare-up that quenches quickly. Maybe the scourge is treacherous; maybe I hurt it unintentionally; maybe it doesn't have a mind or personality at all, simply a function.

Push that musing away. I don't have time for it.

I reach to check on the skinhound, my fingers brushing the cocoon. It's hard like a shell, formed into a carapace. I rap swollen knuckles on it, ignoring the squishy pain. They make the wet-melon *thunk* of a liquid-filled container, like thumping a full jug of milk.

Where did the liquid come from? What is the liquid doing? Is it digestive like a stomach? Or amniotic like a uterus?

I put my fingers in the ends of the broken strap, which lies limp from each end. It feels like the thin, leathery fabric the coat always felt like when I wore it, but there's no life to it. It's just listless against my skin. I don't hear the coat's voice. There is no connection.

It's not dead.

It's.

Not.

Dead.

With a deep breath I stand up. On my feet, I have to take a moment and push down the pain.

Shit. Everything hurts.

I look up, and opposite of where I stand there is a light. It glows around what looks like a raised area in the middle of the darkness, far enough away that I cannot make out the details. Everything else is darkness.

What choice do I have except to head toward the light?

It takes several deep breaths with my hands on my knees before I am ready to take hold of the end of the coat's strap.

I cannot lift it up and tie it back in place.

I can't put it over my shoulders.

My swollen hands refuse to close.

I wind the strap around my wrist and tuck it into itself so that it will stay in place. My joints protest as I begin dragging the hard shell cocoon behind me.

I ignore them.

36

IT'S A BED.

Not just that, it's a bed with a woman on it.

Her back is to me and she lies on her side. Fabric drapes her body in gentle folds that flow over the rise of her hips and down into the dip of her waist. Long, dark hair has tumbled off her head to blend in with the fabric. Her arm lies casually along the upper ridge of her body, graceful fingers splayed along the top of her thigh.

The bed is a perfectly flat platform that appears to be made of the same material as the floor I stand on. The woman is in a nest of fabric and materials that look like matted fur and clumps of leaves held in a cup of branches that have been woven together.

I don't know how long I stare at her.

It could be minutes. It could be months. But I stand silent and still, anchored in place by my fascination as my eyes look over every inch presented to me. The fabric covers her but does not hide her. One leg has escaped from the covering and lies over the crushed folds as an example of how perfectly a calf can curve into the geometry of an ankle that then becomes the artistry of a foot. The limb is covered in flawless ivory, as is her arm and shoulder.

Her shoulder.

It hovers in beautiful contrast to the darkness of the spill of her hair, like an alabaster cliff overlooking an ebon sea.

I finally know the meaning of the word "awestruck": "struck with awe."

I am drawn to her. I want to climb up and embrace her. And I dare not get any closer, for I am not worthy.

I am the pitiful moth. She is the eternal flame.

It takes an eternity to find the strength for me to offer up a whisper of a prayer.

"Satet."

At the sound of her name she *stirs*.

She doesn't roll as much as cascade like river water over rock, the movement as gentle and soft as can be and yet still inexorable and inevitable. Her body rises until she's sitting up. The silken fabric isn't a sheet but a dress, a gown that flows over her body, both covering and yet revealing her form. The nimbus of light that surrounds the bed forms a corona around her, outlining her with a glow as her hands cover her face, rubbing away her slumber. The tangled locks of her hair sway gently around her head.

The corona is cracked, splintered from her brow with the silhouette of antlers that sweep from her forehead in a crown of bone. The main part of them curves up and around, as thick as my arm, tapering to a point that looks sharp as a spear, and that's what they are: arcing spears of bone. Along their length, shorter tines cant and jut at angles, appearing to be just as wickedly sharp. The surface of them is textured with shallow ridges that trace the curves and shapes of the antlers, giving the bone strength in its architecture.

At their base, the thickest part of them, cling tatters of dried velvet that curl away from the bone and blend with the darker, finer curls of the hair beneath them.

Her hands come away from her face and rise into a stretch. Her head is still bowed, leaving the curtain of hair to obscure her visage from my eyes.

Finally, she turns and is revealed.

Above delicate, birdlike collarbones,

atop a slender throat the envy of any Victorian,

beneath antlers designed for war,

and in the midst of silk-spun locks of hair

the lady's face is a skull.

37

"HELLO, CHARLIE. YOU are early."

The sound of my name coming from the Skull-Faced Woman is like a brace of cold water. I don't feel my face react to it, but I cannot hide the shiver that runs from my sacrum all the way up to the base of my skull like mercury rising in a thermometer on a summer day.

"You know who I am?"

"Of course."

She says it as if it were nothing.

"And how is that, since we've never met?"

"We have been next to each other quite often, Charlie."

"I think I would have noticed you."

"Your kind so very rarely does."

I feel like I'm missing something.

I say, "I feel like I'm missing something. How do you know me?"

"I know you very well." Using her arms, she shifts her position toward me, slithering in her gown across the slick stone of the bed with the tiniest hiss of friction. Her legs come over the edge and hang, tiptoes barely touching the floor; fingers curled beside her knees over the edge, she leans forward. She's far taller than I and so she looms over me.

I don't even try to not stare, to not study.

The skin of her neck is taut as it comes up under the jawbone, smoothing into itself there. There is no border or seam where flesh becomes bone, where skin melds to skeleton. The bone that forms her skull face is delicate and she's close enough that my eyes can pick out areas of porous sections, especially where the bone thickens, that look as if tiny insects have been burrowing. There are micro-fractures that form lightning patterns along one of her cheekbones, tracing up and disappearing as they come to the eye socket. Her teeth are set firmly in their sockets; they do not wiggle or move. The edges of her nasal cavity are paper-thin and ragged, but not haphazardly, not as if they had been broken or snapped away or destroyed in any manner, but rather the jaggedness seems to have a purpose and my brain shows me an image, like one found in a medical textbook, of that thin scrim of bone perfectly suturing itself into softer, more flexible cartilage. The hole where her nose would be is dark, the nasal ridge casting a shadow, masking whatever lives inside that skull.

Her eye sockets are the same, shallow but shadow-cast under a heavy brow bone. They are large enough that my closed fists would fill them perfectly. More pitting traces along the orbital bones, almost in a tribal pattern, some sort of primitive design like a tattoo. In the deepest recesses there are openings that go inside, but my sight cannot go inside them, cannot curve into their depths, blocked by the shadows cast there. Her forehead is a smooth bowl of bone bisected with a heavy suture line that forms a ridge between the bases of the two antlers.

Here before me, knowing my name, is Satet, the Skull-Faced Woman. She is Thanatos; she is Hel, Persephone, Santa Muerte.

She is Beautiful Death.

Her head tilts. "That appears to be a kiss from one of the keepers outside my door." Her hand lifts, moving forward of my shoulder.

I pull back and look down, the sharp angle making my neck hurt, causing my eye to vibrate in the socket. Over the top of my shoulder two furrows of angry, red scratch-scabs lie next to each other, souvenirs from the blind murder penguins. The furrows have crusted over since I got them, sealing shut on my trek from the door to here. There's a lot of pain going on in my body, like I'm a radio transmitter and it is a staticky, crackly white-noise station that pours out of me.

It takes a moment for my brain to pick out the signal coming from the wounds on my shoulders, but, once I identify it, the pain moves to the forefront and lies like a hot brand in my mind. The two gouges on my shoulder are joined farther down and back by two more that are not as deep but hurt just as much. It's a hot, feverish pain, a pressure pain. Another glance and I see that the skin around them rises into a ridge and the edges of the wounds separate to reveal infection.

The Skull-Faced Woman drops her hand.

"The spurs on their flippers contain a venom for their protection."

"Their protection? It's not enough that they're huge and have beaks full of teeth?"

"Their size is only impressive to you," she says. Her jaw moves as she talks but not the way my jaw moves when I talk. There is no tongue inside her mouth that I can see, but the words she forms are clear and concise.

I consider the murder penguins and in my mind stack them up against some of the other things I have seen. They are scary, but when I put them next to things like the Hungry Dark or, worse, the Man in Black I see that, in this place, they're practically harmless, very nearly prey.

I smooth the tattered edges of my shirt over the ends of the furrows. My fingertips brush them and even that slight pressure causes pain to radiate deep into the socket and up along the side of my neck in a way that pulls my jaw muscle tight and grinds my teeth together.

"This is not good."

The Skull-Faced Woman shakes her head. "No, child, it is not." She lifts her hand again. "Allow me to help."

The hand hangs there, fingers loose and slightly curled. Her nails are perfectly formed half-moons, the one on her index finger marred by three white hatch marks that lie side by side.

Leukonychia.

My mom calls them milk spots. I know they're caused by injury to the base of the nail where it is formed and part of my mind wonders how the goddess of death injured her finger.

Those fingers flex, drawing me back to her offer of help. Do I want to be touched by Death? There have been many times in my life when I've felt that I have been, but that's in a philosophical, poetical sense of the words. This is real.

Absurd, ridiculous, batshit-elder-god crazy, but still real.

If I let her touch me will I die?

Surely if the Skull-Faced Woman wanted to kill me she would not need to touch me to do so.

She offered help.

And inside me that pull toward her still exists, the draw that I felt when I first laid eyes upon her. And it's not as if I've never sought her embrace before.

I've still got the scars on my wrists as evidence.

I nod, the barest tremble of agreement, and lean slightly forward at the same time.

I don't see it happen even though I am looking at her face, but the bone and enamel somehow morph incrementally, minusculely, into a subtle smile.

Am I projecting that onto the blank slate that is her skull face?

That thought finishes in the same moment her fingers touch the wound on my shoulder.

They're cool, not like ice, not sharp in that way, but comforting. Her skin feels like my skin with no heat. Fever in my flesh breaks apart like a clot of phlegm and leeches away. Her thumb licks across the top of the scab, the edge of it digging into the gap between incrustation and flesh, sending a moist, exquisite pain that ripples and lurches all the way through my torso and makes my knees buckle.

It's all I can do to keep my feet as she picks at the wound, lifting the brand-new scab. Infection runs freely down my arm and chest, soaking into the shirt that I'm wearing. Her fingers push gently, causing me to turn and give her my back. When I'm facing away from her they go back to their ministrations and there's more tearing, more sharp slices of pain, more freely running corruption. On my back it sluices down and puddles in a long, narrow moat where my jeans hang on my hips.

It hurts and yet in that pain I can feel the venom being leeched away and it is a relief. My skin cools and relaxes, and the queasiness that had set up in my stomach eases off.

Her fingers are quick, half-moon nails like scalpels. Her other hand rests lightly on my arm and I can barely feel it. She's not using any strength to keep me there and she's not in the defensive position. Her hand just lies gracefully on my arm because that feels like exactly where her hand should lie.

She begins to squeeze, gently working her way from the bottom of the wounds to the top. It hurts, but in the doctor way, the way that you know it's for the good, the healing way.

I feel like I should make small talk, but it's ridiculous to ask a death goddess how her day has been. *So, have you killed anyone cool today?*

Instead, I ask her, "What name do you prefer?"

Her fingers cross over my shoulder blade and it hurts more.

"With this, you may call me Serket."

"What do you mean, 'with this'?"

"It translates as She Who Tightens the Throat. In this aspect, I prefer bittersweet draughts."

Bittersweet draughts? Where have I heard that before? As she works, my mind goes searching through all the things I've ever read, especially all the poems. "Bittersweet draughts" feels poetical.

Nightshade.

It's sometimes called bittersweet. A draught made from nightshade would be bittersweet, and poisonous . . . like venom.

Random literary allusions for ten points.

Is it an allusion? It's not a metaphor.

She hits a particularly raw spot and the pain sings through me bright and sharp and I lose that train of thought in it as I jerk my head around to look at her.

A curl of black hair hangs over her eye sockets; the rest of her bone face is impassive. No matter what name she has, in my head she is the Skull-Faced Woman.

She pats my shoulder softly and I relax as much as I can. Her hand comes around; she holds it cupped in front of me. The fingers glisten, wet from the same stuff that now coats half my back. It's viscous and thick, like syrup, a mix of plasma and venom and thin, dirty blood.

"Spit into my hand."

Did I hear that right?

"Do what?"

"Your wound must be sealed; spit into my palm."

I don't do it.

Just the thought of it makes my mouth go dry and chalky, my tongue sticking to the roof of it.

She sighs behind me and it passes across the back of my neck, prickling the skin there into gooseflesh. I know my brain can sometimes be overactive, but it feels cemetery cool, like an autumn breeze passing between gravestones.

"Do you not realize that this is how your essence works? You are fluid, born of water, made of water, and when the water leaves you behind there is nothing but ash and dust. There is fluid in every transaction that you do. Fluid when you are born, fluid when you meet me for the second time, fluid when you feel pain, or joy, or sorrow, or anger, or any strong emotion for that matter."

Her words make me think back to the instructions about my Mark. I can picture the Man in Black as he was then, tall, dark, handsome in the same way that a knife is handsome, where you're both repulsed and attracted by the fact that it can cut you, slice you to the bone. I remember being in my kitchen, the linoleum underneath me, my right hand all hot and sore and throbby, feeling as if I'd just put it in a wood chipper. The Man in Black had Marked me, I'd put my right hand in his red right one, and something between us carved the symbol into my palm that is still there embossed in raised scar tissue. When I finally got my hand free my Sight activated for the first time and revealed the Man in Black's true form to me, his monstrous form. I saw the Crawling Chaos.

And it was terrible.

After my Sight broke and I could see the normal world again, he gave me these instructions: *When you need your magick, it can be activated by touching your Mark with any bodily fluid. Blood is the strongest, followed by sexual issue, but any secretion will spark it to life.*

That was the night my life changed and led me down the road

to where I am at this moment, standing in a room of nothing with a Skull-Faced Woman treating a seeping wound that I got from her murder penguins, all in a quest to save the world.

There is a small stab, a prickling, in my heart. It's so tiny and quick that I don't even bother trying to push it aside. It flares and then it goes away, and I am left knowing that the Skull-Faced Woman is telling me the truth, as weird as it is.

Almost as weird as the fact that I trust her to not do me harm.

It takes a long moment for me to work my parched throat into producing even a tiny bit of spittle. I have to circle my mouth with my tongue, working my lips loose away from my teeth, and I'm nearly overcome with thirst.

How long has it been since I drank something?

Finally, I work up the saddest bit and drool it into her palm.

"Can you work with that?" I glance at her over my shoulder.

She pulls her hand back, her thumb rubbing my spittle into her fingers, as she nods.

One of her fingers—it actually feels like her thumb—smooths down the torn flesh on my back. She's humming a tune. I cannot place it; it is alien and unfamiliar and sounds hollow coming from her. It doesn't sound too far off from the voice of the coat when I used to wear it.

The coat is still tied to my wrist.

I had forgotten about it. I may be loopier than I thought I was.

I would reach and untie it from my wrist, but it's actually cinched pretty tightly from dragging the cocoon across the floor, and I can feel numbness setting up in my fingertips. I worry about nerve compression and wrist drop, but I don't want to disturb what the Skull-Faced Woman is doing.

"There," she says, gently turning me back to face her. "'When he had thus spoken, he spat on the ground, and made clay of the spittle, and he anointed the eyes of the blind man with the clay.'"

I move my arm; the skin is tight, but it doesn't hurt. It feels a little soft, like I could tear it open if I move too fast, like I could press my finger into it as I would a soft spot on an apple.

"Why is that familiar?"

She shrugs and from the neck down it is the very picture of listless elegance, and the dichotomy of that contrasted with the placid visage of her face is alluring, and I feel that pull toward her again.

"It is from the story of one of your kind that humans continually find comforting at the ends of their brief lives."

I know this one from when I was a child, the story of Jesus and the blind man. Why is a death goddess quoting from a story in the Bible?

Before I can ask, her head turns and even with the empty eye sockets I can tell that she's staring at the cocoon tethered to my wrist.

"What is that?" she asks.

I begin to undo the wraps knotted on my wrist. "That's the reason I'm here, well, one of the reasons that I'm here."

It's so small a movement as to be imperceptible, but I *feel* her pull back from me. "I should have known."

"Should have known?"

"Humans never come to my chambers. So many of you leave your lives so quickly I see you quite often, but yet you have no love for me."

"Some humans love you."

"Some of you are fascinated by me, some of you choose me, but you all love life far more than you love what I do for you."

The tone of her voice, the sorrow that rides her words, rends my chest open, exposing the hidden bits of me. I have felt the sting of that sorrow before; I've held despair close like a lover. I've told hope to fuck off because I had no use for it in my time of weeping. My sorrow was a candle flame, easily extinguished, compared to hers.

It only takes a moment for me to bring to my mind the words

of Shelley, tragic Shelley, doomed to be haunted by love his entire short life before mysteriously meeting his death at sea, mostly because at the time I suffered my sorrow I found comfort in the more morose and depressive works Shelley penned. His sentences resonated with me across the centuries and I didn't feel alone anymore.

I let his words spill from my mouth.

> "*How wonderful is Death,*
> *Death, and his brother Sleep!*
> *One, pale as yonder waning moon*
> *With lips of lurid blue;*
> *The other, rosy as the morn*
> *When throned on ocean's wave*
> *It blushes o'er the world;*
> *Yet both so passing wonderful!*'"

The second I finish speaking them embarrassment makes my face burn all the way across my cheekbones and up into my ears as I am struck by the foolishness of trying to comfort the personification of death with a poem.

She does not ease my suffering, sitting as still as a statue, no indication that she even heard me.

I bite the inside of my cheek, finding the sore spot from when I was on the Witchstone, to keep from apologizing and making it worse.

"That . . ." She hesitates, her voice dropping to a near whisper. "That was lovely."

"I didn't write it." The confession makes my face burn hotter. *What is wrong with me?*

"It was written by Shelley."

The Skull-Faced Woman nods as if she understands. "You memorized it for me. I know how little room you have to remember things."

I feel like I should correct her, confess that I did not memorize it for her, but for myself.

I will keep that tidbit to myself. I still need her help.

She moves off the bed, sliding past me in her silken gown. It brushes across my skin and it feels as light as gossamer, with as much substance as the barest hint of a breeze. I have to step back to give her space and I am struck by how tall she is, nearly two feet taller than I am and built substantially. I turn as she passes, and watch as she squats beside the cocoon that I have carried so far. With her kneeling, her head is very nearly even with my chest.

Her antlers sweep up higher than I am tall.

Her hands move over the cocoon, caressing its uneven surface, graceful fingers dipping into folds and seams as she examines it.

"This is why you have come here?"

"It's not the only reason. The—"

"Shush." She holds one hand up, quieting me. "One thing at a time."

"Let me tell you about the other thing?"

"This is more important. We will deal with it first."

"It's important," *or I wouldn't have hauled that across this prison,* "but the other thing is important too."

She doesn't look up at me as she says, "I forget that humans are linear."

Every time my brain begins to normalize this stuff I get reminded that I'm only human.

"What do you mean we are *linear*?" I ask.

"It's how you conceive time. For your species time is a constraint, something that defines you. And you consider it to go from the beginning to the end as you see it. It's not your fault; it's in your design. Every bit of you, every cell, every organ, and all of

your connected bits, is made to work that way. You age and it defines your entire existence."

"I don't see that there's another option."

She chuckles. "For your kind there often is not another option.
You are charming in your primitiveness."

I feel insulted. "Should I feel insulted?"

"I would prefer that you do not."

"Were you trying to insult humans?"

"I called you charming."

"And primitive."

"Never be insulted by the truth."

She slaps the tops of her thighs like a plumber who just finished
sealing a leak. "Well, now I know what happened to that."

I would ask her what that means, but the tone of her voice lets
me know that she was talking to herself. She reaches under the
cocoon, lifting it to her chest. She stands cradling it and it looks
so much smaller than it felt hanging from around my back.

"I have something to show you if you will follow me."

I consider it. So far she has been nothing but kind and helpful.
She hasn't tried to eat me or have me beat her bloody.

"I will follow you, not to Mordor, but through the mines."

She nods as if she understands.

Does Death read Tolkien?

Maybe it's the nature of her appearance. A skull allows me to
project my feelings onto her. It is both familiar and alien; we all
have skulls just behind our faces, but rarely do we see them other
than representationally. Humans have been drawn to the skull forever. It appears in art from the classic and sublime to the raunchi-
est of lowbrow. There is power in a skull. Power in the death it
represents.

Mortality.

Shit, she's right. Mortality drives everything we do. I'm here now trying to be the defender of mortality for my loved ones. For all the other people on Earth. The Man in Black is going to unleash his father on Earth and everyone will suffer and die because of it.

But everyone will suffer and die even if I stop him.

It just won't be as dramatic.

The weight of that concept sinks into me, and my bones feel like they are made of lead and trying to carry me to the ground.

What am I doing?

Stop.

Almost. You almost got me. That worm of self-destruction and nihilism, the futility of struggle against the inevitable. You tried.

Fuck off.

I might fail, but I won't quit.

The Skull-Faced Woman is lying on the bed.

Same position, same graceful undulating curves, same spill of midnight hair blending with the silk of her gown.

And she is standing, waiting for me, the cocoon in her arms.

"Are you ready?" she asks.

"There is another you on the bed."

She turns, looking. "I cannot see my avatars unless they are hosted."

"You can be in more than one place at a time?"

"Child, I am always everywhere."

"How does that work?"

"Let me show you what I have to show you and then we can discuss it."

I follow her around the dais and farther into her chambers.

38

I REALLY HATE the lighting here.

Almost everywhere seems to have random diffused lighting. Here in the Skull-Faced Woman's chambers, the lighting stays mostly bluish, sometimes it turns slightly greenish, and once it even takes on a purple tone, but it remains in the cool end of the spectrum and it just exists, so amorphous and undefined that I wonder if there's even light at all. Is this just another trick that my brain plays upon me to make sense of what is actually here?

Why would something like the Hungry Dark need light at all? It has no eyes.

And things that are here that have eyes may not even see things like I do.

I follow her, a foot or two behind so as to not step on the hem of her gown as it sweeps back and forth over her trail, moving in time with the efficient *tick* and *tock* of her hips. Not quite a sway, definitely not a sashay, her walk is *feminine*. It's very nearly predatory, but it's done for efficiency, not seduction. It's a simple matter of body mechanics, using her long levers to eat up the space we are crossing. I am not sprinting to keep up with her, but I am definitely hustling.

I don't see the wall until it looms out of the darkness as we draw close to where it is.

There is an opening with no door to cover it.

The Skull-Faced Woman doesn't hesitate; she just enters in.

I stay close to her. I can sense nothing in the darkness around us, but I have a feeling I do not want to get left behind in it.

The room we enter is simple. The floor remains the same, the walls made of square stone blocks seated atop one another and holding up a low ceiling that looks as if it is made of pitch.

It's a small room, narrow and claustrophobic. A dramatic contrast to the openness of the chambers outside.

Feels like a cell.

Not a cell like the ones in the prison, more like a monk's cell. Spare and sparse, completely functional, with no use for any type of decoration or personalization. On the far wall from where we entered there is a long trough filled with water. Above it, a font spews out a tumble of liquid that splashes on the surface, causing it to rise over the edge and run down the sides to make the floor one big damp spot. The air smells green, the sodium-rich moistness of ocean brine.

The Skull-Faced Woman goes to the tub and looks down at it.

I move around her to see what she is staring at.

And immediately wish that I hadn't.

There is a thing in the tub that doesn't look like a man, but he's vaguely man shaped.

Longer than he is wide, the bottom half split into what could be legs, the upper half with two things that could be arms peeled off the sides, he looks a little like a sodden voodoo doll. He's definitely humanoid, but the joints are wrong where there are joints.

Where there are no joints, the limbs are banded tubes of what could be muscle woven into themselves, separated by rings that look somewhat like cartilage.

Above his shoulders is a densely misshapen head that lies heavy in the water, listing to the side like a wounded ship. Thin strands of what appear to be corn silk are plastered to the skin along his temples. His mouth yaws open, too wide and filled with too many teeth. They crowd together like tiny gray pearls starting from the edge and clustering back along the roof of his mouth. His tongue is flat and fills his lower jaw.

My brain chews on the image of him, trying to figure out how that works, and the only thing I can imagine is that whatever he puts in his mouth is then pressed between the thick muscle of the tongue and the studded roof of his mouth and worked into some kind of paste to be swallowed.

Around the crown of his head are depressions that appear to be eye sockets. They lie, a half dozen in a semicircle, like the radiating beams of a sun. The eyes are crystalline, the depressions filled with crusty granules of translucent material that look like hardened jelly. I look closely, my eyes sweeping down his form, picking out other depressions that look similar to the eyes on the head. The depressions string out along the limbs; the two that sit in the shoulders are similar in appearance to the ones on the face, filled with the same substance. The ones on the lower limbs, the ones submerged beneath the water, are simply depressions spaced evenly down the arms and legs.

The body is covered in interlocking muscles, or what look like muscles. Along their surfaces are raw sores and long, sweeping cuts that lip out, all of them angled down left to right.

The Skull-Faced Woman leans down and says something that I cannot make out.

The thing in the water stirs, lifting himself with a sloshing sound. The tepid greenish-gray water comes up over the edge and rolls down, spreading the stain that surrounds him on the floor.

The thing in the water . . .

The creature in the tub . . .

The more I look at him the more he bothers me, the way that looking at food on a table set out for a banquet that has spoiled would make my stomach turn. There is a revulsion that sits underneath my breastbone because of this thing in the tub.

His movements are weak, as if he can barely lift his limbs. Just enough motion to make the water sloshing around fill the chamber with white noise.

As I look at him struggling, all I can think about is the raw red right hand of the Man in Black. Something about its form reminds me of the thing in the tub.

The revulsion lurches into my esophagus as I realize what it is.

The thing in the tub has been *skinned*.

He lifts a pitiful hand that rises above the edge of the tub, water running between the muscles, in the grooves of them, dripping from the edges of the hand, and I hear him say, "Mercy."

The Skull-Faced Woman makes a shushing sound and leans farther over the tub. Her antlers have begun to glisten in the humid air that fills the room. Little droplets of moisture, like dew on the grass in the morning, cling to them. Shimmering as they threaten to release and fall away in drops.

The same moisture lies on my skin in a clammy sheen that causes me to shiver.

This close the micro-spray from the fountain mists across me. It smells musty, not fetid like rotting vegetation, more animal, more cannibal, like the inside of a mouth where things are stuck in the back molars. I always think of running water as fresh water, but this is not. This water is from some ocean or sea, perhaps a saltwater lagoon, but it is a brine meant for preservation.

This doesn't seem like torture to the thing in the tub. I can only assume that it is some form of comfort, perhaps even therapy.

And I wonder what sort of thing can survive being skinned alive.

The Skull-Faced Woman places the cocoon on the thing in the tub's chest with one smooth motion that is fast. So quick that it is accomplished before I realize what is happening, because my brain has finally tripped over what is so obviously in front of me.

What can survive being skinned alive?

An archangel.

"Is that—"

She is in front of me, fingers pressed against my lips, stopping my words. I jerk back and my tongue darts across my now wet lips before I can stop it, filling my mouth with that taste from the tub water. The flavor is worse than the smell and I gag, choking on it, and I hate the way my throat clenches from the middle of my chest all the way up to the roof of my mouth. I hate the way my tongue leaps against my teeth. I hate the way the muscles under my jaw knot themselves up. I hate the hot tears that run down my face as I try to breathe through it, try to spit the taste from my mouth.

I drag an arm across my lips.

Her hand is moving toward the thing again as I start to say, "What the *fuck*?" and it stops me short and I clamp my mouth shut.

Her hand falls away. She leans forward and whispers, "It is time to go."

She steps around me and moves toward the door we came in through without waiting to see if I follow.

Of course I am going to follow.

Before I do, I look in the tub.

The thing there has wrapped his raw, skinless arms around the cocoon, cradling it tightly to his chest, huddling around it. The coat remains unchanged save for one thin tendril of inky substance that has unfurled from its surface and slithers across the thing's chest and up the side of his neck like a parasitic vine. I watch it cross over the bottom edge of the thing's face and then split into thinner branches that move faster, separating to seek out the thing's crusted-over eyes. They reach them and begin burrowing under the crust, and into the open mouth to curl around the mamelon teeth before they race down the thing's throat.

The thing in the tub rolls to his side, still clutching the hard cocoon, submerging it halfway into the briny, brackish water.

The thing begins to moan and buck like a dog having a nightmare. Water splashes onto the floor, running toward my feet.

Worry for the skinhound rolls through my mind, clashing against the repulsion that keeps growing from what I'm seeing, and the conflict makes me turn and follow the Skull-Faced Woman out of the room.

39

_____

I FIND HER not far from the door, waiting for me.

"They will be a while," she says. "We should get you cleaned up."

I'm about to push that aside, to press her on what it is that is happening in the room we just left, when it hits me just how filthy I am. I feel as if I've been dipped and battered. I'm grimy with dirt and sweat and secretions from my wounds and I feel unclean, more than just my skin. I feel tainted by my uncleanliness.

She motions for me to follow again and I do.

It doesn't take long to come across another door. Like the other, it is a simple opening. She steps inside and I continue to follow.

The room is larger but just as spare. There is no tub or fountain, but there is a pool in the middle of the floor. Light comes from underneath it, diffusing up into the room in a soft blue tone. The floor slopes toward the pool, actually underwater for a few feet around the edges of it. The pool is vaguely round and from the surface wisps of steam curl into the air. The room is warm and humid and smells clean, like a gravel road after a spring rain.

The Skull-Faced Woman stops beside the pool. The edge of her gown trails through the edge of the pool and the material turns dark as the water begins to wick itself up into the fabric.

"Will you bathe with me?" She indicates the pool with a graceful wave of her hand.

"I need to—"

"Whatever it is, trust me, it can wait."

"Stop that," I spit the words at her. "Stop interrupting me every time I go to say something."

Her head drops, dark hair spilling over the light ivory of her bone face. After a moment she looks up. "I apologize. I have allowed my eagerness in this new situation to cause me to be impolite."

Her apology is so sincere that it feels like fingers have reached behind my heart and are tugging it forward.

There is an element to her voice that is unmistakable. I have felt it many times in my life.

She is alone.

And worse, she is *lonely*.

I found her in an empty chamber, sleeping on a bed. I know that sleep. When you just feel disconnected from reality, you're not a part of anything and no one cares about you in any way that matters at the moment. The isolation wraps you like a blanket and the loneliness is a chain around your waist, binding you to the bed, and you lie there in your depression too tired to even sleep.

Yes, I know that *far* too well.

"*What* do you want to do again?"

"I would like to bathe together. You are injured and the water will help. You can tell me of the other thing that has brought you here and I will answer any questions that you have."

"I don't know."

In all of my time spent in gyms and dojos I know that people often will shower together, sit in saunas together, even soak in hot tubs with each other after strenuous workouts, but I never have. It took years for me to change in front of other people, and by "other people" I mean other women, but even that is still uncomfortable. Sometimes, at the apartment, Shasta will come into the bathroom while I'm showering to get something, or to just talk, and the entire time she is in there with me, even though I am behind the curtain, I am tense.

Maybe I have a few hang-ups with being naked in front of people.

I don't think I'm alone.

And shut up.

"It is not a trap nor a trick."

The thought of that makes me snort and I say, "I don't think it's a trick. Why would you need to trick me? You're the goddess of death."

She nods. "I am. But if you're not worried about a trick then why do you hesitate? Do you not like me?"

"Lady, I don't know you that well."

"Don't you operate on instinct? Do you not listen to your 'gut'?"

"I do, but that doesn't seem to do me much good."

"It has brought you this far."

"Not easily."

"Even the shortest life for your species is not easy. I ask you again, will you bathe with me?"

I squat down and reach out, putting the tips of my fingers into the water. It's warm, just a notch under too hot, and it feels slippery but not like oil. This close the scent of it fills my nostrils, all mineral, like zinc and copper. It smells like old pipes carrying well water. It's not unpleasant at all.

I can see the bottom of the pool. It's a simple, clean hole in the rock, nowhere for anything to hide that I can see.

I nod as I stand up.

"Okay," I say. "I'll bathe with you."

The Skull-Faced Woman smiles without smiling and claps her hands. In two shakes of her shoulders, and one tug on the material, she is naked before me.

And I am unprepared.

I turn to avoid looking at her and my face feels hot from my collarbones up.

"There is no need to turn away, child."

"Um . . ."

"You have seen my face; can you not look at my form?"

Slowly I raise my eyes.

She stands before me lit by the glow of the pool. Highlights gleam along the curves and spines of her antlers and lie softly on the tops of the curls in her hair. The highlights along her face are muted, glowing softly rather than shining, the light diffused by the nature of the bone. The gown that she wore before did not conceal much, and yet the rest of her is very nearly overwhelming.

Her arms and shoulders have muscle to them that carries over onto her chest; her breasts are small and one smaller than the other. Her chest narrows underneath and then flares dramatically out to heavy hips that carry the smooth roundness of her tummy, the surface of which is unmarred. She has no navel to mark her birth. The muscles from her shoulders and chest match the muscles that form her legs in long, sweeping, graceful curves. There is strength there.

Looking at her brings to mind both Ashtoreth and Shub Niggurath as the last women I have seen naked. The memory of seeing the fallen love goddess in her true form flashes across my mind's eye, immediately followed by the image of the Black Goat of the

Woods in her raw fertility. Both of them disturbing in different ways, one a corruption, the other alien and primordial.

The Skull-Faced Woman is neither.

Somehow seeing her in the altogether is comforting, weird but not frightening.

Something inside of me breaks, some bubble of tension, and I feel myself loosen just slightly.

The Skull-Faced Woman turns and slips into the water with barely a ripple. She spins and leans back against the edge.

And it's my turn to undress.

I kneel to untie my shoes and as I do the scourge that is tucked into my belt *clickety-clacks* on the floor below and it causes me to stop.

"You can leave that with your clothing. Keep it close enough to reach if it comforts you."

I nod at her words and pull the scorpion tail–tipped flogger out of my belt and lay it gently upon the floor.

"I know the worth of that. It is impressive that you have one."

"I picked it up on the way here."

"Megaera must like you."

The smile that twitches in the corner of my mouth surprises me as much as the feeling that puts it there. It's a dark thrill at the memory of using the scourge on the Fury, feeling it bite into her flesh and draw out the sounds from deep inside her, that runs from the base of my skull to the bottommost point of my pelvis.

The chuckle that escapes me is dark and throaty.

"I think she did like me."

What the hell is wrong with me?

To say that my sexuality is confusing to me is like saying quantum physics is confusing to a goldfish. After all I've been through since that night, that damned night so long ago that my world was shattered the first time, it's been a part of me that I have fought against. I've done it most of my adult life. Maybe "fought against" is the wrong way to say it. I haven't struggled. I've simply ignored any hint of it. Even after years of therapy, I have kept that part of me shut down, ignored, and shut away.

I had conflict and confusion when Daniel came along and for the first time I didn't want to ignore that part of me, but since the Man in Black came into my life things of that nature have gotten downright terrifying.

I go back to untying my shoes, moving my fingers quickly and pulling them off. I stand back up and undo my belt, pushing my pants down over my hips and stepping out of them.

I don't know what to take off next.

Taking off my underwear exposes me, but maybe not so much, because my shirt might be long enough to cover me for another few seconds. Or I could take my shirt off, but then I'd have nothing but my bra and underpants.

Fuck it.

I grab the bottom of my shirt and pull it over my head. It hurts to lift my arms that high. The motion reminds me of how much I hurt. Still, I drop the shirt on top of my pants and my fingers are already undoing my bra before it hits the ground. Moving as fast as I can, I shimmy out of my underpants and slide into the water.

I'm so quick that I slip on the edge and my head is underwater before I can take a breath.

Panic doesn't even have a chance to set in before I am hauled back to the surface.

I sputter and gasp, shaking the water from my face so I can open my eyes.

The Skull-Faced Woman has me by the arm.

She is close.

Very close.

My body touches hers in a long line, my side to her front.

She pushes me gently to the edge of the pool. I use my arms to hold me in place.

"Thank you," I say.

She moves back beside me with a laugh. "Trust me, Charlie, you were in no danger of dying."

"Well, if anyone would know it would be you."

"I don't know the moment of your death."

"Then how do you know that wasn't it?"

"I don't quite know how to explain. You are constrained by your concept of time; you are so brief that you only see your existence as linear."

"Time isn't linear?"

She nods. "It is, for you and creatures like you. You experience each moment one at a time, whereas something like me, I experience all moments equally because a version of me is in that moment."

"So, you're omniscient?"

"In a way, but not in a way that you mean. I am ever present, but the version of me speaking to you here is not the same version of me that will speak to you again, and is not the same version of me that is watching a child die under a star that you will never see."

"How do you know all of the versions of you are experiencing all of the things that they are if you yourself are not experiencing them?"

"I did say it was hard to explain."

"It does not make any sense."

"To *you* it does not make any sense."

"I'm the only one you're trying to explain it to."

Her legs kick under the water, making a current that passes over my legs and hips. The water is hot and I feel it working on the soreness that has set up in my body. As I hang on the edge, with the heat loosening my muscles and tendons, the weight of my lower half, even suspended in the dense, mineral-filled water, begins to work and stretch my spine. Carrying the skinhound in the cocoon compressed me, jammed my spine up, and put a lot of stress on my lumbar region and down into my hamstrings and calves. Even the bottoms of my feet are sore and tender.

I let myself sink farther. The water discolors around me as it washes away all of the sweat and grime and grossness I have accumulated in my time here. It quickly dissipates and the water is clear again.

Gently, I stretch, pushing my muscles to release their cramped strains and knots.

"You have a lovely form, Charlie."

Her words make me draw up and push away from her.

"I only mean that you have an efficiency in your movements that most of your kind do not have."

"Um, thanks."

Please stop. Don't say anything like that again.

"I did not mean to make you uncomfortable."

"It's okay."

"It's not."

"It's my hang-up."

"Where did you happen to find Erathaol's garment?"

What is she talking about?

Oh.

The coat.

"That thing in the tub?"

She nods.

"That thing is an archangel?"

"He was an archon. Now he is a suffering patient."

"Is an archon an angel?"

"That is what your kind calls them."

"How is he still alive?"

"How was his garment alive?"

"This is a weird conversation to have with a death goddess."

She laughs a small laugh. "Who better?"

At least Death has a sense of humor.

"I stole it from the Man in Black."

"I do not know this Man in Black."

"Nyarlathotep."

"The one who cut it away from Erathaol?"

"That's what he claimed."

"However did you get it from him?"

"That is a long story." I hold up my palm and show her the Mark. "He tricked me into being his Acolyte, but he was just using me. When I found out I fought back and the coat jumped on my side."

Holding my palm up, I realize that my magick has been quiet. Thinking about it now, I can feel it bubbling deep inside. It feels like it's getting stronger, but it was really depleted.

"I am surprised the Son of Azathoth does not seek to take back what you have rightfully stolen."

I still haven't told her the full reason why I'm here. Maybe I should have told her before I got naked, and weaponless, into the pool with her.

"I am here trying to find him."

"To give him back the . . . what did you call it?"

"I just call it the coat."

"The coat."

"No, he wants it back, but he's not here for that."

"The Crawling Chaos is here in my home?"

I nod.

"Who told you this, child?"

"No one told me. I followed him from my Earth. Remember when I said he tricked me? The whole time he was taking the essence of other gods to gain enough power to set his father free."

"If he were here, I would know."

"Would you know it? Or would only some version of you know it?"

Silence stretches between us, broken only by the slight chopping noise of the water lapping against the sides of the pool.

"Is it possible he could be hiding from you? Because I've seen him. I chased him into one of your cells."

"You did?"

I nod.

"What was in that cell?"

"The Hungry Dark."

"I do not like this game." She tilts her head, making her hair dip into the water on one side. "Why are you lying?"

"I'm not lying."

"*You* survived the Eldritch Devourer?"

My old friend anger flares hot and bright at her tone.

"I'm here, aren't I? Some version of you didn't have to visit me. I used the magick the cell was made of to drive it away."

And then Marty saved me, but I don't say that part; it would take away from what I did.

"I see."

Damn right you do, lady.

"Even if I believe what you say, Nyarlathotep will never be able to locate his father."

"I've had a very long dance with him. I don't think you should underestimate his ability. He's come this far after killing more than one thing that can't be killed to get here."

"You doubt my ability to contain the most dangerous entity under my care?"

"Somehow the Man in Black snuck past you, so yeah, I have concerns."

"Do you know how this place works?"

"From what I was told, humans kicked the gods off Earth and put them here and this place uses the worship of those things to steal their power, keeping them weak enough to be held."

"Who told you that?"

"It was either the Man in Black or Ashtoreth, possibly a combination of the two."

"This place exists because I exist. I am the building blocks. Every bit of this, all of the cells, all of the worlds maintained here, all of the gates and the walls and the doors, they all come from me. That is why I am always here."

I can't stay in the water anymore. I have to get out. Frustration is making my insides hurt from tension and I feel silly showing that tension while floating in a pool of mineral water. Pushing up on the edge, I swing myself around and sit, leaving my legs in the water. It feels better having my face higher than hers; being able to look down on hers, I argue.

"The Man in Black has the essence of three gods in his grasp."

The words of Cthulhu said to me so long ago come roaring back in my mind and I let them spill from my mouth.

> "*Three to break the seal.*
> *Three to turn the wheel.*
> *Three to loose Azathoth.*
> *Three and all hope is lost.*'"

She is silent for a long moment. "Where did you gain that knowledge?"

"Cthulhu said it to me in my mind while the Man in Black was killing him."

"Great Cthulhu is not dead."

"I know; he's in Raleigh in Slumberland. But there was a version of him, an avatar, that was on Earth. The Man in Black killed that and took a gemstone from out of its head. One of the same gemstones he's going to use to set his father free."

"That's the other thing that bothers me about your tale."

"It's not my 'tale.' It is what's happening somewhere out there in this prison."

"Nyarlathotep hates his father. Worse, he's afraid of his father, not just because of his father's nature but because his father will destroy him."

"Why will he do that?"

"Azathoth is the Primal Chaos. He is the embodiment of the destruction of this universe. He is only here because his son betrayed him, led him into the trap, in exchange for the freedom to wander the universe seeking amusement."

"Well, now he has decided that dear old Dad needs a reprieve and he's the one to grant it."

"And do you think you're the one who can stop him?"

"Someone has to. I hate the son of a bitch, and I've come all this way. But I'd gladly let you do it."

"Charlie, I believe you have mistaken me for a person."

"What does that mean?"

"This avatar, and all of me, enjoys this." Her hand swings toward me and back to her, indicating our conversation. "But I am not a person. I am a function. I am the embodiment of death and all that that entails. Unfortunately, what it does not entail is being any kind of champion or warrior."

"Then I guess it has to be me."

"But are you up to the task?"

"I don't know." I'm being honest, so honest it's actually painful. "I have the will to, and I've hurt him in the past. He still holds a wound that I gave him back on Earth."

"He is extremely powerful."

"I know he is; trust me, I really, really know. But I don't have to kill him, I only have to stop him, and if there's one thing that I can do, I can fuck up his plans."

"How do you plan to do that?"

"If you show me how to find Azathoth, I will be there waiting for him."

"I don't know if I would call that a plan."

"It's the best that I've got. But he and I are connected through the symbol in my hand and the fact that he was once my master."

It never gets any easier to say that word.

"And I have weapons." I point at the scourge. It scratches at the floor in response. "And I have . . ."

The shotgun and the knife of Abraham are still in the coat.

Damn it.

I'll have to make do without them.

"It will not be easy to find where I have hidden the Primal Chaos."

"If I were looking for easy I would have quit by now."

"Then I will show you the way."

"Well, all right then, ramblers, let's get rambling."

I go to stand up; her hand touches my knee.

"Will you do one thing for me before we go?"

"I can try."

"I've never seen myself; will you show me?"

"I don't have a mirror."

"With a very simple working I can use your eyes to see my face."

"How bad will it hurt?"

She pulls away. "Never mind, you don't have to do it."

That spike of loneliness is back.

"Stop. I'm just trying to prepare myself. I'm not saying no."

"You will do this thing for me?"

I feel very put on the spot. "Sure."

"Excellent. Thank you, Charlie."

"Can we put our clothes on first?"

Pushing off the way that I did before, she rises from the pool and climbs to her feet. She looms over me, water running over her like quicksilver.

"Yes," she says. "That, we can do."

40

I FEEL BETTER.

Correction, my body feels better. A fair amount of the aches and pains have gone away. I'm still sore, but it's one step removed, present but without the sharp edge.

But my clothes, they're pretty wrecked. My shirt is useless, torn to shreds by the murder penguin. I still have my bra but nothing to cover it with. It's a modest sports bra, but I'm still uncomfortable without a shirt over it. My jeans are wet, as are my underpants. Both needed a wash, so I did that at the edge of the pool. Without somewhere to dry them I had to peel them on and wear them wet.

They're too tight, constricting, binding me up.

"Is there something I can do?" she asks.

"No," I say. "I just wish I had a shirt."

"Would you like my gown?"

"I'll keep my jeans."

"Allow me to help." She bends at the waist and grabs the hem of her dress. In one swift jerking motion she rips it all the way up to mid-thigh. She tears in the opposite direction and the bottom of her dress comes away in her hands.

Jerking her head, she signals me to come over.

Holding up the fabric, she presses it against my body, her arms going under my arms and around behind my back. She is up against me, my face in her hair. It smells like I imagine the underside of a raven's wing would smell, like autumn smoke and acorns.

It takes all I can do to not bury my face in her neck and lay my lips against the skin there.

It takes all I can do to not shove her away, to put more distance between us.

I don't like to be touched like this.

And I don't like to be held tight.

I don't have the panic or the anger. Instead, I feel my mind sinking away into that staticky place where I freeze up.

I start to count my breaths, giving my brain something to keep it working.

At eight she pulls away, her hands sliding back around, smoothing across my rib cage and then down my stomach. They abruptly flick back up, her knuckles skimming over my abdomen before her hands turn and cup my breasts.

They're gone before I realize what has happened.

She grabs the top of the fabric and tugs it up. It stretches, becoming pliable, and she pushes it up over my shoulders before spinning me around. There is a tug on the fabric that's lying over my shoulders down to meet the top in the back. Her fingers smooth the joining and suddenly I am wearing a shirt. It's a tight shirt, but I can breathe just fine.

"There," she says, stepping backward. "Does that help?"

The tension I held of having no shirt has already lessened.

"It actually does."

"Good. All I ever want for you is that you be comfortable. You will find this material more *resilient* than your previous clothing."

I could use resilient. For a long time I have used the coat to keep me intact; without it I will need something to protect my skin.

She runs her fingers over the hem at the sleeve, knuckles dragging over my skin with a buzzing that makes the taste of metal settle on the back molars of my teeth. It's some small magick. A color, an impure black, spreads from her touch across the shirt, darkening it. I watch it seep from my shoulder across my entire torso.

"There." Her voice lifts in satisfaction. "That suits you better."

"How do you know I prefer dark clothing?"

"You have been crafted into a thing that strikes from the dark, a weapon wielded only by yourself. The assassin's knife needs no flashy blade. Believe me."

The Skull-Faced Woman has been the easiest god to hold a conversation with besides Cthulhu. She's almost normal.

And then she calls me "a weapon wielded only by yourself." Gods, man, they just have to make things weird.

She looks up and away, as if listening to something.

After a moment, her attention comes back to me.

"We should look at each other. The time is growing short."

"I thought time was a human hang-up?"

"Do *you* like to have your statements used against you?"

I lift my hands. She has a point. I hate to have my words used against me. She's right. I shouldn't have done that. Sometimes I just can't help myself.

"How do I show you yourself?"

"It will require a level of intimacy."

This is a bad idea.

"As long as it's not too intimate, then I am okay."

She shifts, moving even closer to me, until we are almost touching. Her right hand comes up between us and her left grabs my wrist, not tightly. Her longer fingers loosely encircle it. She lifts my Marked hand and presses it, palm down, against the center of her chest. My fingers begin to tingle, magick moving in my blood.

Her hand falls onto my chest, pressing hard.

And my world splits in two.

41

I AM TWO parts.

Two parts that are not me.

One part sees me standing at the end of my arm.

Not my arm.

I've lost weight. I knew that; my body has felt tighter, more drawn in on itself, but it feels stronger, pared down, the excess trimmed away. The side of my face is discolored, a bruise that goes from beside my mouth up to the side of my eyebrow. It's not dark, just darker, and I cannot remember what could have caused it.

I look down and see my arm.

My actual arm, touching my chest.

Not my chest.

I hear the Skull-Faced Woman speak from two places, inside my head,

not my head,

and with my own ears.

"Charlie," she says. "I am *beautiful*."

I nod,
not my head.
"Thank you for this," I/she says.
Before I can say "no problem" she says, "I'm sorry."
And then things get truly bizarre.

42

THERE IS A woman I am touching. She lies in the mud made by her own fluids. They leak from her stomach like soup from a cracked bowl. Her eyes widen as she sees me kneeling over her. I watch the light go out from them.

I see it coming, the thing in the dark, the shape of it separating from the shadow, outlined in a thin rim of not-dark. The creature I now stand in front of does not see it. Just before the thing in the dark scoops the creature up into its maw, it raises its heads and freezes at the sight of me. Its blood is hot across my shins.

I am with them all, looking up with them at their sky, bearing witness as the razor's-width scrim of their sun sputters to a deep crimson before snuffing out in the darkened sky. I am with the ones who take this as a sign and fling themselves belly first onto the sharp shards of the crystalline desert their seas have become. Their ink washes over my feet and freezes as they dash themselves into my embrace.

I stay for the ones who choose to suffer through the shriveling starvation and the incremental agony of freezing.

I close the eyestalks of the sandwyrm, pushing them down into the gelatin flesh safely hidden beneath the thick plate of horn that is its exo-skull. They sink beneath my fingers, waving as they do. Once seated, I have to use my nails to grip the nictating lids and pull them together from the sides.

I am alone. There is no one and nothing to embrace. Only me. My time has come. I'm slowly fading. The universe folds around me. In the face of oblivion there is only fear. No peace, no rest. I will cease to exist. All that I have witnessed, all that I have borne, and it is all for nothing. I will be no more, not even a residue.

Vanity of vanities. All has been for nothing.

My purpose has been for no purpose.

I won't even survive long enough to enjoy the joke of existence.

Which is the cruelest joke of all.

43

I'M ON THE floor and I don't know how I got here.

The Skull-Faced Woman bends down toward me.

I roll and scramble from under her, getting to my feet and making distance in the small room. I have the scourge in my hand even though I don't remember pulling it from my belt. I shake it in her direction, snarling over the clackety rattle of the stinger-tipped ends batting against one another, and drop it back low in my grip. My body instinctively lowers into a fighting stance and my left hand is stretched out toward her. I flip the wrist of my right hand over so that the scourge is ready to strike.

"I am sorry, Charlie."

"Don't be sorry," I snarl. "Just back off me."

"Listen to me—"

"No."

"No?"

"No. Listening to you got me zapped." The images I

saw float on the edges of my eyesight. The deaths were sad, but the ending . . .

You want to know why I never took that step when depression had me in its teeth? When it twisted up my brain? When the Beast roared in my bones and tried to drive me over the edge? You want to know what kept me from pulling the trigger, or tying the slip-knot, or swallowing every pill in my medicine cabinet?

Oblivion.

Yes, I know, if I cease to exist then I won't know I have, so it shouldn't be scary.

But it scares the ever-living *shit* out of me.

I would rather die and go to a fiery hell than cease to exist.

There, I said it.

The true horror of an atheist. That even if my consciousness survives all the way to the end of the universe eventually even my atoms will disappear and nothing I ever did will mean anything.

"Listen to me very carefully, Charlie."

Death will even come for Death.

"Charlie!"

Her voice jolts me.

She peers at me with those empty sockets she has for eyes. "I can feel you changing. This is not your moment. It is not time yet for you. But if you do not get a grip on your mind then I will have no choice but to meet you here."

"Nothing else matters."

"Everything matters. Because it may be only this existence we all receive, then it all matters."

I can feel the jaws of the Beast tightening.

But it doesn't have me yet.

If there is no ultimate meaning to life then it has to have the meaning in being itself. No overarching truth, no gods worth wor-shiping, no reward or punishment on the other side.

There is no other side.

But just because it doesn't matter in the long run doesn't mean it doesn't matter at all.

Life is about love, and joy, and peace, and anger. It's about the struggle. It's about the despair.

It's about oatmeal crème pies kept in the refrigerator so they are firm and cool in your mouth.

It's about naps on Sunday.

It's about the perfect cup of coffee.

It's about hot showers after a long workout.

And, right now, it's about giving some payback to the Man in Black.

The Skull-Faced Woman claps her hands. "Yes! Yes, thank you for coming back."

The Beast is still there, still pacing on the edge of my brain. If I show weakness it will be at my throat, but it doesn't have me. I won't curl up into a ball.

I might fail.

But I won't quit.

I ease to standing. "You talked me down from the ledge."

"Good," she says, "because he's near, Charlie, and you have to stop him."

"What changed your mind? I thought you couldn't feel him."

"While we were connected I tapped into your . . . I think you called it 'magick.'" She looks over at me.

"Yeah. Go on."

"In it, I could feel the Son of Azathoth near."

"I told you."

"He has always been a trickster, but being able to hide from me inside my domain . . . it is a level of ability that indicates he might be able to find his father."

"They call him the Crawling Chaos. He seems to be able to do anything he wants with a little effort." The words are bitter, soured by the memory of how he fooled me with the King in Yellow, used me to get what he wanted. Oh, I do owe him.

I hold on to the anger, pull it close. The anger pushes the Beast farther away. The anger keeps me safe from myself.

"So, where is he?"

"I don't know. Near."

"That isn't a lot of help."

"It does not matter where he is. He can wander in this place for aeons untold. It only matters if he succeeds in freeing the Primal Chaos. That is what you must prevent. If he does that then Azathoth will not only tear this place to shreds; he will begin to consume the entire universe. He is the last thing I will see before I see no more."

"Okay. You know where you put him; lead the way."

"I cannot leave this chamber."

What?

"I thought you were in every moment."

"A version of me is in every moment because in every moment I am a function at use."

I sigh. "Something is always dying, so you are always where they are."

"Yes, that is the heart of it. Do you understand?"

"Sure." I don't, not truly, but maybe a little more since the mind-meld vision quest she took me on. "But you are a goddess; what can you do to help me?"

"Why, Charlie." Her skull face does that imperceptible smile again. "Are you praying to me?"

"Pray, invoke, communion, whatever word applies. Help me as much as you can." My fingers touch the scourge and it rattles in response. "Right now all I have is this."

I touch the torc around my throat. "This."

I hold my hand up, palm out to show the Mark. "And this. I think I'm going to need something to give me more firepower."

"Come with me." She turns and moves out of the room.

Why am I always chasing gods, even the ones that are on my side?

44

"Here."

Brackish water runs down her arms, dripping on the floor around her feet, splashing up onto her uncovered legs.

She is holding a misshapen object, soggy and malformed like a bean that has rotted and gone soft with decay.

Even from here I can smell it.

Like a wet dog covered in spoiled milk, a sour musk that climbs down my throat using my gag reflex as a handhold.

It is the coat.

It hasn't opened, but it's smaller now, too small, the size of a duffel bag instead of the size of a person.

Instead of the size it was.

"What happened?"

"What do you mean?"

"Where is the skinhound?"

"I don't know. . . ."

"There was a skinhound, a creature like a dog without fur, inside that when we left it. He's my friend. What happened to him?"

"Everything that was inside this is still intact."

"Why is it smaller?"

"Is it smaller?"

"It is."

"Your friend is not dead. Trust me."

"Then where is he?"

She raises the dripping coat once more.

The thing in the tub groans and rolls in the water. One of his arms flops over the side, futilely pawing the air toward us. The meat of it has gone gray, leeched of the color it had before.

"Trust me," she says.

I do trust her. At least as much as I trust anything that calls itself a god. But looking at the soggy, smelly mass in her hands just makes me want to turn and leave. It squicks me out. I know it's the coat and she says the skinhound is still inside, but that is not the thing I carried all the way here.

It looks like a trichobezoar: matted half-digested hair coughed up by something.

I clench my teeth to keep my gorge down and reach out.

It squelches when I touch it, more fluid seeping quickly from the pressure of my fingers, running down my arm all cold and slippery to drip from my elbow.

I cannot stop the grunt of disgust that escapes me as I take it fully from her hands and hold it straight out away from me.

"Hold it like that for a moment. I will help."

I want to drop it. Under my hands I feel things moving inside the coat, like a sack of bones pressing their knobby ends against my hand through it.

Has the skinhound been . . .

No. I will *not* consider the skinhound digested. The coat is good.

It has protected me and the skinhound this whole time. The Skull-Faced Woman says everything is okay, so I am going to trust that it is.

Although my version of okay and a death goddess's version of okay are not in any way related.

The Skull-Faced Woman tears another wide swath of cloth from the bottom off her dress, raising the hem (unhemmed?) line to the tops of her thighs. Her dress is now not much more than a long shirt, but she doesn't seem even slightly concerned about her exposure.

Moving quickly, she wraps the cloth around the soggy thing I hold, swaddling it like a drowned child. As she pulls the cloth around it, water sluices off in sheets, soaking the bottom of my jeans. She takes it back from me, tugging and pulling and tucking and creating a bundle that is wrapped tightly. She holds it back out to me.

"Take this with you."

"What am I supposed to do with it?"

"You will know when the time comes."

"Do you know what I'm supposed to do when the time comes?"

She nods.

"Then why not just tell me?"

"It is an instinctual thing. If I tell you it would be what I would need to do, not what you will need to do. We are not the same, you and I."

And in the weird wide world of strange gods and weird Mythos, that makes as much sense as anything else does.

I take the bundle and put it under my arm. It is wrapped so tight it is hard to the touch. The binding has shrunk it to the size of a small throw pillow. I know magick makes its own rules. I've done things that defy physics with my own magick. But this still bothers me.

The thing in the tub pulls his arm back into the water with a splash.

"What about him?"

The Skull-Faced Woman turns.

She stares down at the thing in the tub. "He is a tether."

"Is he really the former owner of the coat?"

"He is. He crawled his way here across the cosmos after Nyarlathotep flayed him. He was in agony, his flesh covered in parasites, being eaten away slower than his ability to heal, always providing a fresh banquet for the things that would feast upon him. Without his garment he had no protection. He was blind, his eyes dried up in their sockets without lids to protect them. His archon mind just strong enough to hold the edge of sanity that allowed him to feel every bit of pain and agony that he suffered."

"Why did he end up here?"

"The simple answer, child, is that he came so that I could end his suffering. He sought me and my function."

"Why didn't you kill him?"

"I am not a murderer."

"You're the goddess of death."

"One thing does not make me the other."

I guess she's right. I am not the goddess of death, but I have killed, and if I get the chance to with the Man in Black I will kill again.

"I suppose," she says, "the more complex reason that he sought me out would be to bring him to this moment."

"You're saying that fate brought him here?"

"Do you think that I would believe in fate?"

"You're telling me that everybody has an appointed time that they meet you. I mean, it seems like a fate to me."

"Just because there may be a design to this cosmos does not mean that there is anything like unto destiny."

I can't have this conversation. This conversation will bring the Beast back. This is the slippery road to nihilism.

I try to divert the conversation.

"What happens in this moment?"

The Skull-Faced Woman sighs. "Now I become something that I have never been before."

She leans over and places her hand on the chest of the thing in the tub.

No.

"Peace be with you," she says. "My peace I give to you."

Then she pushes him beneath the water and holds him there.

"What are you doing?" I cry.

Foul water is spilling onto her legs, which are pressed into the rim of the tub, displaced by the mass of the thing being held under it. "Only what must be done."

I grab her arm and it is steel under my hand. I yank and it has no effect.

"Don't do this!"

"It is already done, child."

I shove my shoulder into hers and it feels like ramming the side of a mountain. Even her hair doesn't sway with the impact.

The thing in the tub isn't struggling. Bubbles rise to the surface, breaking as they exit. His mouth is open.

"Please, don't do this."

Before I finish saying the words. I see that the bubbles have stopped.

The Skull-Faced Woman slowly lifts her hands from the thing in the tub. He stays on the bottom. She braces on the edge of the tub, her head still bowed, face obscured by a tangle of hair that falls around the roots of her antlers.

Her voice is hollow when she speaks.

"Could I have a few moments alone, Charlie?"

I nod even though she isn't looking at me and move toward the door.

Her voice rises again, making me pause.

"I won't be long and we are not done. Don't go far."

45

WHY DOES WHAT I just saw bother me so much?

I have killed. The Skull-Faced Woman is the goddess of death. Why does it bother me that she did what she did?

I know that part of it is the way she did it.

There are two ways that I do not want to die. I do not want to burn in a fire and I do not want to drown. I don't have a fear of water. But I do not want to lose my life trying to gasp oxygen from the water as it fills my lungs, causing them to swell and grow heavy and weigh me down to the bottom of whatever body of water has taken me.

I didn't know the thing in the tub. Other than my connection with his skin, I barely spent more than a handful of minutes with him. Yet surely the coat is not its own entity, but still part and parcel of its former owner.

Maybe that's why it bothers me. Maybe that's why

it bothers me to have this bundle under my arm when it didn't bother me to wear the skin or carry the wounded skinhound in it across this place.

I keep seeing the thing in the tub as he asked for mercy.

She walks out of the room, her hands cupped around something.

I lean on the wall. The bundle is still tucked under my arm. With my right hand I pluck at the falls of the scourge, making it rattle and click. The stingers flex, trying to pierce my jeans, and I know that it has been too long since they have stung. They are ripe like fruit, and their venom mixes with the water that has soaked the bottoms of my pants from the knees down. It warms my skin, the slightest burn, and I just let it happen because feeling anything, even something that hurts, especially something that hurts, is better than letting the dead spot inside my chest spread and take more of me.

"Do you want to talk about it?" she asks.

"I don't." The words come out with bite. "I do not ever want to talk about what I just saw."

She nods as if she understands.

"Why did you do it?"

"I thought you didn't want to talk about it."

"I don't want to talk about it. I just want to know why."

"It was his moment."

"It's that simple?"

"It is," she says.

"Okay, fine, whatever. What do we do now?"

"I don't trust that you are truly fine with this."

"Listen, I know we have some kind of bond going on here, but you don't really know me. It doesn't matter if I'm fine with it. All that matters is that I'm done talking about it. Believe me, I can put some shit behind me like nobody else. So please, let's just get on with whatever we have to do."

It takes a few moments of her staring at me with her head tilted before she speaks again.

"If you decide to—"

"I won't."

She sighs like the breeze through a cemetery.

Then, with the flourish of a magician performing a trick, she holds out an opal the size of a robin's egg.

"Do you know what this is?"

I nod. "Did that come from the angel?"

"No, child, this is mine."

"Did that hurt to pull out?"

"It did, but that does not matter."

"Every time I've seen one of those, it's been pulled from a corpse."

She shrugs. "It was not my moment."

"It's smaller than I'm used to."

"It is enough to lead you to the Mad God and nothing more. Tell me, is that collar around your neck a gift of Ashtoreth?"

"It is. Do you know her?"

"We have met."

"She really gets around."

"She is the goddess of whores. It should not be surprising that she knows most of my kind."

"I thought we were friends, and then she betrayed me to the Man in Black."

"She convinced you that you were friends?"

"She did."

"Oh, child, that is cruel, even for her."

"It is what it is."

"Indeed."

There is a moment of silence. I don't know what she is thinking about, but all I can see is the stricken look on Ashtoreth's face when

I realized she had been a pawn of the Man in Black. I don't know if she was forced into it or if she went along willingly.

Truthfully, now that time has passed and so much has happened I feel as if she was simply too weak to stand against him. There were moments of genuine friendship between us. I don't trust. Not easily.

Dammit, Ash.

All you had to do was let me know somehow.

The thought finishes and guilt blossoms, running through me like a parasitic vine. How dare I, of all people, victim blame? I know how much that wounds. To have someone doubt you, *accuse* you of being party to your abuse? It's painful in a way that even the abuse wasn't. It sets fire to your self-esteem, turning it to ashes.

I swear, if I get the chance, I will find out the truth. If Ashtoreth was forced by the Man in Black, then I will apologize to her.

If I can find her.

"Charlie."

I look up at my name, spoken by the Skull-Faced Woman.

"Bring your neck here."

"Why?"

"I need to manipulate your collar."

"I can take it off."

"You have removed it since you were betrayed?"

It takes a second to think. "No."

"Best to assume the next time you remove it, it will return to its previous owner. Possession is ownership."

"Do you know that for a fact?"

"No, but that is how these things generally work."

I know she means that I shouldn't take it off because of the probability of losing it, but all I want to do is pull it off my neck and hope that she is right. The torc has come in handy, but it has also been a curse. It is one of the most unpredictable things I

have . . . no, I take that back, it is 100 percent predictable in that
it will fuck me over if I am anything but vigilant. One casual wish,
one stray utterance that could *possibly* be a wish, and the torc will
grant it, but in the most monkey's paw, destructive way that it could
be interpreted.

She looks at me expectantly, as expectantly as you can when
your face is a skull. She wants me to give her my throat.

I step forward.

"Front or back?" I ask.

"Simply tilt your head down."

I do, putting my chin against my collarbones. The hard metal
circle digs into the front of my throat. Her fingers are in my hair,
gently parting it in the back, lightly caressing my neck, and it
causes shivers to chase down my spine. Those fingers curl around
the metal, pressing into my skin with her knuckles.

It makes pressure on the front.

My eyes leak water. I'm not choking, but it's close enough to it
that I have to fight to not gag or gasp. Her other arm moves along
my peripheral vision, disappearing behind me. There is more pressure on the collar, but this time instead of pulling up, it is pushing
down, the hard edge of the circle bruising against my collarbones,
sinking into the softer flesh that lies just underneath them.

My hands close into fists so that I don't shove her away from me.

The collar begins to vibrate, ringing as if it is a tuning fork that
has been struck. My lips feel numb and my teeth ache in my gums.

There is blood in my mouth.

The vibrations shimmy up my jawbone and crawl into my inner
ear. The drum inside vibrates at a frequency that I can hear like
the whine of a part about to snap and it itches deep in the canals
of both ears, feeling as if a centipede has crawled inside and is turning itself around and around and around, becoming an infinity of
scratchy little legs that prickle dozens of times over and over and
over again.

I want to ram a spike into both of my ears and dig out the itch.

My hands rise, fingers curled into claws, when the pressure just stops and the Skull-Faced Woman steps back with her hands raised.

I shake my head like a dog with an ear infection, working my jaw to try to ease the infuriating, maddening itch.

When it finally begins to calm and I can think about anything other than shredding my own eardrums, I realize that the torc around my throat is heavier.

I touch it with my fingers, finding the smooth stone somehow welded into the smooth metal. Etheric energy crackles between my fingernails and the stone.

"That is actually very pretty on you."

"I don't care about pretty."

"I know that, but it doesn't make it less true."

"Is there anything else you have to do to this?"

"No," she says. "That is your lodestone; use the torc in the way it was intended and that will take you to where you need to be in order to find Azathoth."

I know that wording. "This won't take me to the cell?"

"It will take you where you need to be," she repeats. "The Primal Chaos is not some trinket sitting on a shelf. He is the End. He has been put away as well as he can be. He will take some doing to find, but with my gift and Ashtoreth's in concert you will be able to."

"Nothing can be easy with you people."

"I am not people."

"You know what I mean."

"You have to be outside of these chambers to use the gift that I have given you. In this place it will simply return you to my side."

"So, I have to go back out there with the murder penguins?"

"You will find no harm from any of mine."

"I won't have to fight when I go outside?"

"Not with anything that belongs to me. In fact, they will go with you if you so desire."

I don't know how effective the penguins at the door will be against the Man in Black. I've watched him kill truly scary things.

But any backup is good backup and murder penguins might make good cannon fodder.

I am fucked up. Just moments ago I mourned the death of an angel I don't know, sorry, *didn't* know, and now I am joking about sending penguins to their deaths.

I feel as if I am going a bit crazy.

"Any chance you can magick me back to the exit?"

She laughs as if I told a joke.

46

I SLOWLY OPEN the door, just a crack. The scourge is in my hand. I have the folded coat tucked in the small of my back. I was pleased to discover that the fabric wrapped around it stuck to the fabric of my new shirt like duct tape. It feels secure and out of the way.

The Skull-Faced Woman said the murder penguins would not be a problem, but I'm not taking any chances.

I told you, I don't trust easily.

I white-knuckle the door's handle, bracing to keep it from being flung open if anything grabs it from the other side.

I strain my hearing so much that my blood thrums in my ear canals like the ocean in a conch shell.

I don't hear anything but my own shallow breathing.

I can't see anything through the thin crack.

"They are gone."

The voice from outside sounds familiar.

"Marty?"

I open the door wider and find Marty standing just a few feet away. He looks exactly as he did before: short and squatty, kind of dumpy.

I am glad to see him.

"Did the Skull-Faced Woman tell you to meet me here?"

"Why else would I be waiting for you?" he asks.

"Good point." I look around. "What happened to the murder penguins?"

"Those sightless things?" He waves his hand dismissively. "They are worthless, always wandering away, never able to lift anything because they don't have hands, and if you ever get behind them in a narrow passageway you want to stab them in the neck with their own beaks after watching them waddle to and fro."

I laugh and it feels good.

Marty blinks at me. "I am not speaking in jest."

"I know. That's what makes it so funny."

"You have always been an odd one."

"Only since you've known me, Marty."

He doesn't respond to that.

"Are you ready to take a trip with me?"

"Serket gave you what you needed?"

I tap the stone on the torc with my finger. The vibration of it feels good this time.

Marty leans forward, looking at my throat with his big seal eyes. "She put that right on your necklace."

"She did and now all I have to do is make a wish and go straight to Azathoth's cell. Do not pass Go. Do not collect two hundred dollars."

"This will take you there and not where Nyarlathotep is?"

"Not directly to the cell, but to some place where I can find it."

"Serket has hidden it well." His bottom lip rolls out into a frown. "You do know how dangerous this is?"

"I probably won't come out of it alive, but hey, in the end none of it matters anyway, so why not try?"

Careful with the jokes there, Chuckles.

The Beast is still on the edges.

I shake it off. "So, Marty, want to see what happens next?"

"No," he says. "But I have come this far."

I hold out my hand palm up. The Mark is angry red and feels tight. He reaches over and places his left hand in mine. It feels squishy when I close my fingers; I don't squeeze, but I can feel the bones inside. They feel slender, almost delicate, inside the pudgy flesh.

"Will this hurt?"

"Honestly, Marty, I have no idea."

Fair enough.

To take a deep breath and pull my magic up as I clear my mind.

In through the nose. Out through the mouth.

Everything shushes as my mind smooths out its rough edges.

When everything is as quiet as it can be in my troubled mind, I think one thought as clearly as I can.

Azathoth.

47

THIS TIME IS completely unlike any time before it.

The torc does not constrict or tighten. Instead, it begins to vibrate and shake around my neck. The metal hitting my collarbones sends dull pain shooting into my chest. Little shocks of magick cause my hair to stand on end all over my body. Gooseflesh prickles up my arms and down my legs.

Pressure closes around me like a hand compressing me. I have to close my eyes as I am folded by the magick, impossibly spindled into myself. I am aware of the sensation of it, but it does not truly hurt. Gravity lets me go and I am pulled and flipped and it feels like I have turned a somersault against my will.

My feet slap against the ground, hard enough to send shocks up through my shins and make me stumble.

I open my eyes and I am not where I once was.

Overhead is a turquoise-blue sky that stretches to

horizons that are lost from sight. In front of me is a grassy hill with a gentle slope, but the grass is dark, the same purple you would find in a cabbage. Chunks of gray stone scatter across the surface of the hill. The smallest is man-size and the largest the equivalent of a small house. They are not natural; they have been carved and constructed. The source of them is at the top of the hill. A temple looms at the top. It has fallen into disrepair to the extent that it looks half-destroyed, as if something of size has come along and knocked down part of it before wandering away to find something else to entertain itself.

All that is left of the temple on the hill is a broken crumbling wall, a cracked pillar, and a massive stone dome that teeters across both of them.

Gray smoke wafts from under the dome, curling into wisps that disappear as they rise.

Someone lives in the temple.

And I know that I'm supposed to go up there the same way that I know my name is Charlie.

I look and find Marty leaning against one of the boulders. He motions me over.

Has he been hurt? The wishing was not that bad this time, but maybe that was just for me, since it's my magick and my torc around my neck. He might have gotten a worse trip than I did.

I move quickly toward him. "Mar—"

He waves his hands, shushing me, and then motions me closer to him.

I stand next to him and he whispers, "Now I know what Serket has done."

"Why are you whispering?"

"The thing that lives here will only talk to Serket."

"Why would she send us then?"

"He will speak to you because you wear her sign. But he will not speak to me or any of her servants."

"So what's the problem? We go up there, I'll do all the talking."

"You will have to do that very thing. If you even acknowledge my presence he will never help us."

"You can just wait here."

He shakes his head. "No, that is unsafe for you. I will go with you, but I will stay to the side. I will not interfere unless you are in danger from him."

"I can take care of myself."

"Would Serket have assigned me this task if I were not needed here?"

"I see your point. So I'm supposed to just, what? Act like you're not there?"

"It is the only way he will cooperate and give you the knowledge you seek."

"Why does he hate you so much?

"It is not me. He hates this place. It is a prison."

"Yeah, I'd probably hate the guards if I were in prison too."

48

I DO *NOT* like being under this dome.

Standing just inside the threshold, I see that it should not be able to stay in the air. It is massive, eclipsing the light from the sky.

To my left is a stone wall with gaping holes in it. The blocks it is made of are crumbling, their corners worn away and broken, fallen to the ground at the base in the form of pebbles and shards, tiny things to hurt the bottoms of your feet. The upper edge of it meets the dome in only a handful of places, the lip of it resting precariously on the rim of the wall itself. The blocks curve in their formation, the pressure from above causing them to buckle outward. A dark-hued vine has woven itself all along the lower half, both binding the blocks together and also pushing them apart with its inexorable growth. Flowers droop along its length, their petals soft and fleshy, hanging flaccid, wrinkled, and obscene. Insect creatures crawl in and out of them on too many legs and with too many antennae. The sound of them rustling the folds of the flowers sounds like whispers as it comes off the wall itself.

Marty has stepped to the side, by that wall. If the flowers or the insects bother him he makes no sign of it.

Across the broken mezzanine floor, sharp edges of tile stabbing up like swords in a battle, there is a lone column that stretches from floor to dome. From here it appears to be slender, a thin stalk, although I can tell by the number of squares that it covers at the bottom that I would need at least three other people joining with me to reach around the circumference of it. Along its length are deep fissures and places where some of the stone has shorn away to shatter into gravel on the floor.

It's not just that the column looks too small to support the weight of the dome itself; it's that it is set too far back, coming very nearly even with the rear of the wall opposite, so that the majority of the dome hangs in empty space overhead and any moment it could decide on its own to crush anything that dares to stand beneath it.

It feels malevolent to me.

In the center of the broken floor is the fire that I saw the smoke from. It burns in a fire pit made of jagged broken rocks, bits of the building that I stand in.

There is a person beside the fire, poking it with a stick.

I glance over at Marty without turning my head and he simply stares back at me.

He said I was on my own with this.

Fine.

I walk across the broken tiles, watching where I place my feet so as not to turn my ankle. The tiles are large, easily two to three feet across. Most of them are broken, split by large cracks and missing pieces, but a few of them are intact. These have illustrations carved into them. The artwork is simple, deep grooves to make outlines and scratchy hatch marks to give a depth to the images.

There are people in the artwork and things that are nowhere near human. In between them there is something that feels like writing. The patterns of it repeat enough to feel like a language, but not one that I recognize. The runes and symbols and letters that create it twist around one another and are pointed like flames.

Looking at them makes my eyes hurt.

I concentrate on my feet only and even just having them in my peripheral vision causes my left eye to twitch and water.

"Who dares?"

I look up from the floor and I am closer to the fire than I thought.

The figure beside it sits cross-legged, wrapped in a ragged brown robe made of sackcloth. The edges of it are unhemmed, even along the hood that covers his head. I cannot see his face, but I do see a massive beard that hangs down over his chest. It is dark and shot through with streaks of silver. The hand that holds the stick, poking it into the fire, is large-knuckled and covered with marks that look very much like the writing on the floor around us. They crowd against one another and jumble; some of the marks are old and turning gray, but some look fresh, or at least freshly gone over. They seep clear yellowish fluid that sets up in the wrinkles and grooves of those swollen knuckles. They cover his fingers between the knuckles and the backs of his hands, even going under the edge of the sore that stretches completely across his wrist. The edges of the wound curl with little splits and fissures along the edges. The scab on it is white and looks like ash that has been packed into a fresh wound.

I've seen that kind of wound before.

It takes a minute for my mind to place it.

It's leprosy.ßß

I went a little overboard researching Thomas Covenant in the sixth grade. My teacher did not appreciate the eight-by-ten photos of leprosy that I provided with my report, but she gave me an A, and I learned what leprosy looks like.

Do you want leprosy? Because that's how you get leprosy.

"Do not make me ask again. You will regret it."

His words come from under his hood with a push of magick that ripples the air between us. It's a show of power, a threat. It doesn't hurt, but I can tell where it would.

"I have been sent here by—"

"I did not ask why you were here. I asked who you were."

"My name is Charlie."

He doesn't look up, just continues poking the fire, sending swirls of small sparks like fireflies chasing one another. "That is not who you are."

"It's my name."

"Are you an idiot? Have you been sent here to torment me? Tell me who you *are*."

Fine.

I let my frustration pull my magick up into my voice, giving it power.

"I am Twice-Marked, Chaos Hunter, Kin to the Kindly Ones, Emissary of Death Herself, the Deicide." Each name grows with power. "I am the Godslayer."

My words echo off the walls and the floor, rolling up the surface of the dome to fall back down around us.

Once the last reverberation dissipates into silence he begins to laugh.

"What's so funny?" I ask.

"I have no soup."

"You don't appear to have much of anything."

"I have an entire world inside me."

"I was told that you know where I can find Azathoth."

"Oh, I do know where he is, but I won't be telling you."

"I *need* you to tell me."

"Maybe if you had brought soup."

"I don't have any soup."

"Neither do I."

"Yes, we established that. There is no soup."

"There is always soup, just perhaps not in your bowl."

"I don't have time to talk about soup."

"Then why do you keep bringing it up?" He jabs at the fire harder than he did before. The sparks pop and I watch two of them land in the bottom of his beard. They flare bright orange and send up twirls of smoke before snuffing out in little black nests.

He still has not looked up at me.

I don't want to kneel in front of him. Even with him sitting on the floor I can tell that he is tall, far taller than I; his knees make knobby impressions in the bottom of his robe. His back hunches, matching the curvature of the dome that hangs precariously over our heads, and he is sunk into his robe, but the top of his head is not far below my chin.

"The Skull-Faced Woman sent me to you. She said you would tell me where Azathoth is."

"I would tell you or I would show you?"

"Frankly, I'll take either one at this point."

"Do you ever listen to the stars, Godslayer?"

"I've looked at them many nights."

"You should look with your ears; they scream in a symphony. It is lovely to hear."

"Are you saying Azathoth is among the stars?"

"Aren't we all among the stars if you look at the right perspective?"

A growl of frustration escapes me.

"This is bullshit," I mutter. "A waste of my time."

"Time? What do you know about time?"

"I know all about it. I know I don't have any more of it to waste with you."

He lifts the stick, pointing its glowing end at me. "You are human?"

"I am."

"You should have said that from the start."

"Would it have made a difference?"

"Only another human can hold the secret of Azathoth's cage."

"Well, I'm human, so tell me the secret."

"Tell you?" His voice changes pitch, rising in tone. It's the whine-growl of a wild animal caught in a trap. *I will give it to you.*

In one smooth motion he comes to his feet. He *is* tall, standing close to seven feet. With a toss of his head, he shakes off the hood, revealing a gaunt face made of jutting cheekbones and a hanging brow. More of the flame script is tattooed there, blazing across his forehead in rows that stack up to the shaved part of his head. A strip of hair crosses the crown of him in a tonsure, the skin on either side of it scraped and gashed with long, thin cuts.

His other arm comes out from under the sleeve of his monk's robe. It is a white, ashy, leprous stump. A wide blade takes the place where his hand has rotted away, the straps that hold it in place cutting deep in the disintegrating flesh.

"Finally she has seen fit to send my replacement!" he cries. "Give me your breastbone to split; he is most comfortable between your lungs."

I stumble backward, kicking the fire toward him. I feel the heat of the flame through my still-damp jeans, but he doesn't even notice the sparks or the coals that bounce off him.

I have the scourge out and in my hand when Marty appears out of nowhere.

The Mad Monk spins, slinging the knife around in front of him, slicing the air.

Marty ducks, avoiding the blade with a swiftness I did not think him capable of.

His right hand clamps on the monk's wrist and twists it. I can hear the bones fracture like glass rubbing on glass. The sound of it turns my stomach. The monk jerks, trying to get away, eyes wide. They are nearly white, the pupils of them faded like old paper left in the sun.

He's blind.

Marty's other hand grabs the collar of the monk's habit and then yanks it down. The rotten sackcloth tears with a wet sound and peels away like the skin of a dried onion. More flame script covers the monk's scrawny knotted frame, flowing in and out of symbols that form a frame around one long strip of bare skin that goes from the hollow of his throat to his navel. The only thing to be found in that blank strip is a sutured incision, the stitches thickly corded and starkly black as they weave through the puckered edges of pulled-together skin.

He has an entire world inside him.

"Marty, stop!"

His head turns toward me.

He smiles and his mouth stretches wide, pulling high and up on the sides to reveal a shark-toothed grin.

"There is no stopping me now, Charlotte Tristan Moore."

In one smooth motion, he plunges the monk's knife hilt deep into the man's throat.

49

THE CORPSE OF the Mad Monk slumps to the ground at his feet.

No.

No.

It can't be.

He stretches his arms, blood spattered across his face.

"Finally!" he says. "I thought you were *never* going to solve the problem. Well, part of me thought you were never going to solve the problem; the other part of me had full confidence in my ability to choose an Acolyte."

He's taller than he was, the extra height distorting the features of his face; they pull down like a rubber mask. His feet weave together and he does a spin and a kick with a flourish. He shakes out his hands like a concert pianist preparing for a recital.

My eyes lock on the right one, laser focused on the

four holes from where I lashed him with the scourge that have stretched open with his new length, gaping to reveal a brilliant shining crimson underneath.

He sees where I'm looking and he winks at me.

"I do believe I have had enough of this."

His fingers dig into his mouth, hooking into the lips, and he begins to pull. The skin stretches, growing thinner and thinner until I can see through it. He shrugs and the skin parts and falls away.

And standing before me, smoothing the slick black suit he wears with his terrible red right hand, is the goddamn Man in Black.

"How?" I cry out.

He looks up.

"How?" He cocks one eyebrow. "You are a smart girl, not smart enough to not be tricked, but think back and figure it out. I am not your master anymore." He smiles. "I am just the one who owned you."

"You planned all of this?"

"I am the Crawling Chaos; I have intentions, not plans. Now, see if you can put it together."

I do what he suggests. I think back, all the way to the white room.

"I caught you too fast. I thought you were ahead of me, but you were just in front of me."

"I have been in front of you the entire time. I did not think you had the ability to follow me. I should have known you had something up your sleeve. How did you cross this far?"

Should I answer him? I don't see a reason not to.

"I took the King in Yellow's soul gem," I say.

"I always did hate him."

"I don't think he was a fan of yours either. I know I'm not."

"Now, now, no need to be sore about it just because you have lost. Speaking of sleeves, where is my coat?"

"The Skull-Faced Woman kept it," I lie.

"You have lost both of the things you took from me?"

The coat and the skinhound. "Yeah, I don't know where I put my car keys either."

I send a little charge of magick from my spine into the bundle lodged at my lower back, not much, just a tiny zap. I am rewarded as something small and round, like a finger, pushes back against me.

She was right. I feel like I know what to do.

I hope she was right.

"Why should you care? You kept trying to get me to leave them behind."

"I admit, I wanted them back. I should have known you were too stubborn to let them go so that I could pick them up again."

"If I had known that you were trying to get them, there is no way in hell I'd ever put them down."

"Not to mock you." His red right hand touches his chin as he considers what he just said. "On second thought, absolutely to mock you, if you had known I was trying to get them away, we would not be here right now."

I shuffle to the left, facing him front on.

"And you ditched me when we finally got near the Skull-Faced Woman's chambers because the guardians would have known that you were not one of them."

He claps long and slow. "Very good. Like this sad, tarnished priest at my feet, the Raptors of Leng cannot see, but they would have smelled the skin of one of their own that I had fashioned into a disguise after killing it."

The magick makes the vertebrae in my lower back ache as it leaves me.

"You made Marty from one of the murder penguins?"

"What can I say? I am an artist."

"Why not stay a penguin?"

"You would not have trusted something that was not like you."

"I did trust Marty."

"You trusted *me*!" The Man in Black's face twists with anger, cords standing out from his neck. *"There is no Marty: that was only me."*

His outburst spikes my adrenaline and the magic bubbles inside of me faster than before.

I raise my hands. "Easy," I say. "Clearly you are not over me breaking our connection."

His mouth becomes a pout. "I never said I was not a jealous god."

"What are you doing here?"

He shakes himself, smoothing his suit again like it is made of ruffled feathers. "I am having a frustrating conversation with you, Charlotte Tristan Moore."

The bundle at my back is getting heavier. I drop my arms to my sides in case it begins to widen. "What are you doing trying to free your father?"

"You do not believe it is because I love him?"

The laugh is yanked out of me so fast it shocks me.

"No, I absolutely do not think that you love anything."

"That is simply not true. I told you I love your species once. I do not lie."

"You trick and you deceive, but you do not lie?"

"They are not one and the same, not interchangeable."

"So you love me?"

"I do."

"Then why are you trying to destroy everything that I am and love?"

He shrugs. "My father will escape here; it is inevitable. I did help place him here. I was younger then. I am so much older now and I have seen the folly of that decision."

"He's not free."

"If I had not betrayed him, I could have stayed with him at his side as he tore this cosmos apart. He would have turned on me in the end, but it would have been the end and it would not have mattered."

In the back of my skull, I hear a singsong, alien voice.

"You thought it mattered back then. What changed?"

"Nothing changed. It did not matter back then."

"Why did you betray him, then?"

"I am the Crawling Chaos; what else would I do?"

The bundle at my back begins to pull away, the new weight of it causing it to separate.

"You could do anything. Isn't that what chaos is?"

"Do not dare to lecture me on my very nature. None of it matters."

There is a tone in his voice. Is the Man in Black depressed? Can the Beast take even a chaos god?

Before I can ask the question, the coat bundle hits the floor behind me.

The Man in Black's eyes narrow.

"What did you do?"

I step back and kneel down beside the bulging sack that the coat has become. It keeps changing shape, bouncing on the tile as it grows in pulses and spurts. The fabric that had swaddled it has fallen away in shreds. It is almost the size that it was when I carried it. I press the Mark in my right hand against it and curl the fingers of my left around the gem at my throat.

The second I do, I become a circuit of magick.

My magick, the energy of the stone and the torc, both gifts from goddesses and imbued with their power, and the life force of whatever the coat and the skinhound are becoming.

The etheric energy scorches along my skin, singeing away the hair on my arms and leaving behind a layer of ozone that fills my nostrils. The beat of my heart takes on the power of a hammer breaking stone. I channel the magick back into the sack.

Almost.

The Man in Black drops to his knees beside the Mad Monk's corpse. With one swift move, his red right hand tears the stitches free from the wound along the dead man's chest.

At the same time, my sack splits open and I weep at what is revealed.

50

THE CREATURE IS majestic.

Proud like a lion.

He stands on four legs with the wide-barrel body of a grizzly bear. His shoulders are massive, covered in a thick, dark pelt that is still matted with the fluid of his birth. Each wide paw is tipped with crescents for claws, the points of them sharp enough to puncture the tile underneath them.

I am behind him, looking up at him. Even under his thick fur I can see the definition of powerful muscles. They bulge under his coat, flexing and standing out as he shakes himself.

I pick up the scourge that I had dropped and rise to my feet. The creature turns his massive head and stares at me.

With his one egg yolk eye.

His snout opens to reveal a mouth full of bone-breaking teeth and a long blister-pink tongue.

His throat works and the sound that comes out of it is not a bark or a howl but rather the alien singsong babble I have come to know so well.

The coat and the skinhound have become a new creature.

He turns back to the Man in Black, lowers his head, and charges.

The Man in Black doesn't have time to rise before the creature closes the gap in one bound. He bowls the Man in Black over and they roll across the broken tile.

I am up on my feet and chasing them.

I cannot tell where one begins and the other ends. The Man in Black shape-shifts, his arms and legs stretching long and bending with too many joints. They wrap around the creature, who catches one of the limbs in his mouth and begins to grind it between his jaws.

The red right hand has become a spear tip, a wide, flat blade that plunges into the creature over and over, jabbing deeper and deeper, as more and more blood flows. The creature uses his upper body to throw himself on top of the Man in Black, crushing him to the ground. Nyarlathotep uses handfuls of the creature's pelt to drag himself out from under. He scrambles up onto the creature's back.

The creature bucks, trying to shake him off, but the Man in Black has his fingers twined deep in the shaggy fur. He throws himself sideways, using his weight to drag the creature down to the broken tile floor.

I am almost upon them when the Man in Black picks up one of the rough-hewn blocks of stone that have fallen from the wall.

One too big to lift.

One that is nearly the size of the creature himself.

He raises it high and smashes it down on the creature's spine.

The terrible, stomach-turning crunch of his back breaking echoes across the underside of the dome and falls like thunder.

51

THE MAN IN Black extricates himself from the heaving body of my friend just before I get there.

I scream at the Man in Black; the sound rips out, primal and inhuman. There are no words; there aren't even syllables. It's just raw animal howling.

I lash at him with the scourge as I fall to my knees next to the creature.

The Man in Black easily shifts back to avoid my blow.

My face is all teeth in a vicious snarl.

The Man in Black looks down on me.

I hear his words, but they don't make any sense in the raging that is now my mind.

"I have changed my mind, Charlotte Tristan Moore. You may keep both of them now."

The creature trembles and I am afraid to touch him, afraid to hurt him worse. He bleeds from dozens of places, bright red blood puddling under him.

But worse, so much worse, his spine is creased deeply below his shoulders at an angle that spines are not meant to crease. His limbs splay loosely on the ground and do not move. The only movements in him that are not involuntary spasms are the roll of his eye and his breathing.

Pain flashes across the top of my skull and the Man in Black is suddenly there, my hair wadded in his fist.

He lifts me off my knees, using my hair as a handhold, and leans his face close to mine.

His breath is too warm and smells like a wet iron.

"Do you remember what I said about the elephant and the cardboard box?"

His red right hand comes suddenly into view, clenched in a fist. I see it for only a split second before it hits me between the eyes like a woodsman's axe. My vision goes all dandelion yellow and black static and I can see nothing.

His voice fills my ear again.

"I broke your pet. Now I will break you."

Something presses into my forehead, worming its way through the skin and the bone and sinking into my cerebrum. I feel the bumps of knuckles as it curls and rips my third eye wide open and I see everything.

The walls of the temple and the floor pulse with color that runs like water. The Man in Black is gone, his true form spilling around me in tangled knots of tentacles and spindly limbs that wave their hooked claws in the air. Unblinking orbs dotting his body stare up at me from between dozens of gaping mouths that open and close.

I turn away, unable to look any longer.

In front of me is a quivering thing.

He huddles on himself, his shaggy fur hanging loosely on him, like a blanket. I can hear his heartbeat like a drum over the long, low whine that escapes his jaws. In the center of his face glows one bright orb of butter yellow. Pain wafts off him in wisps of lavender.

Language is gone. All I can do is grunt my recognition of the creature as my mind splays apart.

There is a sound, not unlike the whine of the creature, that grows in my ears.

It's me.

I am making a low, inhuman noise from the middle of my esophagus.

Reality is slipping away.

I feel the first blow from the Man in Black just before my mind gives up and I am in the blackness.

52

I AWAKEN TO my body hitching, trying to expel blood from my lungs.

It feels like someone is doing origami with my skeleton. My rib cage is full of jagged pain that sinks deep inside my body all the way to the organs inside of it.

Ribs are broken.

It feels like nearly half.

Something thick and congealed flies out of my throat and catches in my teeth. It sits there in my mouth as I try to get my jaw open wide enough for it to slither out over my busted lips. It splats on the floor beside my face.

I can barely see.

I try to pull my eyelids farther apart, but there's too much pressure; they're too tight, full of fluid and pain. Both of my eyes have been blackened. I know what black eyes feel like. This is what they feel like.

My throat is lacerated on the inside like I tried to

swallow broken glass. The blood runs down it and my belly sloshes from the internal bleeding.

The Man in Black tried to beat me to death.

And he very nearly succeeded.

I lift my head and try to see the creature, see if he's still breathing. He's right beside me, but I can barely make out his shape.

He is too still.

No trembling.

No breathing.

And I cannot *feel* him.

I need to get up.

The Man in Black can't win.

But I have nothing in me. No strength. No magick. No ability.

The Man in Black is going to win.

The thought is not even fully formed and I can *feel* the creep of sorcery in the air. Dark magic is happening somewhere close by and I know it is the Man in Black freeing his father.

The tears cannot get through my swollen eyes.

A white-hot pain runs up my arm and into my neck.

What the fuck?

I crane my neck and look at my arm. My vision is limited to a narrow line with a black veil over it. I strain to see and find one of the falls of the scourge has punctured the back of my hand. I can barely make out that it is pumping venom into my body.

It slips quickly through my veins like quicksilver.

More pain will make it harder in the long run, but in this early moment it gives me the tiniest, briefest moment of clarity.

An idea half-forms in my mind.

As carefully as I can, so that the stinger does not dislodge, I pull the scourge toward me. Another fall crosses my arm and it too buries its stinger into my flesh. This time I'm more prepared.

My magick is gone, so low that I can't even feel it.

But the scourge is a supernatural item, like a magic battery, a bit of the old sorcery just waiting for someone to use it. Just like I did with the cell of the Hungry Dark, I siphon that magick into my body.

It comes in quick and hot, like a shot of adrenaline.

My own magick surges up to meet it, hungry to be replenished from anywhere. In seconds I have drained everything from the scourge and my blood is on fire with the caustic, acidic nature of the venom.

The swelling in my eyes is less and I can see just a little bit better. My ribs are still broken, but I can almost take a full breath.

I am not healed, just patched.

It still takes me three tries to get up on my hands and knees and another five to stand all the way up.

The little bit of magick that I have absorbed makes my third eye work, not at full strength or I'd become a gibbering maniac.

My magick was at low ebb when the Man in Black tore it open.

Probably the only thing that saved me from insanity.

And now I have to try to stop that sorry bastard from completing his mission.

The creature whimpers. I crawl over to him, glad that he is still alive, even in the state that he is in. Carefully, I stroke his muzzle and make comforting nonsense noises. He tries to lick my hand, blister-pink tongue trembling as he does; then he falls to the side.

My chest hurts. This is so hard.

"I'm going to pay him back," I say to the creature.

He makes a noise in the back of his throat. His eye dims, going grayish.

"You were the best," I say to him.

The egg yolk eye rolls away from me in its socket and goes still. The light is gone from inside it and the creature is still, so still I can feel it like a sinkhole, dragging everything into it.

I hate that I don't have time to weep for my friend.

He gave so much.

Softly I lay his head on the tile floor and kiss the velvety fur on his cheek.

He will die for this.

It feels like it takes forever to crawl over to the corpse of the Mad Monk, but I finally get there. My knees and palms are bloody from the broken tile. I keep wiping my hand off on my jeans and shirt to stop my Mark from activating and eating up my magick.

The Mad Monk is cold and his body hard as a rock.

How long have I been unconscious?

The seam in the middle of the body splays open. There's nothing in there but meat and bone and a deep, dark hole that tunnels down to somewhere else. It's not big, no wider around than the Mad Monk, but it seems to go somewhere deep, not into the ground but into some other dimension like a corpse-framed wormhole.

This close I can hear the guttural sounds of some language long forgotten, and the hot electric buzz of chaos magick plays across my skin like the aftereffects of a lightning strike.

Is it still there?

I touch the torc around my neck and I'm relieved. It is still there.

I try to get myself to a sitting position. It takes a lot of effort to put my legs inside the cavity of the Mad Monk.

I don't have a plan.

But I do have intention.

I give myself a push that makes pain scream across my body, and slip over the edge into that hole.

Let's make some chaos.

53

I THOUGHT I would fall, but I don't. I just slip from being outside the Mad Monk to being inside somewhere completely different.

The ground under my feet is sandy and loose, but there are walls of stone.

I'm in a place that looks like an underground quarry. The rock has been cut away and in a manner that indicates someone harvesting stone. Maybe this is where the stone for the dome came from.

The Man in Black is across from me, his arms moving as if they have no bone structure, fluidly forming glyphs and sigils with his own flesh, or whatever he has for flesh.

The three soul gems that he has float in the air in front of him, glowing with their magic.

A glass wall looms far above him, stretching from the floor all the way up into the shadows out of sight.

Fog and clouds swirl against the glass. In the midst of all of this there is a face looking down, a horrible face.

It sees me, sees me right here. And I know I'm looking upon the face of Azathoth.

I avert my eyes.

Even the few seconds I looked, I could feel my mind trying to slip into madness, like sand washing away on a crumbling beach.

The Man in Black may see me as well, but he cannot do anything about it or he will ruin his spell.

I don't even sneak up on him. There's nowhere to hide anyway. I would saunter, but I don't have the energy.

His eyes cut over at me, but he doesn't stop chanting. The noises coming from his throat sound like small animals being slaughtered.

I stand in front of him, the soul gems floating between me and him.

The one on the left is from the cancer god, the first thing that we killed together. The one on the right he pulled out of Shub Niggurath as she lay dying in a backwoods barbecue joint.

The one in the middle.

That is the soul gem of Cthulhu. In its iridescent surface I can see a shiny image of him looking back at me. Cthulhu was kind to me at the time. He was the one who showed me the true nature of the Man in Black, showed me that he could not be trusted. I accidentally captured his soul gem the first time I fought the Man in Black.

I gave it back to get him to leave in order to buy Daniel and my family just a little more time on Earth.

It only takes a second and I know exactly what I'm going to do.

I step forward, into his spell. His chaos magick scrubs against me like a cheese grater inside my skin. It hurts, but fuck it, what is more pain at this point?

My hands close on the gems belonging to Cthulhu and Shub Niggurath.

The very moment my fingers touch their smooth surfaces, I begin pulling magick into myself from the fertility goddess's soul gem, drinking it all down as quickly as I can.

My third eye opens wider and it takes all my mental discipline to hold it at bay, to hang on to my sanity just a bit longer.

I don't empty it; that would take longer than I have.

By the time I reach the Man in Black, I hope I've taken enough.

I drop the soul gem of Shub Niggurath to the ground and throw my free arm around his neck.

His red right hand closes around my throat at the same time I make my wish.

54

"WHAT HAVE YOU done?"

The Man in Black screams at me, his face distorted and alien.

"I just arranged a family reunion."

He turns and looks around. We are surrounded by the fog and the mist. I watch as his face changes.

As he realizes *exactly* what I have done.

I have wished us both into the middle of Azathoth's cell.

The Man in Black's hand lashes out, crashing into my jaw. I would fall, but there's nowhere to fall. My brain shorts out for a moment and when it stops flickering he is again squeezing my throat with his red right hand.

He leans in close, abattoir breath moist and coppery on my face. "Never forget that I made you, Charlotte Tristan Moore. Without me you would be *nothing* but a mewling scrap of flesh, weak and worth nothing more than the taste you might leave in my mouth."

I slide my right hand under the tails of his shirt, fingers locked tightly together, driving up the skin there until I find it, find the raw, ragged edge of the injury I inflicted before, the wound I left that would not heal.

I find it and I shove my hand all the way inside him to the elbow.

He gasps, rearing back, and I lock my other arm around him, pulling us close with all my might as he rises and bucks and I call my magick into the Mark he carved into my palm what feels like a lifetime ago and I let it loose in a torrent of spellshot that pours inside him like napalm from a flamethrower.

It rushes out of me and the skin of my arm goes hot and burning and the Man in Black gasps and chokes and black sooty smoke pours from his jaw, which keeps slipping sideways and back, disjointing and popping into place as he writhes under my death grip.

My eyes water as the smoke pours across my face and I can't see anymore and it all becomes the whirling sensation of being slung around and the beating sensation of the Crawling Chaos trying to buck me off to get away, to get free, but I am inexorable.

I am irresistible.

I am the motherfucking Godslayer and I will not be denied.

My lips pull back and my teeth gleam in the night. "How do I taste now, you son of a bitch?"

My strength gives out and he pushes me away.

We are surrounded by a kaleidoscope of colors, floating in nothing. There is no ground. There is no direction.

But there is *something* in here.

I feel him. He is everywhere.

Everywhere and coming closer all at once.

The colors swirl and part and reveal the horrible face that was pressed against the glass. It is flat and contains two eyes of mismatched size that sit on the edges of it, rolling outward, the tinfoil pupils spinning in opposite rotation. It has a mouth like an open grave, with moldy tombstone teeth surrounded by a jaw that opens like a sewer grate.

The planes of its face don't make sense as I stare at it. They are a constantly changing geometric pattern.

Stop blinking.

My eyes are blinking rapidly. I want to stare anywhere but at him, and yet I need to stare at him.

The Mad God Azathoth has found us.

The Man in Black moves away, twisting through space, trying to escape. His human form shreds like rotten silk, revealing his true form full of bulbous twisting tentacles, covered in a thin worm-white membrane, and bristling with multi-jointed spindly limbs that end in hooked claws. Unblinking eyes dot his surface between mouths of varying sizes that chew at nothing.

The thing that is Azathoth looks down at me.

I feel his attention in my bones like a marrow transplant.

Please turn away. Go after your son. I delivered him to you.

His voice sears my brain.

I cannot understand him, but I feel his intent. And he moves toward me.

My mind shifts and slips like a joint coming apart. The moorings that hold my personality together fray and stretch, the fibers coming apart.

As he draws closer, who I am fractures more and more.

After all I have suffered, and all that I have done to survive, to avoid becoming a mewling, gibbering thing, I refuse to let that be for nothing.

It matters.

I matter.

But my thoughts

Slipping

There's a thing in my hand. A round thing.

I was going . . .

There's a thing.

My hand.

I peer at it, lifting it close enough to my eyes that it touches my nose.

There is a thing, man, thing, inside it.

Cute-thulu.

The scrap of what I intended whisks across my mind like a bit of ribbon in a sandstorm.

I snatch it, pull it close inside my head even as the insanity begins to boil.

I close my eyes and I make another wish.

The thing in my hand cracks, breaking open as if I'd smashed it against a rock.

My magick races out of my body, in a long golden thread as it retraces my steps through this godforsaken place, guided by the broken gem that I hold.

It runs through the Labyrinth that is this place.

It passes by the Skull-Faced Woman's chamber and drops through the wormhole above the Witchstone.

It trails through the corridors and sweeps past my sisters, causing the blood roses to chime.

It ruffles the hair of the Star Vampire.

And finally it dives into the frigid, salty water in a puddle in a corridor.

It falls like a meteor to the bottom of that sea and crashes into the sunken city of R'lyeh and keeps crashing until it finds there the Dread Dreamer Cthulhu, He Who Will Not Die.

Great Cthulhu so fearsome that he is kept sedated, off-site from a prison designed to hold the worst of the elder gods.

My magick *pulls* and it feels like my insides are being shredded.

The atmosphere of the cell I'm in implodes against me and then explodes against me and I'm driven into the glass with enough force to crack it.

The impact clears my mind, but the darkness closes in.

Cthulhu lies before me, still for a long moment. He looks as he did when I met his avatar, except he is massively larger than before. His form stretches like a mountain range and my eyes cannot take him in all at once.

He turns like the earth moving, rolling his massive body to the side. Black wings the size of an eclipse unfurl from his shoulders. This far away it appears to be a gentle movement, but the clouds and fog between us swirl violently and seconds later I am battered by a backwind that makes me feel like I have been hit by a car.

The glass behind me cracks more. Sharp pain digs into my back, making me wince, and I feel the heat of my own blood spread on my skin.

When I open my eyes everything is red in front of me.

It's his eye.

Cthulhu has brought his face near me and is staring at me.

His eye blazes at me, like flaring neon crimson that I feel against my skin. His presence is overwhelming, like the ocean, like the void of space, like the nothingness that comes after death.

He is inevitable.

Charlie.

His voice *pounds* at me.

You did not stop him.

My mind drowns in him. His avatar was overwhelming. Cthulhu in his full form is obliterating. I claw at my mind. I have to keep it together.

I didn't. I did not.

Brought you.

You summon me as if I am yours to call?

No. No.

Yes.

Help. Friend . . .

He moves back, the motion causing a backdraft that pulls me

forward. I only move a few inches before I am stopped with a jerk, snagged on the broken glass behind me.

I hang there as he moves back, looming over me, impossibly large. Gnarled hands rest on knees covered in thick sheets of barnacles. He considers me with those scarlet eyes, looking down at me over a mouth that is a nest of writhing tentacles.

Something spills over his shoulder. It looks like light but is not; I struggle to place its nature.

It's a *color*.

It runs down his chest in iridescent rivulets. He shakes off the impact, as he watches me.

Somewhere behind him I can hear the gibbering howl of Azathoth.

And I *feel* Dread Cthulhu make his decision a moment before he rises and turns. Cthulhu closes his hoary hand around the Crawling Chaos as he squares off against the Mad God Azathoth.

And then the darkness overtakes me and it all goes away.

Epilogue

"Charlie?

"It is not your moment yet."

It hurts to blink.

Why am I able to blink?

Everything is a blur of light, all shimmery and loose. I reach up to wipe my eyes and pain hitches deep in my back. It shoots from just above my kidney across my body into the bottom of my lungs.

Ho, fuck . . .

I can't breathe.

"Let me help you with this."

The voice sounds familiar and I struggle to place it as hands slide around my back and lift me, supporting me.

Everything in me screams to fight, but I just can't.

I am pulled and tugged and every bit of it hurts. I bite my tongue even though all I want to do is curse and scream. It stops and I feel like I'm in an upright position, propped against something both soft and firm.

"Stay calm," the voice says.

Pressure flattens against my eyes, moving back and forth; my ocular nerve flares into bright speckled lights.

The pressure goes away and I try opening my eyes. They feel raw and abraded, but I'm able to open them and see, even though things are fuzzy at the edges.

The Skull-Faced Woman is holding me.

Her hair hangs just in front of my face, close enough that I can still smell the water we bathed in. I realize we are back in her chambers.

That feels like so long ago.

Her bone face lowers toward mine and her hair tickles the skin on my chest above the collar of my shirt. "This will hurt," she says. "And I am sorry."

She shifts behind me and the lance of pain stabbing through my torso intensifies, spiking high and shrill across all my nerves, making my head go completely staticky. Sweat beads along my skin under my clothes and that *sticky-hot* feeling of nausea runs over every bit of me.

She pushes me forward suddenly and the pain inside me explodes, ripping through every part inside my body, and I become nothing but a vessel holding it.

Am I going to die?

The pain shrinks immediately back to its original place, the original line of it through my body, and it *throbs* there.

My ears are stuffed with cotton, but I hear a clatter beside me. Turning my head slightly, I see a jagged piece of sharp crystal, as long as my arm and covered in blood, settling into place on the hard floor beside us.

My arms and legs are cold and going colder.

Pressure blossoms at the wound behind me. Something burrows partway in and it washes that *sticky-hot* painfever over me again.

Sharp pain hooks inside, tying my lungs into crochet knots that tighten as it slides slowly out of my body. Breathing is not a thing.

The sharp, hot pain slips out of my body and relief floods in behind it. It settles down into a dull throb and I can breathe, kind of.

"There," she says. "That will hold until."

Until what?

"That was a very clever thing you did."

What is she . . . Oh, Cthulhu.

"What's happening with that?"

"Oh, you and the linear thing."

"Just answer the question."

She shakes her head, making her dark hair sway, and her antlers swish through the air. "I have to show you something and then you have a decision to make."

"Can you not just ask me? I can decide right here."

"That is not how things work and you know it."

"I don't know anything except I don't like arbitrary rules on things."

"Some things are some things and they have rules. Not all things have rules and not all rules have things."

"Does this mean you're taking me out of this place?"

"I am."

I sigh.

"Fine. Show me what you have to show me, but I need to make a stop first."

———————————

"Meg."

She turns as if I have startled her. I know it's not the case; not only did I pass the other two Sisters and all of the razor roses leaning in my direction as if I am a magnet, but the scourge at my side has been chattering nonstop since the Skull-Faced Woman ported us here.

She stands beside me.

Meg is sitting on the ground in front of the tree where I whipped her. She turns, looking up at me, her spine twisted in an elegant, impossible curve. Her movement breaks open her wounds and they weep with a clear fluid that looks like pear syrup in a dozen spots.

"You have returned."

She doesn't call me sister and it hurts.

"I have. I promised I would."

"But not to stay."

"I didn't promise that."

She is suddenly standing, even though I didn't see her move from the ground. A small cloud of dust rolls away from her feet. "Now that your promise is fulfilled you can be about your leaving."

She turns away and I lunge forward, grabbing her arm even though it flares the pain up in my torso.

Her face is a snarl as she slashes at my arm with her nails, drawing shallow furrows that well up immediately with thick blood. I send a jolt of magick down my arm into the Mark on my palm and zap her, still holding on.

"Why are you pissed at me?!" I yell.

Tears flow from her eyes as she looks down at me, her lower lip trembling. "I felt you pass by." Her voice is raw. "I felt you not choose me to help you."

"That's not—"

"Do not lie to me. I would have come when you called. I would have been by your side."

"Things were intense. I didn't think."

"No, you most certainly did not. Not of me."

"You would have been hurt." The second they leave my mouth I regret the words.

She glares at me and I know I've insulted her.

"I'm sorry," I say.

"You're still leaving." She indicates the Skull-Faced Woman. "Else you would not be in her company."

"Greetings, Sister of Mercy," the Skull-Faced Woman says. "Be at peace."

"Do not speak to me of peace. I know what your peace means."

The Skull-Faced Woman raises her arms, palms out toward Meg. "I mean you no harm."

"Release me," Meg snarls. "Me and my sisters. Take us with you when you depart. We served you in our function before."

The Skull-Faced Woman stares at her impassively for a long moment. "Perhaps."

"You would set them free?" I ask.

She turns to me. "That depends entirely upon you."

I don't like the sound of that.

"What does that mean?"

"We have to leave this place for me to show you."

I turn back to Meg and the hope that is on her face breaks my heart. I don't know what she sees in my expression.

Whatever it is causes her to say, "I will not ask for promises this time."

Damn it.

"Meg," I say. "If I can, I will."

"I know that about you, sister."

Without another word I turn away. Between one step and the next the Skull-Faced Woman has taken us to a new place.

WE'RE STANDING AT the edge of a room. There's not a lot of light in here and most of it comes from candles and blinking LED Christmas lights strung along the ceiling. The shitty light illuminates stacks of books and piles of paper and cluttered things. The room smells like candle soot, dry-rotted leather, and someone who has been in the same clothes three days too long.

Sitting in a chair hunched over a book that is larger than the table that it sits on is a thin man with long shaggy hair. His shoulder blades jut from beneath a threadbare T-shirt.

I can't see his face. It's shrouded in hair and shadows, too close to the pages of the book.

"What are we—?"

"Hush, child," the Skull-Faced Woman says. "Not that he can hear us; simply wait and all will be clear."

The man leans back far enough to turn one of the huge pages, but his face stays hidden.

The sounds of someone approaching come through the open door. I watch, curious to see what will happen.

"I found it, but I do not think it will be of use to you."

In through the door steps a middle-aged woman, her dark hair swept up with some sort of braided headband, and she's wearing a robe that completely hides her figure. Her features are plain, completely normal to the point of boring. But I would recognize her no matter what face she wore.

Ashtoreth.

The Skull-Faced Woman grabs my arm even though I don't need holding back.

Ashtoreth stops short and slowly turns her head toward us and I can see in her eyes that she can see us.

If this is Ash . . .

No.

Please, fucking, no.

Daniel looks up from the book he is reading.

The Skull-Faced Woman's hand tightens on my arm enough to leave a bruise.

His skin gleams oily in the candlelight and his features have been whittled, pared down, as if he has not eaten in several days. His oh-so-green eyes blaze in dark, smudged circles.

He holds his hand out toward Ashtoreth. "I found a working."

I look and dangling from her hands is a small fluted white bone with what appears to be thin black wire wrapped around it. I know that it's not wire. It's a strand of my hair. And the little bone came from a murdered child. The Man in Black used it to locate Ashtoreth after he first picked me and Daniel up.

Ashtoreth takes the thing over to Daniel and places it in his hand. He doesn't seem to notice that she's staring at us the entire time. The moment she lets go of it, his hand closes and drops back to the book and he goes back to reading.

"What the hell is going on?"

"Patience," the Skull-Faced Woman says.

Ashtoreth moves toward us, stopping just in front of us. She looks from me to the Skull-Faced Woman and back.

"Charlie? Is that really you?"

"Can you hear me?"

"Of course I can," she says. "But are you *you*?"

"I am."

Her head drops to her chest. She takes a deep breath and holds it for a long moment before letting it go and looking up.

"I am ready."

"Ready for what?" I ask.

"You said the next time you saw me you would kill me. You have brought Satet at your left hand."

She leaves the rest unsaid.

Oh, Ash.

The Skull-Faced Woman says nothing.

"I need to ask you something and for you to answer honestly."

Ash waits expectantly.

"When you betrayed me, was it your choice or did the Man in Black force you to act that way?"

"Oh, Charlie." Tears begin streaming down her face.

And I know the answer.

I reach out, pull her close, and let the broken love goddess weep on my chest.

"I forgive you." I say it over and over again.

I don't cry.

I don't.

Fuck you.

I do stop before she does, though.

She's curled into me, tucked into my chest, and so I look over her head at Daniel.

I know there's some sort of magick keeping him from seeing us, but I'm not sure he would see us even without that. He's absorbed in the book that he holds. When he adjusts it, he raises the cover and I see that it's bound in some sort of thin leather that bunches across the front. Stitching holds it all together and, on the cover, is some form of design that is familiar but doesn't make sense. I keep staring at it in the low light, trying to figure it out.

Daniel shifts once more and when he does what little candle-light there is falls directly on the cover and I see a slight gleaming inside one of the depressions and it all clicks.

There is a human face on the cover of that book.

Someone somewhere was skinned to make the cover on that book and their face stares at me with empty eyeholes and screams at me with a hollow mouth.

What?

What is Daniel doing reading a book with a human face on it?

My eyes sweep the room in jerky motions, looking at this and that, and I see what I did not see when we first arrived.

The candles burn, but they do not melt.

The stacks of books are ancient, some of them bound in the

same thin leather as the one Daniel holds. On the thicker spines I can make out the words of some of their titles.

Sefir ha-Razim.

Mafteah Shelomoh.

Le Grande Grimoire ou Dragon Rouge.

Unaussprechlichen Kulten.

And then there are ones in languages that haven't been spoken in centuries, their spines marked by symbols and runes and flame letters that make my eyes water to look at them.

What is happening here?

Ashtoreth pulls back and looks up at me. "It's gotten really bad, Charlie. He's obsessed with finding you."

"He can stop looking. I'm right here."

"He cannot see you, child," the Skull-Faced Woman says.

I push Ash away and stare at the Skull-Faced Woman. "Well, then fix it."

The Skull-Faced Woman shakes her head. "It cannot be."

"Did you bring me here as some kind of joke? Are you getting your kicks off of this Ghost of Christmas Past bullshit?"

"I am not trying to be cruel. I am offering you a choice."

Ashtoreth opens her mouth as if to say something.

The Skull-Faced Woman snaps her fingers and everything around us freezes. The candles stop flickering. Ash is stuck with her mouth open. Daniel has just pushed back his hair, exposing his face so I can see it, study it. He has a fine trace of stubble along his jaw and cheek. He said he had a hard time growing facial hair; if his hair is any indication of how much time has passed, this might be the closest he can come to a beard.

It's cute, and boyish, and attractive, and it breaks my fucking heart.

"The time has come," she says. "I would claim you, make you mine, if you are amenable to it."

"What does that mean?"

"You would become my vessel, an instrument of my function."

I don't say anything, but my head is full of the visions from when
we did the mind-meld.

"I don't think I can be an avatar of death."

"Child." She tilts her head, looking at me with her empty socket
eyes. "You have been an avatar of mine for a long time now, since
the first time you killed a god that was not yourself. This will simply make permanent your function."

"My function?"

"Godslayer." The word reverberates from her with power that I
feel in my chest.

Godslayer. The Deicide.

It sits on me like a mantle. It feels good. Right.

"I would kill gods?"

"There are gods who need killing," she says. "And I would allow you the use of the Sisters."

I could help Meg and her sisters, my sisters, be free.

"What is the cost?"

She turns and looks pointedly over Ashtoreth's head at Daniel.
Fuck.

"If I choose Daniel? Then I get to be with him?"

"That is not the choice." Her voice is hard as granite. "The choice
is accept the role or do not. If you choose to become the Godslayer
then you will be granted a measure of my power. If you do not then
I will return you to your moment."

"If I say yes—"

"Then I will allow you to be there when his moment occurs;
otherwise you must leave him to his own devices."

"What kind of choice is that? Leave the man I think I love to
go hunt down gods or die?"

"You left him before to do that very thing."

I look at Daniel. Frozen like this, I can see the mania in his oh-so-green eyes. I see what being involved with me has done to him. He deserves better than this, better than chasing after me.

Especially if I am not coming back.

Ever.

That will not be the way it goes.

But I will *not* go into oblivion. Not willingly.

"Can you make him forget me? Give him a normal life again?"

She shakes her head and I feel her sadness at the answer she must give.

"There is a price to be paid for consorting with gods. For most humans their sanity is at risk."

"He didn't choose this! Didn't choose to get involved with the Man in Black."

"That does not matter, but in his chase for you he has chosen to engage many of the Great Old Ones."

Oh, Daniel.

"If I accept this then he is off-limits."

"How do you mean?"

"If I take the mantle of Godslayer, then any god who comes for him goes to the top of my to-do list."

"I can accept that." She puts her hand out.

I put my hand in hers, my Mark against her palm.

"Deal."

And everything is never the same again.